The Trials of Alaric

A TWIST UPON A REGENCY TALE
BOOK 9

BY JUDE KNIGHT

ARE YOU SIGNED UP FOR DRAGONBLADE'S BLOG?

You'll get the latest news and information on exclusive giveaways, exclusive excerpts, coming releases, sales, free books, cover reveals and more.

Check out our complete list of authors, too!

No spam, no junk. That's a promise!

Sign Up Here

www.dragonbladepublishing.com

Dearest Reader;

Thank you for your support of a small press. At Dragonblade Publishing, we strive to bring you the highest quality Historical Romance from some of the best authors in the business. Without your support, there is no 'us', so we sincerely hope you adore these stories and find some new favorite authors along the way.

Happy Reading!

CEO, Dragonblade Publishing

ABOUT THE BOOK

To wed her, he'd do anything. Even lose his heart!

When Alaric Redhaven is shipwrecked on the Isle of Claddach in the Irish Sea, he finds himself attending a most unusual house party. The Earl of Claddach is holding a set of trials to discover a worthy man to marry his daughter.

Lady Beatrice Collister, only child of the Earl of Claddach, is committed to choosing a husband who will be her consort when she is the island's countess. But not one of the eligible gentlemen selected to enter the trials makes her heart race.

As Alaric strives to win the trials, and with them, everything he has ever wanted, he also faces a brother bent on revenge, a drunken villager, and a cousin with a mountain-sized sense of entitlement.

But only the man who uncovers the Heart of Claddach can win Bea as his bride.

Chapter One

Off the coast of the Isle of Claddach, June 1819

THE STORM CAME as a surprise to the crew of the good ship *Flora Louise*. They had confidently expected a smooth run across the Irish Sea and into Liverpool.

Alaric Redhaven, their passenger, was not surprised. Alaric had not predicted that a storm would blow up out of nowhere, but he had been waiting for something else to disrupt his journey home.

Nothing had gone right for him since he had allowed himself to be captivated by a lying jade. She had married his brother. He had been exiled to Brazil, to join the staff of the British envoy to the Portuguese court in exile.

Alaric was not cut out for a diplomatic career, a fact he had known from the first. He had tried to tell his father he wanted to be a land steward somewhere. On the lands that would one day be his brother's, for preference. He had been caring for them without the title since he left university. Anywhere else in England if need be.

Instead, the Earl of Elsmouth had decreed a new career for his unsatisfactory second son, who was born too late to become a general in the recent wars, was as unlikely a potential bishop as anyone could imagine, and who refused to be an idle ornament of Society. Alaric was exiled to become a diplomat and reflect glory on the Redhaven family name from ambassadorial heights.

The ship he had taken from London in obedience to his father's command had been blown off course by a storm, attacked by pirates, and saved in the nick of time by the United States Navy. Alaric arrived at his post three months late, after the United States authorities had eventually decided he presented no threat and was, besides, too young to have been involved in the 1812 war.

From his arrival in Rio de Janeiro, he had not distinguished himself in any desirable fashion, and the litany of his accidents and mistakes was far too depressing to think about. His brief eighteen months as a diplomat had been a disaster. When he had inadvertently insulted the Spanish Ambassador at a reception in Rio de Janeiro, it had been the last straw. He, his uncle and sponsor, and the British envoy to the Portuguese court in exile had all been in agreement for the first time since Alaric had arrived.

Alaric had been dismissed and found a berth on the first ship leaving Rio de Janeiro with England as its destination. Now that ship was stuck in a rising storm while the experienced crewmen ran around in a panic, arguing about which sails to reef and who was going to do it.

To make things worse, the captain was nowhere to be found—probably lying in a hidden corner in a drunken stupor. They were without the first mate, too. He came up on deck when the weather first turned foul, was struck by a flying belaying pin, and knocked out before he could take charge.

Which meant they were trying to stay afloat in an unexpected storm, with a minimal crew and the two most senior officers disabled.

Drowning in the Irish Sea was a more permanent disruption than the arrest of their captain in Fortaleza and the shortage of supplies that kept them for two extra weeks in Jamaica. Not to mention the desertion of a good third of their crew in Dublin.

Alaric felt he should do something, but what? He knew nothing about how to sail a ship. Telling the crew to stop bickering and do their jobs was likely to get him hurled over the side. And suddenly, it was too late. First one mast broke, then another, then the third.

And then it got worse.

"We've lost the rudder!" shouted the man on the wheel.

"Rocks!" screamed someone else.

Some of the sailors leapt into the sea. Others clung to the nearest solid object as the ship pitched and yawed with every wave and gust of wind. Alaric tossed a mental coin, shrugged out of his coat, and jumped overboard. He would take his chance with the sea.

FROM HER BEDROOM in one of the castle's towers, Lady Beatrice Collister had a grandstand view of the foundering ship, though only in glimpses, between curtains of clouds and rain.

She could hear the storm bell—the tolling of the treble bell that summoned all able-bodied people to the beach below the castle. All people, that is, other than the Earl of Claddach, his wife and daughter, and the guests at his house party.

Some of the guests trailed upstairs to see if they could see anything through the storm. None of them wanted to go out in the rain for a better view or, heavens forfend, to help.

Which meant that Bea, as the earl's daughter, was going to have to be quick and sneaky if she was to be of any help at all. She dug through to the bottom of the trunk in her dressing room for the trousers, shirt, and jersey she wore for shipwreck rescues, and was soon dressed in wool that would stay warm no matter how wet it got. With luck, those who watched from a distance would take her for a boy.

She pulled a knitted hat over her hair, which was fortunately in a simple crown of plaits. The hat came low over her eyes and should further disguise her identity from the house party gawkers. She hurried down the tower stairs to the door into the top of the mansion that had been built around the bones of the ancient *Cashtal Vaaish*—Castle Death, the stone fort that had protected Claddach and its people from marauding Picts, raiding Irish, pillaging Vikings, and invading Normans.

Bea walked swiftly along the hall and let herself into the servants' stairwell. That was the risky part done. If her parents had come looking for her—unlikely, but possible—they would have stopped her. As it was, she made it to the ground floor and joined the others donning boots and oiled coats and hats.

They hurried down the path from the clifftop to the beach, most of the servants of the castle, joining a stream of people who had come over the hill road from the town. On an afternoon like this, they could not put out the boats, but they could go out into the surf, roped together, to bring in anything the spotters saw from the cliffs.

Not Bea. Her people would not hear of her putting herself in danger. She would stay on the beach, help build the fire, and wait to give aid to those recovered from the sea.

There should have been at least fifty crewmen on a ship of that size, but fewer than twenty were pulled alive from the water, and several of those would need careful nursing if they were to live. One the most alert men explained they'd been short-handed from the beginning and had lost fifteen men in Dublin. "Captain's a drunk," he said. "He shouldn't have sailed without hiring more men. He shouldn't have been drinking when the storm struck." He bowed his head and looked solemn. "God rest his gin-soaked soul."

The doctor had finished bandaging the man's arm, where it had been ripped by something in the water. "You'll do," he said. "Who's next?"

"You said you wanted to have another look at the man who

wasn't breathing," Bea reminded him.

"That's the passenger," the chatty patient informed them. "A gentleman, that one. Name of Redhaven."

He looked like a gentleman. Like the English gentlemen who were currently cluttering up her castle. A particularly nice specimen. Tall, broad-shouldered, handsome, if you liked the chisel-jawed, high-cheekboned, straight-nosed sort. Which Bea did, though her old nurse would say *handsome is as handsome does.*

At the moment, he was not doing anything. Except breathing, which was thanks to the doctor, and an improvement over when they had brought him ashore.

"He has a bump on his head," the doctor discovered. "Probably explains why he has not yet come around. He'll need someone with him at all times, at least until he recovers consciousness."

The rector, who was arranging billets for the rescuees, said, "I wonder who would be best. Mrs. Stephen perhaps. No, she is on the other side of the island at her daughter's place. Perhaps the Quayles?"

"The castle," Bea said, firmly. "He is a gentleman, the sailor said. I will take him, and the responsibility for his care."

It would at least give her some distraction from her parents' despicable house party. Which she had agreed to, with a tiny amount of hope that shriveled as soon as she met the bachelors her mother and aunt had selected.

She was done here. A spotter would remain on the cliffs and a dozen people would keep the fire going and wait in case more people needed to be pulled from the water. There was nothing more for Bea—or most of the other townspeople—to do. Already, those who had been assigned sailors had left the beach.

Most of the servants from the castle had also gone, but enough were left to form a stretcher party for the gentleman. Mr. Redhaven. Bea escorted him up the path from the beach, considering which bed chambers were occupied and which were free.

The single gentlemen's accommodation was fully occupied, and the single ladies' section would be inappropriate. Not the family rooms, of course. Which left either the area normally used by married visitors and widows, when they came to stay, or the smaller and less desirable rooms allocated to companions and poor relations, who could not be put to stay with the servants but who did not merit a finer chamber.

One of those, she thought, as she escorted the stretcher up to the front door, which was the quickest way to the main staircase. She could not in all conscience expect the stretcher carriers to carry Mr. Redhaven up one of the steeper secondary staircases. She would just have to risk being caught, but with luck, everyone would still be preparing for dinner.

The butler emerged from his room as she opened the two big doors and ushered the stretcher bearers inside. "Lady Beatrice! Was it a bad one?" Skelly was a Claddachman, born and bred, and understood the obligation to those cast up on its shores.

"Close to twenty men saved, and I understand there were fewer than thirty aboard. This gentleman was a passenger. I've said the castle will look after him. Can you assign footmen to sit with him tonight? He will need watching until he recovers consciousness, the doctor said." She grimaced. "I am sorry to put a further burden on you when you are already dealing with the suitors."

"I will need to speak with Mrs. Johnson about a room," Skelly began, but was interrupted by the housekeeper herself.

"A room for whom? This man?" Mrs. Johnson sent a jaundiced glance at the stretcher. "You can take him somewhere else," she scolded the stretcher bearers. "Lady Beatrice, come along and get out of those dreadful clothes. You will be late for dinner."

Mrs. Johnson, while not Claddach-born, had known Bea for most of her life and unfortunately often forgot that Bea was now an adult, and no longer to be instructed like a child. Now, Bea decided, was a good time to remind the woman who was in charge of whom.

"Mrs. Johnson, this is Mr. Redhaven, who was a passenger on the wrecked ship. He will be staying here, at least until he regains consciousness, and longer if he needs our hospitality. I think the tapestry room will be suitable to begin with. Close enough to the servants' stairs for those who are watching over him while he is still unconscious. The men will carry him up the main stairs, however, as the servants' stairs are too narrow and too steep."

Wringing her hands, and wailing, "What will the countess say?" Mrs. Johnson nonetheless stepped out of the way.

ALARIC WOKE TO the sound of rain beating on a window. Of course. The storm. But no. He was not still on the ship. The room was not rocking. Nor could he hear ropes rubbing, or the bangs, clatters, and shouts of a busy crew.

He opened his eyes. Sure enough, he must be ashore, for he was in a room with stone walls softened by tapestries. A comfortable room kept warm by a fire, the tapestries, and heavy drapes over, he supposed, the window. The room was softly lit by the fire, a lamp, and a scattering of candles.

The young woman standing beside the bed captured most of his attention. The young lady, rather. She was dressed for the evening in a gown of figured silk, with pearls at her neck and scattered and twined in her dark hair. A *pretty* young lady, with large lustrous dark eyes and a warm smile.

"You are awake, Mr. Redhaven. How are you feeling?"

Alaric thought about that. *Bruised. Sore everywhere.* "As if I have been nailed into a barrel and rolled downhill," he admitted. "What of the ship? The captain? The crew?"

"As far as we could see before sunset, the ship is in bad shape," she replied. "It was lodged on the rocks. Probably, it will be broken apart before daybreak. I have no word of the captain. We recovered nineteen people, including you. There may be more by now. We have left watchers on the cliff and on the beach and will keep a fire burning all night."

"We" was in interesting pronoun from a lady who looked as if she belonged in a Society ballroom rather than a beach in a storm. Perhaps she meant her servants, but clearly, she was more involved in the *recovery*, as she called it, than her appearance suggested.

"Where are we?" he asked. "On the coast of England? Ireland?"

"Neither," she informed him. "You were shipwrecked off the coast of the Isle of Claddach, south of Mann and perhaps halfway between Ireland and Wales. You are in *Cashtal Vaaich*, the home of the Earl of Claddach."

Claddach. He had never heard of it. But she had heard of him, he realized. "You know who I am."

"I know you are Mr. Redhaven," she corrected. "One of the sailors said you were their passenger. You are a gentleman, then?"

"I try to be." A confused gentleman, and one that was as weak as a kitten. "May I be permitted to know your name, my lady?"

She chuckled. "How rude of me. I am Beatrice Collister, daughter of the Earl of Claddach."

"And I am Alaric Redhaven, second son of the Earl of Elsmouth. I am pleased to meet you, Lady Beatrice. I apologize for not standing, but I think I would fall over if I did." His head was pounding. He must have hit it, though he remembered nothing after the decision to leap from the sinking ship.

Lady Beatrice smiled. "Stay where you are, Mr. Redhaven." She stood. "I just popped in to see you on my way to retire. I am so pleased you have recovered consciousness, but I recommend you go back to sleep. Tomorrow will be soon enough for you to try to get up." She gestured to someone behind her, and a footman stepped into Alaric's field of vision. "If you need anything, ask Colyn here, or Gilno, who will be replacing him at midnight."

"Thank you. And please thank your father for his hospitality," Alaric said.

That fetched him another bewitching smile. *"Vaaich* is pleased to offer you refuge. Goodnight, Mr. Redhaven." She left the room in a rustle of silk; it seemed emptier and far less hospitable in her absence, somehow.

"His lordship'd be surprised to be thanked, and so he would," Colyn ventured, after Lady Beatrice had left. "I'd wager our lady hasna mentioned ye yet, sir. An earl's son, is it? Well, perhaps our earl'll be pleased to have ye here, at that. Now, sir, is there anything ye need for yer comfort afore ye sleep?" The accent had a lilt something like Irish. Or perhaps Scots. Halfway between would fit the geography Lady Beatrice had described.

Alaric tried to make sense of the footman's words about his host, but all his attention was required to stay upright, with Colyn's help, to—as the man put it—deal with his comfort. As soon as his head was back on the pillow, he sank back into sleep.

Chapter Two

WHEN ALARIC WOKE again, the room was lit by daylight rather than candles and the lamp. Reluctant daylight—the rain continued to pound the window—but bright enough for him to see the room in more detail.

A different footman was dozing in one of the chairs by the fire. Gilno, Alaric assumed. He jerked awake when Alaric struggled into a sitting position.

"Sir," he said, standing and stepping toward the bed. "Good morning." His accent was thicker than Colyn's—his *d* almost a *t*, and his vowels so different to what Alaric expected that he had to make a mental translation.

"Good morning," he replied, after a moment.

"Be ye more yerself this day, sir?" the footman enquired. "It's a good long sleep ye've been after havin'."

"I am better, thank you." Alaric's reply was untrue. He ached everywhere, and was conscious of bruises on his head, his shoulder, and his thigh that formed the foreground pain against a background of generalized discomfort. Still, nothing felt broken or out of place, and bruises were always worse on the day after an injury.

"Doctor'll be by to see ye, sir," Gilno told him. "Milady, too. I'll get ye cleaned up a bit, if y'feel up to't."

"Lady Beatrice," Alaric said. Her visit last night felt like a dream, but he remembered the name.

"Aye, sir."

Alaric managed to swing his legs out of the bed and over the side but was grateful for Gilno's support when he dropped to the floor—the bed was higher than he expected and his knees were shaking. Various other parts of his anatomy were also complaining.

"Let me help ye to chamber pot," Gilno suggested, "then sit ye down while the hot water comes for yer wash."

With a great deal of help from Gilno, he washed, and dressed in a pair of loose pants, a shirt, and a man's silk dressing robe, with a kerchief knotted at the neck. No slippers or house shoes, for which Gilno apologized and offered stockings as an alternative. "But Lady Bea will find something to fit you, sir," he assured Alaric, who was beginning to acclimate to the accent and easily understood that he owed his current attire to the earl's daughter.

By the time Alaric was done, fatigue was weighing him down, but he refused Gilno's suggestion that he return to the bed. "I will sit in the chair by the fire," he decided. He would feel more confident meeting the doctor, the young lady, and perhaps his host. He accepted the offered footstool. No point in being stupid about it.

Gilno brought him food and drink. A couple of slices of bread that Gilno toasted over the fire and—praise the merciful angels— a pot of hot, bitter coffee. Alaric managed one slice of the toast with some sort of conserve. He had a second cup of the coffee.

The doctor and Lady Beatrice arrived together, but the doctor sent the lady away while he examined Alaric. "I was right last night. Nothing broken," he said at last, after prodding and poking Alaric in uncomfortable places, looking into Alaric's eyes, examining the bruises, and removing various dressings and replacing them. "Rest for a few days, young man. You're lucky to be alive, but you have come away with little more than a bad headache. I'll order some willow bark tea for that."

He repeated his diagnosis for Lady Beatrice when she rejoined them. "I shall send my bill to the house steward," he declared, and Lady Beatrice thanked him.

"I have money," Alaric offered, but no. He'd put his money pouch in his coat pocket before leaving his cabin, but he'd removed his coat before jumping into the water so it would not weigh him down. He shook his head and sighed. "I lost it in the wreck," he admitted. "But if you send me an account, Doctor, I shall pay it as soon as I reach England. I do not mean to be a charge upon the castle."

The look Lady Beatrice gave him was nothing short of patronizing. "*Cashtal Vaaich* is not an inn, Mr. Redhaven. We do not present our guests with a bill."

Maybe so, but neither was Alaric a beggar, relying on the charity of others. Except at this moment, when he depended on the *Vaaich* household for food, clothing, the roof over his head, even his life. The knowledge pinched at his pride.

"You shall allow me to pay my own doctor's bill, Lady Beatrice," he said.

She looked at him, her head tipped to one side and with a thoughtful expression on her face. She was really very beautiful. He wondered why she was not wed, for she must be in her early twenties. But then, perhaps she *was* wed. He really knew nothing about her. "The doctor's bill," she agreed, her tone haughty. "I shall authorize the steward to pay Dr. Bryant, and to give you an accounting. Will that be satisfactory, Mr. Redhaven?" She lifted an interrogatory eyebrow.

"I meant no offense, my lady," he assured her. "I am truly grateful for your rescue and your hospitality."

"You need to rest, Mr. Redhaven," Dr. Bryant declared. "We shall leave you to Gilno's care. Lady Beatrice, you mentioned the kitchen maid's burn. Shall we have a look and see why it is not healing?"

The doctor was correct. Alaric was exhausted. He allowed Gilno to assist him and was soon sinking into the blackness of sleep, his last thoughts lingering on the lovely Lady Beatrice.

Bea had been lucky last night. She had managed to get Mr. Redhaven up the stairs and into his bedchamber without being seen by her parents or any of the guests and had even been able to dress for dinner and arrive downstairs before her mother became testy.

It was midafternoon before Bea's mother discovered that the household had acquired a guest. Bea had been meaning to tell her, but the countess did not emerge from her bedchamber until after eleven, and then immediately summoned Beatrice to her sitting room.

Before Bea could introduce the subject of Mr. Redhaven, her mother said, "This rain means we cannot have our planned excursion into the town, Beatrice. We will need to make alternative arrangements. I thought some games in the long gallery. Archery, perhaps, dear, and skittles. You know the sort of thing. Then we can have music and perhaps charades in the large drawing room. Make the arrangements, there's a dear."

"Mama, I need to tell you—"

"Not now, dear. Our guests will be looking for amusement soon, and I have no time to waste, and neither have you. I must dress, and you must pass on my instructions to the servants. Hurry along, Beatrice."

What instructions? Mama gave no thought to what was possible or how to put her ideas into practice. That was Bea's job, with Mrs. Johnson and dear Skelly as her lieutenants. Bea had, of course, made contingency plans for poor weather, but archery and skittles had not been on the list, so she would have to scurry to make things happen.

Ah well, she would tell Mama about Mr. Redhaven later.

But first, she must speak to Cook, for they had been planning to purchase food at the town market while they were out, and now the kitchen would have to add a range of savory and sweet delights for those guests who had not fully satisfied their appetites in the breakfast room, where most of them were now gathered.

Once refreshments were organized, she moved on to the long gallery where she rallied some footmen to move any furniture, ornaments, or paintings that might be damaged by a stray arrow or ball from the long gallery into adjacent rooms and set up the room into zones for the planned activities. Skittles at one end, archery at the other, with the contestants facing away from the middle of the room, and the doors at each end of the gallery locked and bolted to avoid accidents.

Then lawn chess in the middle, and also space for blindman's bluff and musical chairs. For which they would need an instrument, so she sent for one of the small harpsichords. She would ask Aunt Joan to play.

She left the servants hurrying to and fro marking out the boundaries of each activity and setting up the equipment and moved on. The drawing room was simple enough. Enough chairs for those assembled, all set up and facing the row of doors to the music room, which she opened ready for music and then charades.

She had better tell Mrs. Johnson that a second round of comestibles should be served with tea and coffee in the drawing room in time for people to arrive from the long gallery. And then, perhaps, a glass of wine or some other such drink after charades before people went up to change for dinner.

The small drawing room was her next destination. The guests gathered there at around noon every morning. Mama would greet them all, once she was dressed, confident that she could announce the changed program to her guests, and that everything would proceed without a hitch.

Which it always had, though Mama had never troubled herself with ways and means. Aunt Joan had always been the moving force behind Mama's successful house parties, and she had trained

Bea to take over from her.

After that, her time was taken up with The Suitors, all of whom wanted her attention, or, rather, the attention of the Heiress of Claddach.

There were five of them, all invited so Bea could choose one to be the next lord of Claddach—in fact, if not in name. Her father had been firm. "You must marry, Beatrice, and you have consistently argued against going to London, so we have come up with a solution."

He had held up a hand to silence her when she would have protested. "Your mother and her sister will select appropriate candidates to come here for a house party. It is my hope you will find one of them suitable. You are in your twenties. Your mother assures me your marriageability decreases by the year. Your breeding potential is also reducing, and it is your task, your most important task, to give birth to the next Earl of Claddach. Preferably while the current earl is still above ground."

Mama would never have been so blunt, but the cattle of Claddach were Papa's pride and joy, and clearly, he thought of her, too, as he did of his prize heifers.

Her father had been happy enough to encourage her to follow him and his land steward all over the island, to study the books, to argue the time of planting and the best new bull for the herd. He had even, in recent years, handed many of his local tasks over to her so that he and Mama could spend more time in Mama's beloved London.

But Bea would never be the boy Papa had wanted. At best, she was only a place holder for her eldest son, the next Earl of Claddach. Ach, she was being unfair. She knew her father loved her, but he had no confidence in her ability—or in any woman's ability—to protect Claddach from the politicians in London without a male to represent her at court and in the clubs where the gentlemen gathered.

She understood why Papa was anxious about what he called her breeding potential, too. Papa had delayed marriage until he was in his forties and had then married a childless widow in her thirties. Several months later, Papa's older brother had died in a shipwreck with his wife and two sons, and Mama's age became a matter for concern. Papa was convinced Mama's age was the reason she had given birth to only one child. Disappointingly, a girl.

And now Papa was unwell. She did not wish to believe him mortal, but she would not shy away from reality, either. The doctor said a cancer was eating away at his gut. She would be Countess of Claddach sooner than any of them had hoped.

Bea sighed. Papa was right. Producing a son should not be put off much longer, definitely not for more than a year or two, and if it had to be done, why not do it now? And to produce a son who could be her heir, she had first to marry. And, to have a male who could represent himself as her protector when her father was no longer in this life, she would have to marry. There was no way around it.

So, the house party went ahead, with the possible candidates for her hand plus a few other people to make up the numbers. She had already told her father her opinion of the candidates. Her father had told her she was being picky.

Papa had investigated the twenty names on the list Mama and Mama's sister Aunt Lewiston had written. "I removed the town fops, the idiots, and the fortune hunters," he had said. "Any of the five who have accepted your Mama's invitation would be a suitable father for your sons and consort for the Countess of Claddach when I am gone. Pick one. Draw a name out of a hat. Hold a contest."

"Perhaps we should have a tournament, like the knights of old," she had retorted. "Or you could chain me to a rock for a dragon to eat and give me to man who kills the dragon."

"Trials of some kind are not a bad idea," Papa had mused, ignoring her sarcasm. "See what they are made of. We'll do that. But if you have not chosen by the end of the house party, my girl, I will expect you to have an extremely good reason for putting us through this exercise again."

As she smiled her way around the long gallery, fielding florid compliments and refereeing pointless disagreements, she asked herself, *Is Papa correct? Am I being too picky?*

But no. Surely it was not too much to ask that she respect the man she would be bound to for the remainder of her life? That she actually liked the man?

Respect and liking would do. She did not demand love. Papa and Mama had fallen in love. They loved one another still—she supposed. But they were so different—had such different lives and interests—that their lives barely intersected. Bea wanted more. She needed more, for she was choosing not just a husband, not just a father for her children, but the man who would be lord of Claddach in all but name.

Sir Henry Dashwood hurried up to ask her when the archery contest would begin, and proceeded to explain to her exactly how the point system would work. The point system she had organized. Sir Henry, he was happy to explain, was not too modest to declare that he was a champion archer.

So far, all the suitors fail to impress.

"I have a small objection to the way the contest is organized, Lady Beatrice. I hope that does not offend?" said Sir Henry.

"Please," Bea said, trying to modulate her tone and not let him know that internally, at least, she was rolling her eyes, "give me the benefit of your wisdom."

The man was so dense that her sarcasm prompted a satisfied smile. "I am sure you are doing your best, my lady," he assured her. But then he frowned. "Lady Beatrice, the ladies should not be permitted to enter today's contest."

Oh dear. "It is a friendly contest, Sir Henry. Some of the ladies wish to join in. Some, I know, are excellent archers."

"Yes," Sir Henry complained, "but they are ladies!"

And you, sir, are a cork brained twit.

Sir Henry obviously would not do. When the contests began in earnest, Bea was going to have to find a way to make sure he failed, although she was reasonably confident that he would manage failure without her intervention.

As the thought crossed her mind, Mama and Aunt Lewiston came hurrying up.

Uh oh. Mama was doing her best to keep her temper hidden, and to smile at the guests, but Bea could see she was in one of her states. "You will excuse Lady Beatrice, Sir Henry, will you not? I just need her for a moment."

Aunt Lewiston smirked.

Bea kept her own smile in place and followed the two ladies out of the room and into one of the adjacent parlors. *One. Mother has discovered I responded to shipwreck last night. Two. She has found out about Mr. Redhaven. Three. Both.*

Aunt Lewiston shut the door. Mama, keeping her voice low, demanded, "Who is this man you have been hiding in the tapestry room? Where does he come from? Who is his family?"

Aunt Lewiston chimed in, "Beatrice Elizabeth Meave Collister, what have you been up to?"

"Mama, the gentleman was a passenger on the ship that was wrecked last night. I told Mr. Kinred we would look after him." Which was true, even if it did skate over the fact she had been on the beach, and that bringing Mr. Redhaven to the castle was her idea.

"And who is he?" Aunt Lewiston demanded.

"His name is Mr. Alaric Redhaven," Beatrice replied. "He is the second son of the Earl of Elsmouth. I have no further information, Aunt, except that he speaks like a gentleman, and the sailor who identified him as a passenger said he was one. I daresay he will be able to tell us all about himself now he is conscious. Dr. Bryant says that none of his injuries is life-threatening."

The sisters exchanged glances. "The Earl of Elsmouth," Mama repeated, the name clearly taking some of the wind from her sails.

Not so Aunt Lewiston. "Why did you keep this man a secret

from your mother?" she demanded. "You take too much on yourself, Beatrice."

"Not a secret, Aunt. I had not yet told Mama, it is true. She has so much on her mind with the house party. Last night, he arrived just before dinner, and this morning, Mama had all the worry of the rain, and the activities to replace the picnic."

Mama nodded. "That is true, and the last thing I needed to worry about was some shipwrecked sailor."

"It was very thoughtless of you, Beatrice," said Mother's one-woman Greek chorus.

Beatrice ignored her aunt and answered her Mama. "He is a gentleman, Mama. Not a sailor."

"I shall be the judge of that," Mama pronounced. "Come, Dorrie. We shall meet this so-called gentleman and decide for ourselves."

Aunt Lewiston contented herself with a harrumph of displeasure and said to Mama, "We shall see what this Mr. Redhaven has to say for himself. Even if his name is, in fact, Redhaven, Mary, that is no guarantee he is related to the earl. Why, England must be full of Redhavens who have no more claim on Elsmouth than Skelly!"

Beatrice sighed once they had left the room. She had visited her father this morning, in his study, and had explained the events of the previous evening. He had already heard from the rector with a report on those rescued and those believed to be lost. He approved her actions, but she would not use that trump against Mama unless she had to. Mama had subtle ways of making her daughter uncomfortable that Bea's father would do nothing to prevent.

She hoped Mr. Redhaven was awake, but he would have to fend for himself this afternoon. Beatrice was needed in the long gallery to judge the archery contest. She wondered what sort of an archer Mr. Redhaven was when healthy. Surely, with those shoulders, he would be able to beat Sir Henry and probably the rest of her guests.

Chapter Three

A LARIC SLEPT FOR several hours and woke to find Colyn moving around the room with exaggerated care, obviously trying not to make a noise. "What time is it?" Alaric asked.

Colyn, who had been bent over the open drawer of a clothes press, jerked upright, then turned to Alaric with a smile.

"It is early afternoon, sir. Or not early so much as first part of the middle if you take my meaning."

Two or two-thirty, perhaps. Depending on what Colyn regards as the middle.

"What have you there?" Alaric asked next. He certainly didn't need to worry about servants rifling through his things. He had no things! Perhaps the usual occupant of this chamber had left something he needed in the clothes press, though the room had the look of a chamber that was little used.

The footman held up a stack of white cloth. "Shirts, sir. You now have trousers, coats, and neckties. Also stockings, sir. Lady Bea told us to see what could be found in the attics. To dress you, sir, since your own clothes went down with the ship." He looked entirely delighted with himself.

It went against the grain to accept such charity, but Alaric could not walk around in his borrowed silk banyan until a letter to his father could be written, sent from the island, delivered, and result in a return missive with money to pay for a new wardrobe and a ticket on a ship out of here. He forced a smile and said, "That was kind of Lady Beatrice."

"Do you need to get up, sir?" Colyn said. "Shall I help you?"

"I shall try on my own, Colyn." Alaric had to do something to assert his independence, and his pride held him up as he got out of bed and crossed the room to the dressing screen and the washstand behind it. He was pleased to lean against the washstand once he'd arrived, but he was out of Colyn's sight, so he would count it as a win.

I will feel better tomorrow, he promised himself. Rounding the side of the dressing screen again a few minutes later, he asked Colyn, "Could you lay out something for me to wear, and then help me change? I will just sit here by the window for a minute."

A desk was under the window, and its straight chair looked as if it would be much easier to get up from than the chairs by the fire, which had presented quite a challenge earlier in the day. He was pleased to know nothing in his thigh and knee was broken, but they hurt as if there were, especially as his knee, which had no interest in bending.

Colyn looked overjoyed to be given the task, and hummed happily around the bedroom collecting an item from here and another from there until he was satisfied. "Very well, sir. I've the blue coat, the buff breeches, and the cream and blue waistcoat. Also, the cream stockings with the blue clocking, and the dark blue cravat."

Alaric nodded his approval. "That sounds splendid." Colyn was clearly in his element.

And yes, when Alaric approached the bed where the described glories were neatly laid out, he discovered that the blues all matched and so did the creams. The styles were well out of date—presumably the reason the items had been relegated to the attic. But at least Alaric would be tidy and respectable. And grateful, he reminded himself. Lady Beatrice and her servants had been very kind.

What of Lady Beatrice's parents? Were they in residence, and did they know their daughter was being generous with the contents of their attic?

As Colyn helped him into the coat, with protests from his scraped and bruised shoulder, there was a knock on the door. Colyn gave the coat one more tug then went to answer the knock, while Alaric did up the buttons on the double-breasted front.

Two matrons bustled into the room. "The Countess of Claddach and the Countess of Lewiston, Mr. Redhaven," Colyn announced.

The two countesses were too much alike to be anything except sisters, and either one of them could have been Lady Beatrice's mother. The thought crossed his mind that they were evidence Lady Beatrice would keep her good looks into middle age.

"My ladies," he bowed, calling on his training as a gentleman and a diplomat. "May I be permitted to know to whom I owe thanks for the hospitality of this house? I am very grateful."

The slightly shorter of the two ladies dimpled when she smiled. "I am Lady Claddach," she informed him, graciously.

He bowed again. "I owe my life to your townspeople, my lady, and the fact I continue to breathe to your daughter, for welcoming me here, and your servants, for making me comfortable and watching over me while I slept."

Lady Claddach accepted a heavy helping of his charm with a simper, but Lady Lewiston was examining him as if he had been carried in on the gardener's boots instead of being scraped off at the door. Time to drop a name. In fact, *the* name. "I know my father, the Earl of Elsmouth, will also want to express his gratitude." Now that Tarquin had a son, Elsmouth would probably be quite happy for his spare to drown, but no need to tell the ladies that.

"Elsmouth's son, are you?" Lady Lewiston's tone was rich with suspicion. "The second, you told my niece. Of course, with this dreadful weather, you could lay claim to any name and lineage, and we would not be able to prove you a liar."

"Or a truth-teller," Alaric pointed out, trying to keep his irritation out of his voice. He was not accustomed to being called a liar. "I am the son of Elsmouth, my lady. Though I cannot prove it at this moment, I believe I can at least take your comments with the courtesy a gentleman owes a lady."

"Bravo!" declared Lady Claddach. "He has you there, Dorrie. He looks like a gentleman, you must admit. Smoothly shaved. Clean hands, if a little scratched, but that will be the shipwreck. Let me see the palm, Mr. Redhaven. See, Dorrie? No calluses."

Alaric was tempted to ask if they wanted to examine his teeth, but he kept his tongue still.

"I think we should ask him to join us," Lady Claddach announced. "The trials will soon show us what he is made of."

Trials?

"Mary, no!" Lady Lewiston appeared horrified. "Another suitor? I thought we were agree..." She shut her mouth mid-word, leaving Alaric to wonder what the two ladies were plotting, but the words "another suitor" gave him pause.

He spread his hands. "Ladies, I wish only to recover from my ordeal and continue my journey to England and to my home. I do not wish to be any trouble to you."

"You will be less trouble if you are part of the house party," Lady Claddach said, decisively. "You can join whatever activities you are well enough to enjoy. Of course, I do not expect you to compete to win my daughter's hand. She has suitors enough. But I do expect you to show you are a gentleman." She held up a hand to stop whatever complaint her sister was about to voice. "No, Dorrie, my mind is made up. It does not change anything. Good day, Mr. Redhaven. We shall excuse you from dinner this evening, but after that, your valet shall be given the day's program while you are at breakfast."

The two ladies left the room. Colyn caught Alaric's eye. "I take it the valet would be me, sir," he said, his voice full of suppressed laughter.

"This is not funny, Colyn," Alaric warned.

"Well now, sir," Colyn told him, "it is after being just a little bit funny. Lady Lewiston wants Lady Bea for her own son, you see. But Lord Claddach said Lady Bea's husband cannot be anyone with his own lands and title, for when Lady Bea is countess, she will need her husband to manage the lands in her name. His lordship might spend most of his time in London on account of his lady, sir, but he is a Claddachman, born and bred. He don't want an Englishmen putting his English lands first, see you, ahead of our sweet island."

"I see," Alaric commented. So, Lady Beatrice was an only child, was she? And her father's heiress for title as well as estates? Unusual, but it made it all the more surprising she was unwed when she must be in her twenties.

"Lady Bea never wanted to have her Season," said the chatty Colyn as if reading Alaric's mind, "and her ma let her be, thinking she would be more likely to marry Lord Beverley if she hadn't met anyone else."

Lord Beverley? Alaric had been to school with a Viscount Beverley. Come to think of it, that was where he had heard the name Lewiston. The despicable viscount was only too happy to tell lesser mortals he was son and heir to the Earl of Lewiston. And according to Beverley's view of the world, all other mortals were lesser.

Colyn continued, "When my lord decided it was time for Lady Beatrice to find a husband, he told Lady Claddach and Lady Lewiston to make a list of suitors. The list had twenty names, I hear tell, and Lord Beverley was one of them. My lord struck the name off and ordered his lady to produce another younger son or the like."

"Annoying for Lady Lewiston," said Alaric. No wonder she had already decided she did not like him. In her mind, at least, Alaric was a rival to her son. Not that Alaric had any interest in these contests, or in marrying Lady Beatrice. Lovely though she was. And little though she deserved a husband like Lord Beverley.

"The earl had them investigated," Colyn continued, "and picked his five preferred candidates, but downstairs, we think the ladies chose twenty men Lady Beatrice won't want any part of. For a more dismal lot you could not hope to meet. Four of them without a skerrick of sense and one who doesn't want to be here. That's what we think downstairs, anyway. She won't have her cousin though. She cannot stand the man."

In that, Lady Beatrice showed herself a woman of sense.

It was nothing to do with Alaric, in any case. He would dutifully attend any house party activities he could not gracefully avoid and leave on the next available boat. Or, since he would have to send to his father for the money to leave, on the next available boat after his father replied to his letter.

Which he would have to ask Lord Claddach to frank, since he did not have a bean to his name.

Alaric shuddered.

THE SUITORS ALL entered the archery contest. So did three of the four young lady guests and Mr. Maddrell, Papa's secretary.

Bea's cousins, Dorothy and Lucy Hetherington, were more interested in giggling, and in admiring the young men than in hitting the target, but Lucy had a natural aptitude that left her in the game after Dorothy, Mr. Maddrell, and one of the suitors, Mr. Ambrose Howard, failed to survive the first three rounds.

The Fairweathers, brother and sister, were leading on points going into the fourth round. Lady Eleanor Fairweather was at the house party to make up numbers, but her brother, Mr. Martin Fairweather, was a Suitor.

They ended the fifth round still in the lead, though Lord Lucas Versey and Mr. Ambrose Howard were not far behind. Lucy was still in, but Sir Henry went out in the fourth round and

Mr. Francis Meadowsweet in the fifth.

Those dropped from the game stood with the other guests, cheering for their favorite and commenting on form. Sir Henry added to the negative impression he was making on Bea by complaining loudly about all the factors that had prevented him from showing his usual form. He then tried to talk some of the other gentlemen into going off and playing billiards with him.

Mama and Aunt Lewiston arrived back from their visit to Mr. Redhaven halfway through round six. "I have told Mr. Redhaven he is to join the house party," Mama said, when she came up with Bea. "See to it, Beatrice."

"It is a mistake, Mary," said Aunt Lewiston. "You mark my words. We do not know for certain who this young man is. I can only imagine what Lewiston will say when he hears."

Bea doubted her uncle would do more than raise a sardonic eyebrow, and his reaction did not matter, in any case. Her father had approved Mr. Redhaven's presence in the castle, and her mother wanted Mr. Redhaven in the house party.

Bea supposed it was remotely possible that someone—some gentleman—had boarded the ship under a false name and then carried on with the ruse after being shipwrecked. Mr. Redhaven seemed a pleasant enough person, though. He was certainly handsome. And charming.

It might be quite amusing at that to see what the suitors and the other house guests made of him. Especially in the clothes the poor man would be forced to wear. With her father's permission, she had made Conyl and Gilno—both of whom aspired to be valets—free of some old trunks from the attic. Clothes her father had worn when he was younger and, as he put it, *slenderer*.

The two footmen had been looking forward to making some changes of clothing for their castaway gentleman from her father's castoffs. They would no doubt be delighted to meet the challenges of a house party.

Lucy had been outshot in round six and Mr. Howard in round seven. Lord Lucas and the Fairweathers were evenly matched,

Bea thought. The honors would go to whoever didn't make a fatal mistake. And there. Mr. Fairweather had shot wide.

He bowed out with a smile. "I muffed it," he said to his groaning supporters. "Eleanor's still in though. Ten pounds says she can take Lord Lucas."

In the next round, the three arrows the remaining pair shot were so close it was impossible to pick a winner. With an eye on the clock, and conscious that Sir Henry was not the only person who was becoming restless, Bea made the decision to declare them joint winners.

She would need to find another prize for the charades, she thought, as she presented a vase to Lady Eleanor and a silver goblet to Lord Lucas, both from the attics.

"Now to the drawing room for refreshments and then charades," she said, trying to sound happy about the prospect. To think that this was just the introductory week. She and Papa had decided to give the suitors a week to decide whether or not to join the contests. What would it be like when the real trials began?

Chapter Four

THE RAIN STOPPED late in the evening, and by the following morning the sky showed no trace of the storm. Bea woke early and scrambled into her riding habit. Normally, after a big storm, she would ride out with Papa and his steward to see what damage had been caused to the farms and the roads, but when she saw Papa in the stable yard, he shook his head. "Better stay with the house party, Beatrice. I shall probably be out most of the day."

One of the grooms brought out Papa's big stallion, and he mounted without another word, and rode off in the direction of the main gate. Out all day? In his condition? *If I were male, would he have dismissed me so easily?*

Bea walked off her feelings along the clifftop, from which she could see what remained of the wreck on the reef offshore. The garden, too, showed damage from the storm, with broken trees, flooded hollows, and several miniature landslides along the paths on the steeper slopes.

As she stopped to look up at one bank where soil had slumped, leaving the roots of a tree exposed, a male voice called her name. "Lady Beatrice!"

She suppressed a sigh. Could she not even have this quiet morning hour without having to entertain one of the suitors?

Apparently not, for Mr. Howard was walking toward her with a pleasant smile.

"You are out early, Lady Beatrice."

Mr. Howard had lost yesterday's match with grace, she reminded herself. And he was certainly easy to look at, even if he did go walking in the morning before breakfast dressed as if he had stepped from the pages of Ackermann's Repository. Perhaps she should take this opportunity to get to know him better. "I am surveying the damage from the storm," she told him. "I suspect that tree will have to be brought down, and the upper path rerouted."

He cast a cursory glance up the slope, and then his smile widened and turned patronizing.

"Such matters are best left to the gardeners, I am certain, my lady. I am sure your parents would not want you worrying your pretty head. Perhaps, if you were particularly fond of the tree, they will order another planted?"

Not worry my pretty head? Fond of the tree? Was the man a complete dunce? Bea understood from her cousins that her upbringing was unusual—she had been raised knowing that Claddach would be hers and taught what she would need to do to be a good steward of the land and people. She supposed she could not blame Mr. Howard for treating her like any other unmarried lady of his acquaintance. But did he speak to all ladies as if they were children? And witless, careless children at that?

Could the man adjust his attitude, though? "You misunderstand, Mr. Howard. As future Countess of Claddach, all this island is my concern, from the garden here at the castle to the crops in the fields of the meanest tenant farmer. I should be riding with my father as we speak. He will be gone all day, reviewing the storm damage across the island." She sighed. "But it would be rude to our guests for both of us to desert them, and so here you see me. Carrying out the least of my duties by cataloguing tasks for the gardener."

He was staring at her, uncomprehending. He blinked hard

and gave his head a little shake. Clearly, it didn't work to reorder his thinking, for he adjusted his expression to another empty smile and stepped closer to her than she liked, almost touching. "My dear Lady Beatrice, how delightful that you try to help your father. You must long to lay such unwomanly burdens on the shoulders of a husband. How fortunate that man who wins your favor."

His voice dropped to a husky drawl on the last sentence, and he stepped even closer. She had only a brief moment to evade his hands as they came up, presumably to hold her shoulders.

She ducked away from them, stepping backward and sideways in time for the kiss intended for her lips to fall on empty air.

"I daresay food has been laid in the breakfast room, Mr. Howard," she said, as she walked away, but the man hurried after her and had the temerity to take hold of her hand in such a firm grip she had to stop or engage in an undignified tugging match.

"Mr. Howard," she began, crossly.

But Mr. Howard had a speech to deliver, and no intention of allowing her a word in edgewise until he had delivered it. "Lady Beatrice, from the moment I first saw you, I have been consumed by admiration and, dare I say it? Desire. Such beauty! Such poise! Such grace! I cannot believe I am alone in this passion. Say you feel it too, dearest, most glorious Beatrice. May I call you Beatrice? And you shall call me Ambrose, and your own."

"No," Bea said, decidedly, and tugged at her hand, hang how undignified it appeared.

The stupid, stupid man looked decidedly bewildered, but kept tight hold of her.

"But I esteem you," he insisted. "Greatly."

They both turned at the sound of slow clapping. "Yes, we heard," said Mr. Redhaven, who was leaning against the concrete corner plinth at the bottom of a flight of steps, just a short distance away. "Such beauty. Such poise. Such lands and house. Do release Lady Beatrice's hand, Mr. Howard. You are gripping it tightly enough to bruise."

Bea was released so suddenly she fell back a step, and Mr. Howard curled his hands into fists. "Sir, I do not know who you are, but I beg leave to tell you that you are impertinent. Get you gone, sir."

Mr. Redhaven inclined his head. "Alaric Redhaven, and it would be insincere, I fear, to say at your service. At Lady Beatrice's service, however. May I escort you into breakfast, my lady?"

"You may," Bea said, and was surprised to find that her voice was shaking.

"I will escort Lady Beatrice," Mr. Howard insisted.

"You will not," said Bea. "I do not wish to see you, Mr. Howard, until you have amended your discourtesy. When I say 'no,' I mean 'no.'"

She took Mr. Redhaven's offered arm and walked away, Mr. Howard's voice following her. "I do not despair, Lady Beatrice. It is a lady's privilege to change her mind."

ALARIC HAD COME out to the gardens because Gilno said he would be able to see the wreck from the clifftop. He had stopped partway to rest, leaning against a handy wall. While he felt a lot better today, he was still a bit shaky on his legs.

Lady Beatrice's irritated voice saying "Mr. Howard" had attracted his attention. It came from just around a bend in the path he had been following. When a gentleman spoke over her to declaim his undying passion, Alaric had a hunch that the lady might need rescuing. In ten paces, he was around the corner and though within sight, figuring he could retreat as quietly as he'd come, if the lady was receptive to the posturing idiot's advances. He'd found another bit of concrete wall to lean against and discovered he was glad he'd decided to overlook the situation. She was trembling as they walked away, and he wanted to go back and plant the man a facer. Perhaps she expected him to do so?

Before he could ask, she spoke. "That man," she said, her voice sounding much calmer now, "is an idiot. Two, at least, of my suitors have straw for brains. How could my mother and aunt possibly think they would make an acceptable consort to the Lady of Claddach?"

The trembling, Alaric realized, was as much anger as residual fear. "If they are all as bacon-brained as that one, none of them will do," he said. Should he warn her the servants thought her mother and aunt were conspiring to make her marry her cousin? He did not want Colyn to be reprimanded. Nor, for that matter, did he want to lose his own source of intelligence. No, he wouldn't say anything just yet. Best to see how things developed.

In the breakfast room, Alaric was introduced to a Mr. Maddrell, a Mr. Whittington, and a Mr. Meadowsweet. Maddrell, it transpired, was the earl's secretary, and Whittington his chaplain. Meadowsweet, then, must be one of the five suitors from the infamous list.

Lady Beatrice was the only lady in the room, and it soon became clear that Meadowsweet had risen early in order to monopolize her attention. Alaric's presence put an unexpected spoke in the man's wheel, as did Lady Beatrice's determination to include all four gentlemen in the conversation.

Alaric wondered if Meadowsweet was the other man that Lady Beatrice had referred to as having straw for brains. It was a little disturbing that he felt compelled to prove his own intelligence. He found himself asking questions about Claddach, starting with its most notable products—a specific breed of sheep and another of cattle, cider, and woven woolens.

Maddrell, Whittington, and Lady Beatrice were all happy to contribute to the answers. Meadowsweet objected that the conversation was unsuitable for ladies, to which Lady Beatrice said, "What I find unsuitable, Mr. Meadowsweet, is ignorance. I suspect most ladies are glad to know about the sources of their family income. As for me, I have been raised to be Lady of Claddach, and such matters are very important to me."

To give Meadowsweet credit, he rallied, and offered a few questions of his own. He showed poorly even in that, since what he knew about animal husbandry, brewing, and weaving could all be inscribed on his signet ring with room remaining for the seal.

When the conversation turned to Claddach's history, however, Meadowsweet came into his own, having some pertinent and thoughtful facts to offer about the impact of the Vikings, the Scots, the Saxons, and the Normans in the county of his birth. All four, plus the Irish and the Manx, had contributed to the history and culture of the island.

The islands, rather. Though the name was the Isle of Claddach, there were two major islands, one slightly larger than the other, separated by a narrow sea channel with a walkable causeway at low tide, plus dozens of smaller islands ranging in size from a large farm to a rock fit only for seals and seagulls.

Howard arrived just as Lady Beatrice was finishing her breakfast, listened for a moment, and then broke into the conversation as if none of the other men were here. "Lady Beatrice, you cannot possibly be interested in a conversation about fishermen and their catches. Gentlemen, do none of you know the proper topics of conversation with a lady?"

Alaric listened to Meadowsweet's response with some enjoyment. "Lady Beatrice is not an empty-headed ninny, Howard. She enjoys talking about the topics that are important to Claddach, such as its farming, its fishing, and its history. Do you not, Lady Beatrice?"

"I do," the lady confirmed. "Mr. Meadowsweet, Mr. Howard, I have much to do to prepare for the day's activities. May I leave you to look after Mr. Redhaven? He is a late arrival and does not know how to find the drawing room, the billiards room, and other places of interest."

The secretary and the chaplain also excused themselves, and Alaric found himself subject to an interrogation on his lineage, his arrival, and his intentions.

The arrival of an older lady and her daughter promised a respite, but it was a false promise. The ladies proved to be Howard's mother and his sister, and the interrogation resumed, with added questions designed to probe into his marriageability. It seemed that Lady Beatrice was not the only bride on offer to the bachelors at this house party.

Alaric was reasonably certain Lady Beatrice would scorn to entrap a husband using any of the tricks that had been employed against his older twin, their father's heir. He was not so certain about the other ladies. He took the precaution of making certain Mrs. Howard knew he was unemployed, had only modest means, had been replaced in the line of succession by his brother's son, and was out of favor with his father.

Even so, he would be certain not to accept any invitations to a private meeting with any of the ladies present.

Chapter Five

F ROM MR. REDHAVEN's appearance in the garden the second
morning after the storm, he became as much part of the
house party as if he had been there from the beginning. They
made the postponed excursion into the town of Bailecashtel that
day, and he walked down the hill from the castle with the others,
showing no sign of weakness or pain.

Bea's friend Reina Ransome had accepted her hasty invitation
to balance the numbers. She joined the visitors on their explora-
tion of the market and the other sights offered by Bailecashtel and
returned to the castle with them in the late afternoon.

Mr. Redhaven took a seat in one of the carriages for the uphill
trip, Bea noticed. Sensible man. He did not feel the need to show
off how fit he was, as some of the suitors were doing, turning the
simple walk up the hill into a feat of courage and daring by
walking the top of stone walls and ascending vertical banks rather
than going around by the zig-zagging road.

For the last few days of the introductory week, the two new
guests joined in all the activities as if they had been there all
along. Mr. Redhaven's presence bothered the suitors. Bea had
expected it. Though his borrowed clothes were out of date, they
fit his form well. He was taller and more handsome than any of
them. Also, he was more clever, and more charming, and

absolutely more capable of outcompeting them at billiards, charades, and the evening card games.

Mr. Howard and Sir Henry were hostile—not openly, but in their body language and in finding reasons to disagree with anything Mr. Redhaven said. Mr. Meadowsweet, by contrast, looked up to him, and was inclined to copy what he said and did. Mr. Fairweather was cautious. Only Lord Lucas treated him with neither reserve, nor excessive adulation.

Bea was also not surprised by his impact on the unmarried ladies. Bea's cousins were making complete cakes of themselves over the man, searching him out with impudent questions and giggling when he spoke to them. Lady Sarah Howard was more subtle, but just as persistent. Mr. Redhaven managed to deflect all three without giving offense, treating them much as he did the matrons, with charming courtesy.

Even Reina Radcliffe, who was betrothed to Papa's secretary, blushed when Mr. Redhaven paid her a compliment, as did Lady Eleanor, Mr. Fairweather's sister. Bea was almost certain that Lady Eleanor and Lord Lucas, who had been smelling of April and May since the archery contest, would make a match of it.

Those parents who were there with their offspring fell into two camps. Aunt Lewiston continued to regard Mr. Redhaven with the utmost suspicion, and Lady Dashwood, Sir Henry's mother, concurred entirely. The Earl of Lewiston and Mr. and Mrs. Howard declared him to be a fine young gentleman, and Bea's mother agreed. What Bea's father thought he kept to himself.

To Bea's annoyance, what she was beginning to think of as "the Redhaven Effect" extended to herself. How dare Mr. Redhaven cast all her suitors into the shade, when he was not one of them?

On the day before the trials were to begin, the first ship into the harbor since the storm brought her cousin William to Claddach. William, Lord Beverley. Whom her father had clearly told Aunt Lewiston and Mama would not be permitted to marry

Bea. Not that she would have him, even if he won all the trials. Not even his sisters liked Lord Beverley. Only his mother, and to a lesser extent, her mother. To them, he was perfect.

However, here he was. He presented himself at the castle and was shown to the drawing room. "My entire family is here, dear Aunt, so I thought it fitting to join them," he drawled.

"You are very welcome, Beverley, of course," Mama cooed, exchanging a conspiratorial glance with Aunt Lewiston.

The three of them had planned it, Bea realized. Papa looked at each of the conspirators in turn, and then at Uncle Lewiston, whose face showed no reaction. Had he, too, just realized that his son's presence here on this day was part of an audacious scheme to put Beverley in the running for Bea's hand. Or was he one of the conspirators?

The potential family altercation had an audience, too. Most of the house party guests were gathered for predinner drinks. Would Papa turn Beverley away? It was not beyond him. The Lord of Claddach was the law on Claddach, and he was not accustomed to being deliberately defied.

Bea found herself holding her breath.

"Ah, Beverley," Papa said. "You are just in time. After dinner, I shall be announcing the rules for the trials of the suitors. You will not want to miss it, I am certain. Beatrice, dearest, do we have a closet or some such left in which we can stow your cousin?"

"I think we can do better than a closet," Bea told him, both relieved and disappointed to miss a bout of paternal fireworks. "I shall make arrangements. Cousin Beverley, do you wish to freshen up after your travels? Dinner is in thirty minutes."

Beverley followed her out into the hall. "Cousin, you are looking more delectable than ever. Are those fellows back there your suitors? Hardly the pick of the litter. What was Mother thinking?" His smile was smug.

Bea ignored him. The housekeeper must have heard about Beverley's arrival, for she was coming up the stairs. "My lady,

Lord Beverley," she said. "My lady, I have sent maids to prepare the green room, and his lordship's valet will be waiting there for his lordship."

The green room was an excellent choice—one of the best rooms still available, but not in the family quarters, where Beverley would be far too close to Bea for her comfort.

"Very good," Bea said. "Beverley, Mrs. Johnson will show you the way. I will see you at dinner."

Who could she invite to balance the table? Mama would have to put up with an uneven table this once, but she would not take the offense quietly, so Bea had better think of a suitable female, and send the invite before Mama began to fuss.

There was really only one possibility—Dr. Bryant's daughter Christina. She had only been on the island for eighteen months and was more of a friendly acquaintance than a friend. But all of Bea's close friends except for Reina were married.

Would Christina be insulted at being invited to make up numbers? Bea had better visit her in the morning and explain the situation in person.

After dinner, when Mama gave the signal for the ladies to leave the table, Papa stood and asked the gentlemen to also proceed to the drawing room. They all obeyed, of course, though some gave lingering glances at the port decanters. Not Mr. Redhaven, she noted. He followed Mama with a pleasant smile that suggested he would like nothing better.

Those who feared missing their port need not have worried. The decanters and glasses were presented with the tea trays while the guests were still settling into chairs and onto sofas.

Skelly supervised the delivery of glasses of port, brandy, or other libations, while Bea poured tea, chocolate, coffee, or herbal tisane for a maid to take to those who preferred such a beverage.

Papa waited until the drinks had been served and the servants had left the room before taking up a position before the fireplace and clearing his throat.

Instantly, he had everyone's attention.

"My ladies, my lords, gentlemen. You all, I think, know the reason for this house party. Apart from the pleasure my wife and I take in your company."

He paused to permit the polite chuckle the assembled guests obligingly produced.

"The rumors are true. My daughter has agreed it is time for her to marry."

"She could have been presented at Court and enjoyed a Season in London at any time for these past five years," objected Lady Lewiston. "And so I have said before, Claddach."

After a considering look at his sister-in-law, Papa replied, "Beatrice felt strongly, and I agreed, that she was needed here on Claddach, and that those gentlemen who were most likely to make her a good match were also busy on their estates or fighting for our safety or otherwise engaged in productive work."

"Gentlemen," sneered Beverley, "are not required to work."

What a chaw-head Beverley is.

Papa lifted an eyebrow at him. "I am not referring to manual labor, Beverley, though such work is not to be scorned, but the labor of the mind and spirit. It is that which makes our class fit for government. Gentlemen with healthy estates and investments had better know that kind of work. Younger sons who take up a profession had better know that kind of work."

He allowed his gaze to roam the room, focusing on the younger gentlemen. "Even younger sons who are independently wealthy had better take an interest in the investments on which their wealth is based, or they risk destitution. When I attend events in the London Season, I see that each family has a few idle wastrels supported by the labor of someone else in their family, either living or in previous generations. None of them will do for Claddach."

He took a sip of his port before continuing. "I decided, and Lady Claddach and Lady Beatrice agreed, that anyone who wishes to wed Lady Beatrice must first compete in a number of trials. There will be twelve in all, and they begin tomorrow."

He once again focused on the younger gentlemen. "You have until noon tomorrow to decide whether you are a competitor for the lady's hand. After that, you may refuse any trial you wish, and your reasons for doing so will be considered in the final accounting. You may remove yourself from the list of contestants at any time. Are there any questions?"

ALARIC HAD MORE questions than answers. What were the trials? Was Lord Claddach the sole judge? What attributes would he be looking for? How would the winner be decided? Was Lady Beatrice bound to marry the winner? Could any of the unmarried men at the house party enter?

More to the point, did he want to enter?

He listened as others spoke the questions he was thinking.

"You will sometimes be informed a particular activity is one of the trials," Lord Claddach was telling someone who wanted details about what he would be expected to do. "On other occasions, it will simply be something on offer as one of the activities for house party guests. I encourage you to involve yourself in as many of the activities as possible."

Lord Beverley was clearly taken aback. "Then how will we know whether or not we are competing, Uncle?"

"You will not, Beverley," replied Lord Claddach. "This is not a tournament, where the person with the best seat on his horse and largest sword walks off with the prize. This is a test of the attributes I believe will make the best husband for my daughter, and the best consort for her when she is Countess of Claddach. If you only put forward your best when you know you are being tested, the whole exercise is futile."

"Then I take it, Claddach," the Countess of Lewiston said, "you are prepared to include Beverley in this… exercise." She wrinkled her nose as if she scented something foul.

Lord Claddach's smile was predatory. "All the young unmarried gentlemen guests are welcome to compete. I hope they will. Redhaven, that includes you."

Lady Lewiston opened her mouth with an expression that presaged an objection, but her husband touched her hand and shook his head, and she subsided. Their son had a thunderous frown but said nothing.

"Will you decide the winner, my lord?" asked Meadowsweet, then gulped, as if his own temerity terrified him.

"Lady Claddach, Lady Beatrice, and I shall consult on points to be awarded," Lord Claddagh replied. "We shall also agree between us the list of those who will be permitted to pay their addresses to Lady Beatrice. The final decision shall be hers. It may be that no one proves to be suitable. It may be that Lady Beatrice cannot see living the remainder of her life with any of the successful candidates. I am not promising the winner or winners my daughter as a bride. You are merely being given the chance to show your mettle before my daughter and, in fact, the other eligible ladies."

A few other minor questions on process were quickly dealt with by way of referral to the earlier statement. They would not always know an activity was a trial, but they would sometimes be told. The earl would say no more.

Most of the young men were looking thoughtful. Fair enough. Alaric was feeling the same way. He should be arranging his passage to Liverpool and on to Hampshire, to his father's seat, but the more he thought about the trials, the more he understood this to be the chance of a lifetime.

His own place. Lands and their people to care for, to cherish. He had been hoping for a position on the land, working for the benefit of someone else's family, since his father would not permit him a place on an estate belonging to the Elsmouth demesnes.

How much better to be giving his energies to the lands and people of his wife, the lands that would one day, God willing, belong to their eldest son, and his descendants down through the ages?

Wasn't marriage a cheap price to pay for everything he had ever wanted?

None of that was confusing. What was giving him pause were his feelings about Lady Beatrice. Feelings made the whole matter more complicated. He would welcome a civil and affectionate marriage. One in which he and his wife both gave value. A marriage of friends and partners who supported one another.

As far as that went, he thought he and Lady Beatrice could rub along rather well.

Nor did he see it as a problem that he desired the lady. Far from it. He would relish the process of producing the sons Claddach required, and he'd make sure she enjoyed it, too. Even the thought had him shifting in his seat.

But Alaric knew himself to be in danger of falling in love with the lady if he hadn't done so already. He recognized the symptoms. He had been in love before, and it had ended in disaster every time. Furthermore, he had seen marriages that began as love matches and devolved into misery. *Love is a game for fools.* Hadn't he seen—hadn't he found that it only led to heartache. When he married—if he married—love was the last thing he would look for.

Countess Lewiston's daughters were asking their uncle what they were to do while the men were busy with the trials.

"You shall not be neglected," Claddach assured them. "Many of the activities will be open to everyone, and if you choose not to join in, or if the activity is not suitable, Lady Claddach or my daughter will ensure you are suitably entertained."

"We can be part of the trials, Dorrie," Miss Lucy told Miss Hetherington, smiling broadly.

"But I am certain, dear ladies," said Mr. Howard senior, with an avuncular smile, "that Lord Claddach will not require you to marry Lady Beatrice, even if you win."

Everyone laughed at that, though Lady Beatrice looked

pained. Poor lady. The "husband hunt," as Alaric's brother used to call the Season, must be bad enough for unmarried ladies, with all the pressure on them to find a suitable husband, but at least other young ladies were facing the same challenges in the same places at the same time.

At this house party, all the focus was on Lady Beatrice and who would win her. The five other young ladies might also be interested in some of the men, but at least any courtship that might develop could do so in relative private. By choosing this path to marrying off his daughter, Lord Claddach had ensured his daughter's wooing would be the main topic of interest here in castle and undoubtedly across the entire Isle of Claddach.

Which didn't make Alaric feel any better about being part of it.

And yet... *Can I bear to miss the opportunity?* He could not have said, even to himself, whether the greatest attraction was a place to call his own or the lovely Lady Beatrice.

Chapter Six

A LL THE UNMARRIED gentlemen were present in the drawing room at noon the following day. Alaric, who was one of the last to arrive, took up a position leaning against the mantelpiece from which he could see and hear the others but was not part of any group. Maddrell and Whittington hovered to one side, talking neither to each other nor to anyone else.

Beverley was holding forth to Ambrose Howard and Sir Henry Dashwood about how he was certain his cousin would choose him. "She has always admired me," he boasted. "I will exert myself to charm her, and the job will be done."

Dashwood snorted. "She doesn't respond to charm," he claimed. Which meant Dashwood had tried, Alaric noted.

Beverley was not impressed. "She will, to mine."

"You still have to pass Lord Claddach's trials," Howard pointed out.

"I am a master of any gentlemanly skill," Beverley declared. "Foils, pistols, boxing, riding, driving. I have no concerns."

The other three of the original suitors were closer to Alaric, so he heard Lord Lucas Versey's response to that boast, which was pithy, vulgar and—in Alaric's view—entirely apposite.

"Ignore him," Martin Fairweather advised. "He's all mouth."

Francis Meadowsweet nodded. "True. I have seen him box."

Perhaps Beverley heard them. If so, he did not feel inclined to challenge the three.

Instead, he addressed Alaric. "Don't you have other places you ought to be, Redhaven? You just turned up in the storm, they tell me."

"I have no urgent engagements," Alaric replied, resisting the urge to point out that Beverley was another person who had not been invited.

Lord Claddach spoke from the doorway. "I have welcomed Redhaven to my home and to the trials, Beverley." He crossed the room to his usual chair. "If you are unhappy about my decisions, you are not obliged to stay."

Beverley flushed red, and the sore look he sent Alaric behind his uncle's back promised retribution.

"I take it, gentlemen," Lord Claddach said, "that you have all decided to enter the trials?"

He waited for a chorus of murmured agreement. Except for the secretary and the chaplain, they all expressed their intention of competing in the trials.

"Very well. A short while ago, your valets were given your first clue in a treasure hunt. I expect the hunt to take several days—perhaps the full two weeks remaining of the house party. You will therefore be undertaking the treasure hunt while completing other trials and continuing to please my lady wife by entering into her planned activities in the house party, any one of which might, or might not, be a trial. As to the treasure hunt, you will be given a new clue every time you bring me evidence you solved the last one."

Clever. Those who decided the known trial needed all of their own attention might be neglecting an unknown one. Indeed, Alaric would not be at all surprised if one factor in judging the trials would be whether a contestant failed to take Lady Claddach's feelings into account when setting their priorities.

Alaric wondered how many of the others had figured out that every one of Claddach's servants would probably be feeding information to their master to help him judge each trial. Every servant? Every islander, more likely.

Colyn's gossip had made it clear they were all anxious about the choice that Lady Beatrice must make. Whatever local custom and Claddach's last will and testament said, and whatever papers the lady's groom might sign before the marriage, in a court of law, a husband had absolute power over his wife. Even if, as in this case, he would not hold the title of earl when Lady Beatrice became countess, he would still be his wife's legal guardian, and anything she owned in her own right, rather than as countess, would belong to him, as would the children she bore.

Of course, every islander would care about the trials, and would tell the earl anything they observed.

"That is all," Lord Claddach said. "May the best man win."

The gentlemen stampeded upstairs to ring for their valets. Alaric did not bother to run. Given Claddach's words, he fully expected Colyn to be waiting for him. Gilno had returned to his regular footman duties, but always had a smile for Alaric when he saw him.

Sure enough, Colyn was waiting patiently in Alaric's bed-chamber. "Did ye enter the trials, sir?" he asked, as soon as Alaric entered the room.

"I did," Alaric said.

Colyn grinned, broadly. "Well, then. That's good. I have a clue for ye, sir. For the treasure hunt."

He handed over a piece of paper that, when opened, proved to have a short piece of doggerel written on it.

"Watch time crawl by with leaden feet.

The son of night reigns, as is meet.

But hark, young man, as time takes flight.

Beneath, a picture of delight."

The son of night was the god of sleep—Somnos in Greek mythology or Morpheus in Roman. He couldn't make head or tail of the rest of it. Unless... "Colyn, do the grounds have any sundials?"

"Yes, sir. Four. No, five, for there is one at the top of the southern watchtower." Colyn explained where they could be found.

It had to be sundials. *Or clocks. Clocks mark time as well.*

"I suppose there are many clocks in the castle," he said.

"That there are, Mr. Redhaven, to be sure. The one in the drawing room. The one in the great hall. Her ladyship has one in her private sitting room. There's one in the kitchen, too, and in the butler's pantry, so he can make certain the meals are on time."

He was counting on his fingers as he stared into the middle distance, his eyes half-closed. "The earl has a clock in his study. Does the stable block count? The tower of the stable block has a clock."

Alaric supposed he would have to work his way around them all, and hope he saw something that triggered another idea. He hoped he didn't meet all the other contestants doing the same thing.

"This afternoon, sir, will be an archery contest," Colyn told him. "Luncheon will be served at one o'clock, and the archery contest will be at two."

So much for an immediate tour of the castle's timepieces. Still, Alaric would surely be able to look at the clocks in the drawing room and the great hall on his way to the dining room, and he'd find a way to take a look at the stable clock and the sundials before sundown.

"Thank you, Colyn. Am I presentable?" He spread his hands and stood still for Colyn's inspection.

The footman/valet brushed at some invisible dirt and mused out loud about whether Alaric's cravat should be retied or even changed, but when Alaric said he wanted to investigate clocks for the treasure hunt, stopped his fussing and wished Alaric luck.

But neither of the clocks Alaric found gave him any bright ideas. Except that none of the other suitors gathered in the parlor next to the dining room were showing any interest in the clock.

Was he the only one to think of time devices after reading the poem? Did that mean he was wrong?

Or was it possible they all had different clues? Alaric wouldn't put that past Lord Claddach, though it would take a great deal of work. Not work he could give his secretary, either. Not if the young man had been permitted to enter the trials.

Beverley was monopolizing Lady Beatrice, ignoring everyone else who was in the group where she had been standing. Lady Beatrice kept trying to bring others into the conversation, but Beverley kept talking over them, addressing all his remarks to the lady of his choice, and ignoring everyone else. What a knob-head the man was.

Lady Claddach and Lady Lewiston strolled into the room together and almost immediately, the butler announced that luncheon was laid out in the dining room. "We will serve ourselves," said Lady Claddach. "Delightfully informal. And you may sit anywhere for this meal. Beverley, will you take me in, dear?"

Beverley looked furious to be drawn away from Lady Beatrice, but he obeyed his aunt, however reluctantly. Alaric moved quickly across the room. "Lady Beatrice, may I have the honor of escorting you to the dining room?" he asked, offering his arm.

"Thank you, Mr. Redhaven," said Lady Beatrice.

"Shall I escort you to a seat and fill you a plate, my lady?" Alaric asked, as they made their way through the double doors. "Or shall I hold a plate for you while you select what you prefer from the sideboards?" He'd noticed that no servants remained in the room, so his bright idea of co-opting a footman to carry a tray would not work.

Lady Beatrice shot him a look of startled appreciation. "The second," she said. "Can you hold a plate for each of us, Mr. Redhaven? And I shall serve you and myself."

Lord Lucas and Lady Eleanor had followed their example, Alaric noted, as Lady Beatrice filled their plates while he followed faithfully behind her. The other gentlemen had led their ladies to chairs at the table and were roaming the sumptuous selection of cold meats, salads, fruits, pastries, breads, and other delights, either balancing two plates or filling one with the intent of going back for another.

Alaric saw Lady Beatrice to a pair of chairs and assisted her to sit. "What will you have to drink, Lady Beatrice?"

She chose an ale, and Alaric collected a jug and two glasses and returned to find Beverley had taken the seat next to Lady Beatrice, having abandoned her mother, whom he had led into lunch and seated farther up the table.

Alaric put the jug and glasses before Lady Beatrice, smiled at her, located an unused chair and brought it over, squeezing in between Lady Beatrice and Miss Radcliffe, who obligingly moved her chair to make more room.

"I say," Beverley said. "You cannot squeeze in like that."

"Evidently," Lady Beatrice noted, "Mr. Redhaven has squeezed in. So, I take it you meant to say he may not, rather than he cannot."

Beverley glared at her. "His manners are outrageous," he told the table at large. "No wonder he was sent home in disgrace from the British Embassy to Brazil."

He sneered at Alaric, triumph in his eyes. "I remembered this morning where I had heard of you. Sent off to Brazil to make a career in the diplomatic service."

Uh oh. Alaric supposed it was inevitable that news had reached London. It was too much to hope the toffee-nosed prawn hadn't also heard of the former scandal. The one from before Brazil.

Did Beverley just remember the gossip this morning? Possibly. But certainly, he had waited for the largest possible audience.

"Funny. He left London in disgrace after a fight with his brother at his brother's wedding. You are that Alaric Redhaven, or you not?" He raised his voice to be heard around the table.

"I am," Alaric replied. He met Lady Beatrice's eyes with a rueful smile. "One does wonder at my father, does one not?

Thinking I was cut out to be a diplomat?"

"You must have had a reason for fighting your brother," Lady Beatrice said. It was not quite a question, but one was implied.

Alaric said, his voice quiet and his answer for her alone. "It was more that he fought me, but yes, there was a reason. I am afraid I cannot share it, however. It is not my story alone, you see." Tarquin had punched Alaric in the nose. For an insult to Tarquin's wife, he had said. Alaric assumed Eloise had denied she had been the one to jilt Alaric. And the fight at the wedding was nothing to the explosion the following morning, when Tarquin involved their father. Truly, Alaric could not altogether blame his twin. Falling in love did terrible things to a man's judgement. Another reason for him to eschew the emotion altogether.

"I daresay," sneered Beverley, who had leaned closer to hear Alaric's reply. "How convenient that honor prevents you from telling us the reason for such dishonorable behavior." The rest of the company had hushed to hear the scurrilous hound. "I suppose the same excuse applies to your ejection from Brazil. It was over a woman, I heard."

My, my. How stories grow in the telling. Though technically, the rumor was correct. "There was a woman," Alaric conceded. "But not in the way you imply." He made an instant decision to be open about the whole debacle. Undoubtedly, rumor had painted his actions every shade of black, whereas the truth was farcical rather than villainous.

He addressed his next remark to Lady Beatrice, though in a loud enough voice for everyone to hear. "There was a slave. Though she was heavily pregnant, she was serving drinks after dinner at the home of one of the aristocrats of the Portuguese court in exile. I was present, as were other members of my embassy. She slipped in a pool of wine and fell, splashing the wine she was carrying on a young Portuguese gentleman. He kicked her where she lay. In the stomach. When he went to do it again, I punched him."

"Good for you," said Lady Beatrice. "And the ambassador

sent you home for that?"

Alaric shook his head. "Sir Edward, the British envoy, sent me away from the party for that. He said I should have left it to the Portuguese to deal with the matter. In his opinion, her status as a slave made my reaction unworthy of an international incident."

"A fine tale," Beverley said, in a voice that implied he believed none of it. "And I suppose you will tell us you were not thrown out of Brazil at all? Or perhaps you went down to the marketplace and freed all the slaves waiting for auction?"

"Nothing so grand," Alaric conceded, grinning at Beverley as if the man had made an amusing joke. Bullies found such a response very confusing, he had found. He glanced around the table. Everyone was waiting for him to speak. "I *was* thrown out of the diplomatic mission and sent home from Brazil," he admitted. "Sir Edward said my inability to smile at a villain or a knave for England meant I was not cut out to be a diplomat, and I believe he was absolutely right. To be fair to Sir Edward, the final straw was by no means the first time I had shown my incompetence in diplomacy."

"What was this final straw?" The question came from Lady Joan Collister, Lord Claddach's sister.

"It was at another reception, my lady," Alaric explained, speaking over Beverley's claim that no one was interested. A clear bouncer since the room was silent while Alaric spoke and indeed Lady Joan was leaning forward with an intensely rapt expression on her face. As were the rest, he noticed.

"A few days after the incident with the slave, at a different reception. Dom Duarte, the slave kicker, made aspersions. I ignored him, as I had been instructed to do. He then pretended to trip, so that his wine splashed all over me."

He met Lady Beatrice's eyes and chuckled, hoping she would see how funny it was. "I probably should not have picked up a nearby bucket of icy water—we had drunk the wine that was in it. And, I definitely should have checked that nobody else was within range when I threw it."

He spread his hands and shrugged. "Duarte ducked. The Bishop of Rio de Janeiro did not. The bishop was not pleased, and neither was the king. And so, Sir Edward sent me home and told me to find another profession."

There was, of course, a great deal more to the story. But some of it needed to be kept secret and none was for public consumption. Perhaps, too, Alaric had done the wrong thing. Or several wrong things. Sir Edward had certainly thought so. But, he reminded himself, Alaric was not one to accept cruelty to anyone, and especially not to someone of lower status by someone of a higher status—in society's eyes. He found such a tendency appalling and was content in the knowledge that he was the better man—at least in character—than the man he'd punched or even, the bishop. If that meant he'd failed at his task, so be it. Hang anyone who cherished status over sympathy. He had no use for them.

"A member of a diplomatic mission cannot go around diso-beying the laws of his host country, Redhaven," Sir Edward had said, "however appalling those laws might be. Sometimes, it is our duty to tolerate, or at least ignore, an injustice for the sake of king and country. You are an honest man, my boy, and that is to your credit. It makes you a bad diplomat. A pity, for your habit of making friends wherever you go would be useful, if you could just learn not to make just as many enemies."

Alaric did not set out to make friends any more than he tried to make enemies. "I just try to be honest, sir," he had told Sir Edward.

The envoy had nodded thoughtfully. "Indeed. Just remem-ber, though, that honesty, when carried to extremes, is a kind of arrogance." Alaric had thought a lot about those words during the long journey back to England and had still not come to any conclusion. Sir Edward had a point, but was Alaric's honesty of that type? He didn't think so, and he didn't want to be in a profession where he would feel disgust at himself.

For now, Beverley's plan to ambush Alaric had backfired.

That was obvious from the approving looks Alaric was receiving. It was obvious to Beverley, too, for he was scowling. He opened his mouth, but before he could speak, his uncle said to him, "You came in with your mother, I believe, Beverley. It is the custom on Claddach to sit with the lady you escort into the dining room. That was still the practice in London last time I was there, I believe?"

I should watch my back, Alaric thought, as Beverley made his grudging way around the table but not before he shot Alaric a look that boded nothing good. Predictably. But then, Beverley had been disposed against Alaric from the first, so nothing had changed.

Miss Radcliffe asked a question about Brazil, and for the remainder of the meal, Alaric's part of the table engaged in a lively discussion, starting with the places he had been and the things he had noticed, and moving from there to the travels of others.

When the meal was over, Alaric asked Lady Beatrice if she would excuse him, as he planned to walk in the garden before the archery, though in truth, he was on a hunt for sundials. Lady Beatrice declared herself ready for such a walk, and what could Alaric do, other than express his delight in her company?

By the time they were strolling out through the garden door, he had decided to show her the clue and tell her what he was looking for. He was sure she could be trusted, and if she couldn't? Then she was not the wife for him.

"I would like to see as many sundials as I can before two o'clock, my lady," he said.

She looked puzzled, but she pointed to a diagonal path that led from the little courtyard outside the door. "This way, then."

Alaric obediently set off down the path with Lady Beatrice on his arm. He said, "I have my treasure hunt clue, and I have an idea of what it might mean." He took the clue from his pocket and handed it to Lady Beatrice.

"Should you be showing this to me, Mr. Redhaven?" Lady Beatrice asked, not opening the folded paper.

"I am not competing with you, my lady," Alaric pointed out.

"Why shouldn't I share the clue with you? And what I think about the clue?"

"You do not fear I will tell the other suitors?" she insisted.

"I do not," he assured her. "For two reasons. First, I judge you to be trustworthy. Second…" He shrugged. "If I win, my lady, but do not have your regard, there will be no marriage, nor should there be. I do not believe you will lose my regard, my lady, but if you did, a marriage between us would be a mistake. If you prefer another suitor, then I wish you the very best."

"How delightful," Lady Beatrice commented. "A trial of my very own."

For a moment, Alaric was concerned his frankness had offended her. He was relieved to see her chuckling. Just in case, he added, "I do not mean any offense, my lady."

"None taken, Mr. Redhaven. I find your honesty refreshing, as well as your trust in my…" she paused a moment, "my intellect. In spite of the fact that I am a woman." She pursed her lips in a scowl that didn't fail to be pretty. Alaric reminded himself to focus on that intellect and not allow himself to be distracted by her appearance, for that would set him apart from the other suitors. "Let me read this clue, then tell me what you are looking for. *Hmm.* Yes, I see why you are looking at sundials. Or clocks, perhaps?"

"The first couplet seems to say that, when things are boring, you'll sleep," Alaric offered. "That is, assuming the son of night refers to the god of sleep in the Greek pantheon."

"When time drags. Yes, I see. But what of the second?"

Alaric had no idea and said so. "I am hoping something will occur to me when I see the correct sundial. Or clock. As you said, it could be a clock."

Such a moment of epiphany did not occur with either of the sundials they were able to examine before they needed to go to the north lawn, where the archery butts were set up and some of the other guests were already selecting their bows.

On the other hand, Alaric had, he thought, made significant strides in winning Lady Beatrice's esteem.

Chapter Seven

M R. REDHAVEN WAS excellent company. Bea enjoyed her walk with him and was flattered he had taken her into his confidence. Now on the range, she discovered he was a competent archer, but not as good as some of the others. They had split into heats this time, since there were more competitors, and Mr. Redhaven was knocked out in the second heat.

He then joined the onlookers and spent the remainder of the match cheering impartially for whoever struck the targets, and making light conversation. Charming conversation, but since he spread his charm equitably amongst all the ladies, and never trespassed into flirting nor gave a compliment that wasn't true, Bea acquitted him of insincerity.

She wondered about the story he had told over lunch. Trust Beverley to try to make trouble for one of his rivals. He would have done himself no favors with her father! Papa, she knew, was seeing the entire house party as part of his trials. And, unless she was very much mistaken, every servant in the castle—no, probably every inhabitant of the island—would be reporting back to Papa on how the suitors behaved when not under Papa's eye.

Which was frequently. With the excuse that he was busy with his duties to Claddach, Papa spent much of his time sleeping, presumably in his study, for he had not yet shared the seriousness of his condition with Mama. The situation made her sad, and she turned her attention back to the archery.

Her cousin Beverley was predictably patronizing to the other archers, particularly the women. When someone else shot better than he did, he muttered under his breath and scowled. At least he was less vocal about his irritation than Sir Henry, who once again had all sorts of reasons why his shots had been impaired by some factor beyond his control.

Lord Lucas won, with Lady Eleanor running a close second. "As winner," he declared, "I beg a boon of the ladies. Will you walk along the cliffs with me? Perhaps to the beach? We have plenty of time before dinner, do we not, Lady Claddach?" His eyes were on Lady Eleanor, who smiled and blushed. *Why is Lord Lucas courting me, when he is clearly taken with Eleanor?*

Mama said, "Yes, of course, Lord Lucas. Beatrice, dear, you would love to walk with Lord Lucas, would you not?"

Bea could have laughed at Lord Lucas's expression. The poor man. She took pity on it. "We shall all go," she proposed. "Or, at least, anyone who is interested?" She looked around at the young ladies, and then the gentlemen, most of whom were nodding.

So, it was quite a large group that set off down the cliff path to the beach. Bea had time to have a quiet private word with Mr. Redhaven before they left. "I cannot show you the other items you wanted to see, Mr. Redhaven. Do you know where to find them?"

He nodded. "I do, my lady."

But when she saw him in the drawing room before dinner, he reported he'd not found anything to help in his hunt. "Perhaps it is right in front of me, and I cannot see it," he fretted. He had more to say, she could tell, but he would not speak where they could be overheard.

It suddenly occurred to her to wonder if some of the others would make her their confidant. She hoped not. It would be too awkward to keep track of which man had told her what idea. On the other hand, perhaps they did not all have the same clue. She had not seen any of the others examining clocks or sundials.

Mama had paired her tonight with Sir Henry Dashwood. She allowed him to escort her into dinner and prepared to be bored.

BEA WOKE TO another splendid day, which promised well for the day's activity. Papa had planned a steeplechase—a horse race in which the riders would travel cross-country, choosing their own path, from village to village around the island, using church steeples as their guide point. Those who did not choose to compete could travel from lookout to lookout, watching progress, or could remain in the town to amuse themselves and receive the racers when they returned to the town square, which was both starting and finishing point for the race.

"My riding habit, Eunys," she told her maid.

"You are never competing, my lady!" Eunys exclaimed.

Bea would like nothing better, but neither Reina nor Christina were competent riders and Bea's Hetherington cousins had been horrified at the idea of competing with the men.

"No, Eunys. I am taking out the big shooting brake with some of the ladies."

All of the young ladies, in fact, she discovered when she came out into the courtyard beyond the stables. Also, Aunt Joan, who had agreed to come along as chaperone when Aunt Lewiston had objected to her daughters traveling in an open carriage on her brother-in-law's land without one.

Aunt Lewiston was upset that Papa had continued with his trials rather than welcoming her son with open arms and handing Bea over as his bride. Bea giggled at a sudden picture of herself, bound and gagged, so she could neither run from the church nor protest at the altar. For that was what it would take for a wedding between her and Beverley the Beast. Not even if Papa requested it of her, and he wouldn't.

There Beverley was now, mounted on a restless stallion, telling everyone else he had the best mount in the stables. Lightfoot Lochinvar didn't have the stable name of *Looby* by chance. It was a corruption of the word *Lhoobeyr*, the local word for a trickster, and a trickier more self-willed beast one couldn't wish to find.

The beast—the four-legged one—was undoubtedly handsome, though, and the pair looked the part. It remained to be seen whether Cousin Beverley would look as smart and as smug after Looby had landed him in a stream or the thickest part of a hedge. Looby had the strength and the stamina for a steeplechase, and could fly over hedges as if on wings—if he felt like it. He lost interest quickly, though, and if the ride bored him, he was prone to tossing his rider just to add some excitement.

Should she warn him of the probability? Only Papa had ever succeeded in making Looby mind his manners for an entire ride, and the fact that Papa had been choosing a quieter horse was a measure of his slow decline.

But no. She would not warn Beverley. If she said anything, he would take it as an attack on his ability as a rider, and not as an expression of honest concern.

Crebbin, the stable master was standing by the shooting brake. "How did my cousin Lord Beverley come to be riding Looby?" she asked him.

The stable master cast a glance heavenward, as if praying for patience. "He came down last evening, my lady, to choose a horse. Looked right through the stables and declared that yon demon-sprite was the best horse in the stable, and he would have him for the steeplechase."

He shook his head. "We tried to tell him what the horse is like, my lady. He wouldn't listen."

As she had thought. No point in her repeating the same warning, then.

Several more men emerged from the house and attracted the stable master's attention. Then Redhaven walked out of the stable with Woodpecker Bay, affectionately known as *Dhone*, which meant *brown*. Dhone, a big and muscular gelding, was a good choice.

Dhone was steady. He'd be as determined and focused at the end of the day as he was now. His alert ears were turned to Redhaven while his eyes surveyed the courtyard. "Yes, my fine gentleman," Redhaven was saying. "We are off for a ride. Do you like being in front? I imagine you do. You shall have your chance, Dhone."

He paused when he looked up and saw Bea and changed direction to come to her. "Good morning, Lady Beatrice. A lovely morning to see more of your beautiful Claddach."

"We have been fortunate with the weather," Bea told him. "Though here on Claddach we insist we have better weather than any of the nearby lands." *Is he well enough to ride?* No point in asking. He would certainly not tell her that he wasn't.

He chuckled. "Yes, Colyn was telling me that on Claddach, it only rains between midnight and dawn, and a man can walk around na—in shirtsleeves—all year around."

"But of course," Bea agreed, laughing with him. "I see you chose our Dhone for your mount."

"I think he and I will suit," Redhaven told her. "He seems like a sensible fellow."

Mr. Redhaven somehow seemed to use up the air in his vicinity, so she felt breathless and a little dizzy. It was very annoying. To give herself something to do, she gave Dhone a pat. "Any luck with your treasure hunt?" she asked.

"Not yet. I feel I am missing something. Fortunately, none of the others are crowing about completing the first clue. They would, would they not?"

"Are you so determined to win, Mr. Redhaven?" Bea asked, and then wished she had bitten her tongue before she asked the question. He would think she was flirting or asking for a compliment.

He took her seriously though, regarding her with his face

open and his eyes frank before he said, "Increasingly so, I find. I hope that is acceptable to you, Lady Beatrice." But he did not wait for her answer, twisting his mouth in a self-deprecating way and saying, "I beg your pardon. I should not ask. We have days of trials yet."

They were interrupted by the arrival of Aunt Lewiston and her daughters. "Is this our conveyance, Beatrice? Well, girls, up you go and take a seat. Use your parasols to shade your complexions." She gave Beatrice a smile that was closer to a baring of the teeth. "We are happy to wait while you encourage all of the competitors, dear Beatrice." Her expression as she turned her gaze on Mr. Redhaven was closer to a glare.

Mr. Redhaven seemed to find it amusing but managed to change a bark of laughter into a cough.

Bea admonished him with a frown and obediently went to speak with the other riders.

TODAY'S STEEPLECHASE WAS one of the trials. Lord Claddach had told them so last night, after dinner, and several of the men had hurried down to the stables straight away, anxious to pick the best horses. Alaric left them to it. He had dropped by the stables before dinner to take another futile look at the clock, and had fallen into conversation with the stable master, who turned out to be Colyn's uncle.

He'd been given a private tour of the stables, which were admirable. Clean, spacious, organized, and all the horses in magnificent condition. The stable master must have been pleased with his compliments, for when they came to Dhone, the big bay he was currently astride, the man had said, "I'll reserve this fellow for you for tomorrow's steeplechase, Mr. Redhaven. He has a steady temperament and great heart. He'll do you proud."

Alaric had almost refused. A steeplechase? When he hadn't

ridden since Brazil and was still recovering from the shipwreck? But what if it was a trial. Though he had been given the right of refusal, stubbornness perhaps, or maybe an unwillingness to give in to a weakened condition, made him say, "Thank you," instead. Just as well, as it turned out, for after dinner, Claddach confirmed it was a trial, and he might have lost his choice. Not that Claddach had any slugs in his stables. All the men were well-mounted, and they were currently comparing horses.

"You got the big bay!" Versey commented to Alaric, admiringly. "I asked for him last night, but the stable master said he was not available. You sly dog!"

"He is not as fine as Lochinvar here," Beverley claimed, then his participation in the conversation was halted because his mount objected to the proximity of the other horses. He tried to take a bite out of Dashwood's chestnut and did his best to unseat Beverley when he curbed the attempt. To give Beverley credit, the horse's efforts failed.

"He's going to have trouble with that one," Fairweather predicted.

Beverley was riding in circles around the courtyard. "He will settle once we are away," he assured anyone who cared to listen.

Perhaps. The stablemaster had warned Alaric against Beverley's horse yesterday evening. "Lord Claddach can ride him, sir, but he'll unhorse anyone else." *Did Beverley ignore the advice or was he not told?* Alaric had already noticed that none of the servants liked the young viscount.

The men were all mounted, and all the young ladies were in the shooting brake with a groom at the reins and Lady Joan as chaperone. "Lord Claddach will meet us at the market square, my lords and gentlemen," said Maddrell.

"Why didn't you say so before?" Beverley demanded, and without a further word, he wheeled his horse and headed off down the carriageway.

"Papa will not start until we all arrive," Lady Beatrice commented.

"What of Mama and the other parents?" Dashwood wondered.

"Their carriages were leaving from the front of the house as we came out," Lady Joan informed him.

"Then lead on, Lady Beatrice," said Versey, touching his whip to his top hat, and the men formed up around the shooting brake, so it progressed down the carriage way with a guard of honor.

The town was clustered around a harbor on the opposite side of the castle from the beach where Alaric had washed up. The castle crowned the top of the bluff between the harbor and the beach, and a wall winding around the hill halfway up marked the extent of the castle's park.

On the town side, buildings sprawled up the hill as far as the wall, but the town square was across the bridge at the bottom of the hill. As the cavalcade passed the gatehouse, Alaric could see Beverley crossing the bridge. Even from this distance, it was obvious his horse had not settled.

Nor was it any calmer when they arrived in the square. Indeed, both horse and rider were agitated—the one dancing on the spot and the other casting baleful glances at the other riders and longing looks at one of the streets from the square. The crowd that had gathered to watch the start of the race was giving them a wide berth.

The other riders, Alaric among them, rode to the corner of the square where Beverley waited, and Looby's dance became more frantic.

From his raised platform in the middle of the square, Lord Claddach lifted his hands, palms out. Everyone—riders, townsfolk, castle guests—stopped talking to listen to what he had to say.

"Gentlemen, the street you will take out of town has been cleared for the start of the race. You have all been given maps of the island, and you know the rules. You must check in with a race steward at each church on the island. You are free to make your own route once you reach the town boundaries. Be courteous to my people and respectful of their lands and livelihood. I warn you, the first rider back may not be the race winner if they lose points by breaking any of the rules. Good luck to you all."

He nodded to the man who stood beside him, arm raised with a flag in his hand.

"At the drop of the flag, the race starts," Claddach declared.

The flag dropped. Several of the riders left at a gallop. Looby danced in a complete circle before taking off after them. Alaric and Versey held their own horses to a trot. They had a long way to go before the day was done.

THE OTHERS WERE still in sight, leaving the church as Alaric and Versey rode into the first village. The man who must have been the race steward waited at the lychgate of the church and gave them each a soft leather bag and a numbered disk. "The bag can go in a pocket or be tied to your belt, sirs. Put the disks you collect at each church into the bag and present it to the race steward in the square at the end of the race. Also, if I might have your names, please."

It was the same at the next village, except the other riders must have chosen a different path, for the race steward told them they were the first to claim a disc from him. After that, they went cross-country down a ride away from the road, leaping hedges and a couple of streams. Dhone took the obstacles in his stride, as did Versey's mount.

At the fourth village, they paused to let the horses take a drink from a trough outside a tavern, and the proprietor brought them each an ale. "On the house, gentlemen," he told them, when Alaric tried to wave his away. He accepted it with thanks, feeling his lack of money keenly.

From that village, their planned route would have taken them through fields of hay ready for harvest. After a moment's

consultation with the farmer who happened to be on the path—
and the realization they'd interrupt the haying process and
perhaps damage the crops—they changed direction for a different
village.

Maddrell and Whittington arrived at the next church at the
same time as they did. They were participating in the steeplechase, even though they had made it clear in the dining room
they were not suitors for Lady Beatrice's hand. Alaric wondered if
they were there as observers to report back on the suitors. It
would not surprise him.

"Have you seen the others?" Versey wondered.

"We lost sight of Beverley and Fairweather after the first
church," Maddrell said. "The others went a different way." His
voice was heavy with disapproval.

"Through the hay," Whittington explained. "Not good form."

The village was on the slope of a hill, and the road to the next
led over the crown, where the ladies in the shooting brake were
waiting. Alaric and Versey reined in for long enough to exchange
greetings and to admire the view from the lookout they had
chosen. They could see Maddrell and Whittington on their way
to the next village in the valley they had just left—one that Alaric
planned to visit as he came back around the island. Down in the
next valley, two groups of riders galloped through fields, the
smaller group some distance ahead.

"We have pies," Lady Beatrice offered. "Would you like
one?"

They accepted, and let their horses graze briefly while they
ate the offered food. The snack for both men and horses went
down well, and then they were off again.

The course took them right around the main island. Claddach
was a little jewel of a realm. From what Alaric could see, the land
was rich and fertile, the people healthy and happy, the sea never
far away and often visible, with the breeze off the water scented
with salt and swirling over the fields to make the climate
comfortable.

Alaric and Versey stayed together. Time enough, as Versey said, to make a race of it between them for the last two villages, but for now the key was to stretch the horses, not strain them.

Now and again, they caught sight of the other riders, and spoke to two of them. Dashwood was sitting at a table outside a tavern at one of the villages. He was drowning his sorrows in the village ale. His horse had bruised his foot on a stone and pulled up lame, he explained, and so he was out of the race.

Fairweather had parted company with Beverley. "That horse of his is a devil," he said, when they met him while collecting a disc from one of the churches.

He chuckled. "It dropped him in a stream, you know. It has been trying to unseat him all day, but it finally succeeded. I swear to you, gentlemen, that devil-horse folded its legs and slid out from under him, leaving him in mid-air before he splashed down into the water." He chortled at the memory. "After that, the pair of them were in a fine temper, and I decided my horse and I were better off taking our own route."

Fairweather rode with them for a while, then struck off again on his own.

Then there were the spectators. The ladies in their shooting-brake came into view several times, and so did carriages with others of the house guests. In the villages, and outside farmhouses and cottages along the way, people turned out to watch the riders go by and call encouragement.

At several villages, refreshments were waiting. More ale. Cider. Lemonade. Cold meadow tea. Pies and buns with cheese. Grass and water for the horses.

At one church, the race steward offered to sell them disks for three of the other churches. Alaric and Versey both turned him down. Two villages after that, they came upon an overturned cart. It blocked the lane they were following, and a woman sat beside it, weeping into her apron.

Alaric swung down from his horse, and Versey followed a moment later.

"May we help you, ma'am?" Alaric asked the woman.

She lifted her head, her eyes wide with hope. "The cart," she said, gesturing toward it. "I canna set it right. I don't have the strength, and that's the truth of it. I don't suppose two fine gentlemen such as yourselves...?"

"Of course," Alaric agreed, and Versey nodded.

It was hard to see how it had happened. It must have hit a rut at speed, but even so it seemed impossible. It was turned so it was almost at right angles across the road. The woman must have released the horse, for it was grazing peacefully a little farther along the lane.

It took the pair of them around half an hour to right the cart and to put the horse back in the shafts. While it was still blocking the way, Beverley came along.

"Give us a hand, Beverley," Versey called to him, but Beverley just laughed.

"Out of the way, woman," he told the cart's driver, and he set Looby to the narrow gap between the hedge and the cart and galloped away.

Once they had the cart back on its wheels and had checked to see there was no damage, they worked together to set the horse back in its traces while the woman expressed voluble thanks.

"It is no trouble at all," Versey assured her.

"Are you sure you will be safe to continue?" Alaric asked.

The woman smiled. "I shall be fine, sirs, and grateful to you kind gentlemen."

Alaric swore he could feel his bones creak as he mounted. His body had not appreciated the effort needed to right the cart. The muscles used for riding for the first time in months were complaining loudly. Some of the deeper bruises from the shipwreck were singing counterpoint. And the headache that had dogged the first few days of his recovery was threatening again though it was just an ache at the moment. With luck, it would not get to the pounding, nauseous stage before he'd collected his final four disks.

Chapter Eight

A LARIC AND VERSEY reached the next two villages without any trouble, continuing the easy pace they had adopted all the way through. They were approaching the castle again. It sat on its hill in the distance, between them and the town. The ride they were on curved toward the coast, but the fields in the straight line had been harvested.

"Race from here?" Versey proposed.

Alaric nodded. If the worst came to the worst, he'd cling to the horse and hope Dhone had the sense to follow Versey's steed. And that he didn't fall off at Lady Beatrice's feet.

It wasn't too bad. Only two hedges to jump until the next village, and Dhone's gait at the gallop was as smooth as a man with a splitting headache could want. Alaric even arrived a few seconds before Versey and had his disc and was on his way before Versey could remount and follow.

He lost the advantage as they climbed the spine of hill that terminated in the cliffs holding *Cashtal Vaaich*. The English translation of the name was Castle Death, Colyn had told Alaric. It was on his right as Versey passed him and drew slightly ahead, but Dhone objected to the other horse being in front and put on a spurt of speed as they came down the slope on the other side. They galloped into the last village neck and neck. Versey was a stride ahead to the race steward at the church, but only because Alaric had to pause after he had dismounted, clinging onto the saddle to let the dizziness subside.

That meant Versey led off, and despite Dhone's best efforts, he kept the lead along the road that led into *Bailecashtel*—Castletown, in English.

Two other riders joined them, leaping a hedge from the left. Fairweather and Howard. They thundered into town, jostling for position, but a child darted out of a house after Versey had passed, and Fairweather and Alaric pulled up to avoid him. Howard put his horse into a leap without slowing, the horse's hooves clearing the little head by fractions of an inch.

He looked over his shoulder as he rode to see that a woman ran out of the house to retrieve the boy, who was laughing as if it had been a game. Fairweather and Alaric raced the few hundred feet to the square, Alaric just in the lead as they arrived. Alaric all but fell from his horse but remained conscious enough to praise Dhone for his magnificent efforts. Versey hurried to his aid, and so did Lady Beatrice, but Alaric assured them he would be fine if he could just sit down for a minute.

One of Claddach's grooms led Dhone away, and Colyn materialized from somewhere to offer him a shoulder. Lady Beatrice accompanied them to a chair, and Alaric sank into it with a thankful sigh. "We are waiting for the rest of the riders," she told him. "And for the race stewards and others to report to Papa so he can decide the winner."

Alaric had lost. He knew that. But he could hope he'd garnered enough credit to carry him through. He'd lost the archery, too. *Please God, may I do better in some of the other trials.* Especially now, as he beheld Lady Beatrice, he wanted to win the right to propose. He did not think she was impervious to him.

She was not fussing over him. She was chatting to the other ladies. But he caught the glances she aimed his way every minute or so, just checking on his welfare without being obtrusive or embarrassing.

He wanted her. More, perhaps, than was good for him. He was, he realized, seriously in danger of falling in love. Or perhaps it was already too late.

BEA HAD A long wait. Papa had people arriving every few minutes to give him information about the gentlemen and their conduct. In terms of who had arrived in the square, Lord Lucas Versey held first place. Beverley had arrived second, coming into the square only a few paces before Mr. Howard. Beverley was not on Looby, but on another horse. Looby, it turned out, had arrived at the stables riderless and appearing quite pleased with himself, long before any of the other horses or riders. The stableboys had groomed him and put him out to pasture, and then set about informing the rest of the household staff that the mischievous horse had come in first, though not as Lord Beverley had expected, much to their amusement.

Beverley told his mother that he'd borrowed another horse from someone who was watching the race. "He was reluctant to lend it to me, Mama, but I informed him that I was the earl's nephew, and he would be rewarded for his trouble. Though I don't know how a great gawk of a farmer had such a fine horse."

Oh dear. Bea recognized the horse, which belonged to Viscount Stowell's son, Hugh. How Hugh must be laughing at Beverley's mistake!

Mr. Redhaven was fourth into the square, and then Mr. Fairweather. Misters Maddrell and Whittington arrived together some ten minutes later, and Mr. Meadowsweet was not far behind them. They were waiting for Sir Henry Dashwood, and his mother was becoming anxious.

Bea was more concerned about Mr. Redhaven. He had been deathly pale when he rode in and needed Colyn Mugtin's help to stay upright and to walk to a seat. He was recovering, though. He had some color back in his cheeks and no longer looked as if he were about to swoon.

At last Sir Henry arrived, in a farmer's gig, with his horse tied to the back. The horse was limping. "Oh, poor Henry," said his mother. "His horse has let him down. Perhaps it was unfit when he took it out."

Mama was offended. "Claddach would not offer an unfit horse to a guest," she told Lady Dashwood.

"I daresay the poor beast was injured in the chase," Aunt Joan commented. "I understand that these steeplechases are hard on both men and horses."

"That is true," Lady Dashwood decided. "Indeed, I was very concerned poor Henry had been injured. I must go and speak to him. Lady Joan, Lady Claddach, you cannot know how we mothers of sons suffer. Our boys will do these dangerous things, is that not so, Mrs. Howard?"

She bustled off to where Sir Henry was explaining to anyone who would listen about the stupidity of his horse and his own superior riding skills, which had saved him from a nasty tumble.

Papa finished conferring with his stewards and stepped up onto the platform. Everyone stopped talking to hear what he had to say. "Here are the results. Lord Beverley and Sir Henry Dashwood failed to finish the course on the horse with which they started, an automatic disqualification. Five gentlemen—those two, and also Mr. Howard, Mr. Fairweather and Mr. Meadowsweet—are disqualified for failing to comply with the rules, as laid out by me at the beginning of this trial. I am happy to meet with each gentleman individually to explain which rule they infringed and how."

There was a buzz of comment, but the crowd hushed again when he held up his hand. "The winner is Lord Lucas Versey. Mr. Redhaven was second. Congratulations to those gentlemen and to all who successfully completed the course."

Alaric had his hand pumped by an ecstatic Versey and then by various others. He had lost interest in the whole event. He just wanted to go back to the castle and go to bed, and when Colyn came to tell him that a carriage was available to take him back up the hill, he was only too happy to leave.

He took some of the laudanum the doctor had left on the first night and woke up three hours later. He was still groggy, and he couldn't have named any part of his body that wasn't sore, but Colyn was waiting to dress him for dinner.

"Perhaps I should make your excuses, sir," Colyn said, looking worried.

That was enough to get Alaric out of bed. He wasn't going to have the other suitors thinking him weak. Or Lady Beatrice worrying about him, for that matter, though it warmed him to be certain she would. "Nonsense," he said. "I haven't ridden for a while, Colyn, that's all. A bit of pain is inevitable." At least his head no longer felt as if someone was inside it with a hammer and a pickaxe.

He was glad he'd made the effort. Not so much at dinner, though he'd hate to have missed walking in with Lady Beatrice. It was Versey's reward for his win, but he had declared he was already committed to Lady Eleanor Fairweather, so the privilege fell to Alaric as the second-place winner.

"Interesting," Lady Beatrice murmured to him, inclining her head to indicate the other couple as they walked ahead of them into the dining room.

Alaric leaned close to her once they were seated, keeping his voice low to avoid being overheard. "A match, do you think? Lord Lucas and Lady Eleanor?" *It would be one less rival for me to beat.* The thought took him by surprise. Had he made up his mind, then? His own thoughts jeered back at him. He had gone and fallen in love. Again. After he had sworn he would not. But perhaps it was not so bad. Perhaps it was just infatuation, and he would fall out of love with her as soon as he knew her better.

Lady Beatrice said something, and he had to swim up from the depths of his own thoughts to figure out what it was. An answer to his question. "Yes. I think so. She certainly has a high regard for him, and he requests her to partner him at every opportunity."

She showed not a hint of chagrin that one of her suitors was looking elsewhere. In the same circumstances, Delphine, the first woman he had fallen in love with, would have been smiling sweetness on the surface but with barbs and poison in every remark. She could never stand anyone to have even the attention she herself had rejected. As for Eloise... No. He would not think about Eloise.

"They would be a good match, I think," Lady Beatrice said.

Alaric nodded. "They have similar interests, from what I have seen. That bodes well for a happy marriage, does it not?"

"I note," she commented, "you don't say they are from the same level of Society, or some such."

"Is it blasphemy to say I'm not certain how much that matters?" Alaric asked, and they exchanged smiles. They were of one mind on that, though as the second son of an earl, Alaric was certainly qualified to be on Lord Claddach's list. And there he was again, thinking of himself as husband material, if the wife in question were Lady Beatrice.

She was not his usual sort. He had to admit he had previously been attracted to women who seemed to need him—fragile creatures whose helplessness made him determined to defend them from all storms. Lady Beatrice would scorn to be considered helpless. Indeed, her practical good sense and her competence were evident at every turn. He rather liked it.

Enough self-reflection. He exerted himself to converse, first with Lady Beatrice and then, after the first remove, with her cousin, Lady Lucy Hetherington, who was on his other side. The contrast was edifying. Lady Lucy was younger, of course, perhaps by four years. He'd had to force himself to listen to her prattle about the clothes she'd worn to the race and the music piece she would play after dinner and the items she bought in a village during the day out. No. Lady Beatrice had surely never been so shallow.

Later, he would acknowledge he owed Lady Lucy a debt of gratitude, for he might have gone straight up to bed had she not begged him to come and listen to her play, "...for you are such a kind gentleman, Mr. Redhaven, whatever Beverley says, and I know you will be nice about my music."

So, he went with everyone else to the music room, to listen to the ladies take it in turn to showcase their talents. Some sang, some played on the piano, Lady Eleanor played the harp, Miss Howard declaimed a poem.

Lady Lucy played competently, but without a real feeling for the music. He clapped enthusiastically anyway, and she beamed at him. His enthusiasm wasn't for her, though. He had just noticed the mural that ran all along one wall—two scenes from the story of Persephone and Hades. It was the words above those scenes that had set his pulse racing. They belonged to a long frieze of sayings, but these two spoke straight to the poem from the treasure hunt. *Tempus serpit. Tempus fujit.* Time creeps. Time flies.

In the flickering candlelight, perhaps he was seeing what he wanted to see. But no. He was certain. He had found the answer to the clue, or at least where the answer to the clue lay. He couldn't study it properly tonight, with everyone else around, but tomorrow, as soon as he could, he was returning to the music room.

→》》》《《←

BEA HAD HAD a revelation last night. The frieze in the music room! It had proverbs in pairs all the way around the room, each pair containing opposites. They were written in Latin, which Bea had never learned, but Papa's previous secretary had translated them for her one afternoon.

Absence makes the heart grow fonder. Out of sight out of mind.

Birds of a feather flock together. Opposites attract.

The pen is mightier than the sword. Actions speak louder than words.

And on and on around the room, including the pair, Time creeps and Time flies.

This was what Mr. Redhaven's clue was pointing to, but she couldn't tell him, in front of everyone else. Besides, perhaps she was wrong. She had been unable to check without drawing attention to the frieze, but she was on her way there this morning, as soon as she was washed and dressed, before even breaking her fast.

She was careful not to be seen, staying away from the break-fast room where servants would be coming and going, and early risers might be making their selections. Early as she was, it was easy to glide down the secondary staircase from the family quarters and take the long way around via the great hall to reach the music room.

She let herself inside and shut the door firmly behind her, then stopped. Someone else was examining the mural below the frieze. The momentary indignation at being beaten to the answer faded as she recognized that Mr. Redhaven was before her.

He was intent on the mural and didn't see her until she was right behind him, and she spoke. "You saw it too," she said.

He turned with a smile. "Last night. But I could not see properly by candlelight. This must be it, don't you think? *Time creeps*, here on the right, and on the left, *Time flies*."

She nodded. "But does the poem refer to the paintings on the ceiling or on the wall?"

"*Beneath*, the last line says. And look. In the second picture, beneath the words *Time creeps, the maiden is asleep. The son of night*, the poem says. The god of sleep. In the myth of Persephone as I heard it, she is awake and picking flowers, but here she is in a darkened field fast asleep, while Hades approaches in his chariot."

"Yes," she agreed. "It must be, for under *Time flies*, it is a sunny day and Persephone is picking flowers. It is Persephone, is it not?"

"You can tell by the pomegranate, the seeds, the flowers, and the deer," Alaric explained. "They are her symbols. See? In both panels. And see here, in the second panel, near Hades? A screech owl, the chariot, a dog, and a serpent."

"Then is 'Persephone' the answer?"

Alaric wasn't certain. "These two panels are the answer, I am sure of that. But is it Persephone, or Spring, or something else?" He turned to look at her. They had both bent in to see the symbols of Hades in the corner of the second panel, and his face was only inches from hers. His eyes dropped to her lips, and his pupils grew huge, darkening his hazel eyes.

Was he going to kiss her? Was she going to let him?

He blinked and the moment was gone. "I shall take what I have to your father and see what he says." His voice was huskier than usual.

Bea's breath had been stolen by might-have-beens. She swallowed hard and told him, "At this time of the morning, he will be in his study."

He nodded and took two steps away, then turned back. "Colyn tells me today is a recovery day. Will you take a walk with me after? In the garden? I will show you my second clue, if your father gives me one."

"Meet me in the breakfast room," Bea said. "You need to eat to regain your full strength. You are still healing. Then we shall walk."

His smile was warm. "In the breakfast room, then."

Chapter Nine

WHEN ALARIC ENTERED the earl's study, the man was, as his daughter had suggested, already at work behind his desk, a steaming cup of coffee at his elbow.

"You asked to see me, Redhaven," the earl acknowledged.

"Yes, my lord. I believe I have solved the first clue in the treasure hunt."

The earl's eyebrows twitched upwards in an expression of surprise. "Indeed? You are the first, then. One moment, young man."

He opened a drawer and pulled out a folded piece of card, from which he extracted a sheet of paper. "Ah yes. 'Watch time crawl by with leaden feet.' Very well, Redhaven. What have you discovered?"

"Two panels in the music room, sir, with the words *Tempus fugit* and *Tempus serpit* in a frieze above them. I believe the first shows the reign of the son of night, who is the god of sleep in Greek and Roman mythology. The second shows Persephone as the goddess of Spring, so I suppose that the answer to the clue is either Persephone or Spring."

"Hmm," said the earl, which was not helpful. "You will, I hope, work out the significance of that panel, or those panels, as you solve further clues. However, you have identified the panels, and that is enough to win you the next little rhyme. Let me see…" He dug around in the folder for a minute, and then brought out another sheet of paper, very similar to the first.

"This one, I think, is for you."

Alaric accepted it, glanced at it, folded it again, and put it into his pocket to think about later. Another piece of verse.

"Thank you, sir. I won't take up more of your time."

"I will, however, command a few moments more of yours," the earl replied. "Did my daughter give you the answer?"

"No, my lord," Alaric answered, pleased he could say so. However, in all honesty, he had to add, "I think she would have done so, though, if I had not thought of it. She came down to the music room this morning to check what she thought she saw last night and found me already doing the same thing."

That seemed to amuse the earl. "Ah. So that was the way of it? You have consulted her, then?"

"I have, my lord. I initially thought of timepieces like clocks and sundials, and I asked her where to find them, then showed her my clue. We plan to meet later so I can show her this one. Is that against the rules? If so, I apologize."

The earl waved off his apology. "Not at all. I find it interesting, but it is not forbidden, and I am not offended." He leaned back in his chair, steepling his fingers in front of his chin as he fixed Alaric with a stern look that somehow reminded Alaric of Lady Beatrice's expression when she was puzzling out the frieze. "Mr. Redhaven, will you tell me the full story of why you were asked to leave Brazil?"

Alaric thought about that. "Perhaps, sir. If I am successful in the trials and you and Lady Beatrice are amenable to my suit, then you will have a right to know. At the moment, though, it does not feel right."

Lord Claddach nodded. "I accept that. Well done on the clue, young man. I wish you well with the second. Good day to you."

That was a dismissal, if ever Alaric had heard one. He left the earl's office and went into breakfast.

※»※«※

MR. REDHAVEN ARRIVED in the breakfast room looking pleased. His interview with Papa must have been successful, then. Bea itched to hear what had happened but was not going to ask in front of the servants and the other guests. Only Lord Lucas and Lady Eleanor were up, and when she and Mr. Redhaven spoke about their planned walk, they announced their intention of coming along.

"If you do not mind, Bea," Ellie said. The young ladies had all moved to first-name terms during their travels yesterday.

"It solves the problem of a chaperone," Bea pointed out. "The older ladies are all still asleep, and I don't wish to wait." And she did not wish one of the older ladies hanging on every word that she and Mr. Redhaven exchanged. Whereas, unless she missed her guess, Lord Lucas and Ellie would be absorbed in one another, giving her and her escort all the privacy one could decently require.

It turned out just as she expected. They took the path down to the beach again, and the other couple lingered behind, clearly seeking their own privacy. "You seem to be none the worse for yesterday's exertions," Bea commented to Mr. Redhaven, as they scrambled down the steeper sections of the path. In truth, he was still being careful with some movements, but he no longer looked as if he was bruised in every bone and about to pass out.

"Colyn's uncle has a liniment that is good for muscle strain," he replied. "I can now swear by it, having put it on before I went to sleep yesterday. I might have applied more this morning, but it is rather pungent, and I would not wish to offend the company."

She managed a shallow curtsey on the awkward terrain. "The company thanks you, Mr. Redhaven."

"Could you be persuaded to call me Alaric?" he asked. "Just when we are alone. We are becoming friends, are we not?"

Friends, and perhaps something more. The trials—and the

choice at the end of them—loomed large in her mind. Perhaps a great deal more. "Very well, Alaric. And I am Bea."

"A charming little name," he commented. "Very useful things, bees." He gave her a sideways smile that she found rather charming. She smiled at him in return.

"I hope I am useful," she retorted. "How did you get on with my father, Alaric?"

"I have the second clue. He said the panels were collectively the correct answer, but that the meaning of the answer will become clear with later answers. Or, at least, that was the substance of it."

"So, the solution to the treasure hunt is the sum of the clues," Bea guessed. "How devious!"

"Clever, in any case. He wants to be sure your suitors are worthy of you, Bea. I cannot fault him for that." He took a piece of paper from his pocket and gave it to her. "Let's read it together," he invited.

She looked around to see if anyone else was close enough to interrupt them, but even Lord Lucas and Ellie were out of sight. Then she held one side of the paper and Alaric held the other.

"Roses 'neath moon's silver light
Golden stars behold the sight
The flower climbs the mansion wall
For fleeting joy before the fall."

Bea could not make head nor tail of it. "Something in the garden? At night? We do not have climbing roses against the castle. I do not understand, Alaric."

"Me neither," Alaric admitted. "I am prepared to guess the simple answer will not be the right one. Look how long I hunted for clocks and sun dials, and all the time, I should have been looking for the words."

"But which words?" Bea wondered.

Alaric studied the paper again. "It isn't necessarily the same type of riddle, but I must confess, at the moment I am stumped. It could be at night, as you suggest, and in the garden. It could as easily be another ceiling or perhaps a tapestry somewhere."

"Yes, or a painting. Here. You had better put it away. I see the others coming."

Ellie and Lord Lucas had been out of sight together for some time. Talking? Or something else?

Ellie was looking flushed, and her lips were redder than usual. She and Lord Lucas kept exchanging smiles and then looking quickly away.

Bea might have her suspicions, but their behavior was none of her business. Except that Lord Lucas had entered the trials. She hoped he was not kissing one girl while intending to marry another, if he won.

"Shall we walk to the end of the beach and then back again?" Alaric asked, and everyone agreed. Bea's concerns lessened as they walked, Bea with Alaric and Lord Lucas with Ellie.

"It must have been fun growing up with a beach on your doorstep," Alaric said.

Bea agreed. "My governess and I had many a fine walk on the beach, and when I was older, I used to help the stable hands exercise the horses here. There is a ride down the hill on the side away from the sea, and a path that leads to the beach."

"Do you spend most of your time here at the castle?" Ellie asked. "Or do you go to London with your parents?"

"I have never left Claddach," Bea told them. "Mama wanted me to make my come out, but I was determined not to do so, and Papa supported me."

Ellie stopped in her tracks. "You did not make your come out?"

Bea chuckled. "I did not. My cousins consider me very odd."

"What made you so determined?" Lord Lucas asked. "I thought all girls dreamed of gowns and balls and the like."

Ellie poked him in the side. "All girls are not the same, Luke."

Lord Lucas yelped. "Ouch! Note to self. Turns to violence

when annoyed."

Ellie tossed her head. "When provoked," she corrected, laughing, and he laughed back. "There is not a girl in the world like you, Ellie." If Lord Lucas was serious about winning Bea, he would surely not be flirting with Ellie right under her nose. And they were calling each other by their first names. Not even that. Their nicknames.

"Did you dream of gowns and balls?" Ellie asked Bea.

Bea thought about that. "Not really," she decided. "I have some of that with public assemblies in the town and when the local gentry invite us for dinner or a ball. I enjoy dressing in lovely gowns, and I love dancing. But it isn't real, is it?"

Ellie frowned in puzzlement. "It isn't?"

"I think I know what you mean," Alaric said. "It is like sugared violets on a cake. They're fun to have, but you can do without them, and still enjoy the cake. You would not like an endless diet of sugared violets, though."

Bea nodded. She hadn't known how to explain it, but Alaric's example made sense to her.

"The life of a diplomat is almost all sugared violets, is it not?" Lord Lucas asked Alaric.

"A thick layer of them," Alaric groaned, "and what's underneath is not cake, but stale bread."

That made them all laugh. Perhaps the metaphor was being stretched, but the comment certainly disclosed Alaric's feelings about his former career.

"I see," Ellie mused. "So, what do you regard as 'real,' Bea?"

Bea didn't hesitate. "The Isle of Claddach and its people. I am to be the Lady of Claddach. I need to know my land and my people. What of you?"

"My family. Had I found a match in my one Season, it would have helped my sisters. Perhaps even my brothers, if I had married a man with influence or wealth." She shrugged. "As it is, I helped my sisters by staying at home and letting them have their chance. Papa has six girls to settle, without impoverishing the family. It was best to stay home." She colored slightly.

"But when Lady Claddach invited my father to send one of his daughters to this house party, we had a family meeting, and father and my brothers and sisters decided I was to come." She glanced at Luke again and away. Bea understood what she had not said. Ellie's family had assumed a house party might give her the opportunity to find a match without the expense of a Season or weeks of balls requiring many changes of clothing. How good it would be if whatever was developing between Luke and Ellie was, in Ellie's words, real.

In fact, the sugared violet analogy worked very well. "I know what you mean, Ellie. I help teach at the dame school in the village. That is real. And I visit sick tenants and new mothers with Mama." Or, these days, without Mama. "That is real, too, in a way that dances and gowns are not. But I think a sugared violet now and again is very pleasant."

"What of you, Lord Lucas?" Bea asked.

"Luke, please, my lady," he begged. "I hate all this milording. It is not, as you put it, real. What have I done to deserve being called a lord? I was born third son to a duke, that's all. It is a courtesy, particularly since Thorn, my brother, has three sons. And if you want to know what I think, the courtesy's target is my father, rather than myself."

He chuckled. "That was a little impassioned. Luke, if you would, Lady Beatrice."

"I am Bea, and this is Alaric," Bea told him.

"Not Al?" asked Luke.

"Definitely not Al," said Alaric, firmly, and Luke laughed again.

Bea was not going to let him away without answering the question. "Your 'real'?" she asked.

Luke turned serious then. "I'm still working on it," he said. "Being a gentleman is mostly candied violets. I am tired of it. I thought perhaps Claddach? But…" He paused, his eyes holding Ellie's. "My ideas have changed. There are not many jobs for gentlemen. I would make a terrible vicar. I do not know enough to be a land steward and I am not particularly interested. So, what is my 'real'?"

He put out his hand toward Ellie, and she put her hand in his. "A wife. A family. And that means some way of making income. Ellie thinks I could be a politician. A lot of candied violets in that profession. But it is cake underneath, Alaric, to use your image. A member of Parliament can make a difference, I believe. We will think of something, won't we, Ellie?"

"My dowry will help," Ellie declared. "It is not huge. My father has ten children and needs to set three sons up in professions that will support them, without impoverishing the estates my eldest brother will inherit, so we girls have only modest dowries. But it will help."

"In fact," Luke said, "between my allowance from my father and Ellie's dowry, I probably don't need to work. We could live in genteel poverty. But..." He smiled and shrugged. "Candied violets. I need something to do that will feed my soul. Gad, that sounds so pretentious."

Lord Lucas, Bea realized, was much more than the polished society gentleman than showed on the surface, and he was also embarrassed about showing his hidden depths. He turned the attention from himself now by saying, "Your turn, Al. What is your real, so to speak?"

Alaric was looking at the ocean, watching the waves. At the question, he turned his attention to Bea. "The land, I believe. When I was a boy, I was the one that trotted around after my father and his land steward, not my twin—who is the older and the heir. After university, I helped the steward, who was getting old and could no longer do all he used to. I thought that would be my life. I would stay on and take his place when he retired. I was happy." He bent to pick up a pebble and tossed it to be swallowed up by a wave.

"So, what happened?" Luke asked.

"There was a girl," Alaric said. He threw another pebble. He was avoiding their faces, Bea thought. "I was courting her. I brought her and her older brother on a visit to meet my father, and my brother."

Another pebble soared over the waves and disappeared. "She married my older brother. The heir. My father decided I should leave. The envoy to Brazil is an old schoolmate of his, and my uncle is on the diplomatic mission, so…" A fourth pebble went the way of the rest. He turned to look at her, brushing sand from his palms by rubbing them together.

"Anyway, that is my story. If I win the trials and Bea will have me," he sent her a lop-sided smile, "I shall gladly serve her and Claddach for the rest of my days. If not? I will look for a place somewhere as a land steward. The land is my real. I am tired of candied violets."

Did he still love that girl, Bea wondered? For that matter, was his story true? He certainly seemed honest and sincere. But Aunt Joan had warned her that Society gentlemen were clever at dissembling. That was one reason Bea had never made her come out. Bea knew where she was with the men of Claddach. She'd known them all her life, for one thing. For another, most of them were simple folk who said what they meant and meant what they said. But how well did she know Alaric? Did he mean what he said, or was there more to his story than he'd allowed her to learn? And if so, when did he intend to tell her?

Chapter Ten

B EA WENT TO see her father after they returned from their walk. She collected his usual morning tray from a footman who was approaching the door at the same time and allowed him to open the door for her.

"Beatrice, my dear," Papa greeted her by rising from his chair. "Have you come to take tea with me?"

"I came to ask you for something, Papa. But I would like to join you for tea. I shall send for another cup."

She put the tray on Papa's desk before requesting an additional setting from the footman who was waiting outside. She returned and settled into one of the chairs in front of his desk.

"Did you enjoy your walk on the beach?" Papa asked.

"I did. I think Ellie—Lady Eleanor Fairweather—is becoming a good friend, and I learned more about Lord Lucas and Mr. Redhaven."

"Ah." He inclined his head before asking, "I assume young Redhaven showed you the second clue?"

"Yes," Bea admitted. "How did you know?"

"He asked me if it was against the rules. It is not, but I wonder if you have a reason for favoring him in this way."

Bea could feel herself blushing. "He is the one who has made the most effort to get to know me, Papa, instead of assuming I am a paper cutout of a fashion doll. Also, he's the only one who has asked for my advice on his clues."

"And you like him," Papa commented.

It was a statement, not a question.

The footman arrived with the other cup, and Bea stood and busied herself preparing the tea. It gave her something to do, rather than meet her father's eyes. He might have read her thoughts. *Yes, I like him, but what has that to say to anything, Papa? I have committed to choosing from the men who win the trials. Who is to say he will be one of them?*

It had been her choice, she reminded herself. And for good reason. She needed a husband, and soon, so he had time to learn what Papa could teach him.

Perhaps Papa did read her thoughts, for he said, "I wish I could give you more time, Beabea. Time to go to London or to a few house parties. Time to choose for love instead of practicality."

She put his cup down beside him and gave him her hand. "I know, Papa. I understand. I hope you have more time—doctors have been wrong before. But we cannot take the risk. We need to safeguard Claddach."

He clutched both her hands and kissed her on the forehead. "I am very proud of you, Beatrice Elizabeth Meave Collister."

"I love you, Papa."

He gave her hands a squeeze, let them go, and picked up his tea. "What did you wish to ask me?" he asked.

Bea returned to her seat and, following his example, picked up her own cup as camouflage for her feelings. "The boxing tomorrow, Papa. I wanted to ask if you would change it for another activity."

"This is about Redhaven again," he deduced.

"Yes, it is about Mr. Redhaven." Bea heard the irritation in her own voice and deliberately calmed it again. "He was injured in the shipwreck, Papa. He was exhausted by the end of the steeplechase. He almost fell from his horse. If he is hit in the head again tomorrow—Papa, we cannot take the risk."

"A sensible young man would stand down," Papa commented.

"There cannot be very many sensible young men, then," Bea suggested, thinking of the men she knew, all of whom would rather die than admit to a weakness.

Papa laughed. "You have a point. Very well, Bea, I shall make a bargain with you. I shall change the activity tomorrow to something more within the capacity of the young man."

Bea gave a sigh of relief. "Thank you, Papa."

"And in return, Daughter, you will spend an equal amount of time with all your suitors and give them a chance to show you who they really are. Agreed? I want you to have as wide a choice as possible, not to set your heart on one man at the beginning. And it will do Redhaven no harm to have to work for your esteem."

Bea thought about it for a moment. "I accept your bargain, Papa," she said.

➤➤➤◄◄◄

"MAY I HAVE your attention?" Lord Claddach said to the family and house guests, all of whom were gathered in the drawing room. Colyn had found Alaric and alerted him of the time to be here. He assumed the others had all received such invitations.

"My lords, my ladies, and gentlemen, the next trial I wish to announce is a charity fête in two days. The fête will be held in the grounds of the castle and will be open to anyone who wishes to come."

He looked directly at the younger gentlemen. "The role of the suitors will be to take over the organization and run the event. You are not starting from the beginning. Mr. Maddrell has a list of merchants, peddlers, and entertainers who have agreed to participate in the fête, and Mr. Whittington has a list of local parishes and other groups who will also have stalls or assist in other ways with the fête's events. A schedule has been posted. You will have plenty to do, but it should be possible in the time."

His smile was somewhat predatory. "You have forty-eight hours, gentlemen. The fête starts at two in the afternoon on the day after tomorrow. I suggest starting you repair to the green parlor and get started."

Was Alaric ever going to have time to think about the latest clue? But then, did the others? He supposed he wasn't the only one whose time to think and explore was compromised by this current task. Perhaps time management was one of the trials. He shrugged and left with the others.

The first few minutes of the meeting were a waste of time. Beverley insisted that he would be in charge, as he had the highest rank. Luke scoffed and asked whether he had ever organized a fête, which Alaric thought was a good point. "A ball? A Venetian breakfast? Any event more complex than a drunken night in a wine cellar?"

Beverley, who had been admiring his reflection in the window, turned at that and drew himself up, lifting his chin. "I'll have you know I was born to command," he insisted. "I shall be an earl one day."

What a pillock Beverley was.

Luke pointedly ignored him and turned to look at the rest of the group. Beverley scowled, probably put out that no one was admiring him in the window—or out of it—either. "Has anyone any actual experience of organizing a fête? Or anything to do with a fête?" Luke asked.

Fairweather put up a tentative hand. "I run the children's races each year at my father's harvest fête," he offered.

"Make a note of that, Maddrell," said Luke. Maddrell, predictably, had chosen a seat at a writing desk and had access to paper and quill. As Lord Claddach's secretary, he was the obvious choice of notetaker in Alaric's opinion, though the grumbles moving swiftly around the group argued otherwise.

"Who put you in charge, Versey?" demanded Beverley.

"Yes, Versey," agreed Dashwood. "Who?" And Howard nodded his agreement.

Alaric had had enough. "Gentlemen, please remember that the earl said our role is to organize and run the event. The suitors. Collectively. No one is in charge. We work as a team. The only way for us to win this trial is together. The only way to lose is to refuse to contribute."

He let his gaze move from one person to another.

"See, Versey?" Dashwood said, smugly.

"To get all the work done in the time available," Alaric pointed out, "we shall each need to take charge of a particular aspect. Luke has made a start on chairing this meeting, and an excellent start. I propose he continues to do so. Please indicate by raising your hand if you agree."

Only Beverley and Dashwood refused to raise their hands. Even Howard agreed, after a cautious look around the room at the others.

"Right," said Luke. "Motion carried. And I would like Maddrell to make notes. If you don't mind, Maddrell."

"Not at all," said the secretary, with a shallow bow.

"Who normally organizes your father's fête?" Luke asked Fairweather.

"My mother and my sisters," Fairweather replied.

"The same with ours," Luke said. "We do one at midsummer, but Mother is in charge. I'm usually a marshal, managing all the carts and carriages so nobody is blocked in, and escorting important guests to Mother or Father."

Alaric commented, "Another important thing to remember. Make a note of that, please, Maddrell. Gentlemen, we have two lists to consider, as I understand it. Shall we try to organize those in some way, and then see what the gaps are?"

"Good," Luke agreed. "At our fair, we have the charity stalls mixed up with the local merchants and the traveling peddlers. You, Fairweather?"

"The same," Fairweather agreed. "Oh. That reminds me. Put security on the list of things to do. I don't know how many thieves and pickpockets there are on Claddach, but they'll all be at the fête."

"They all have to come through the gates in the outer walls," Maddrell offered. He explained that the fête was to be held in the jousting grounds—a long flat patch of land outside the inner walls that enclosed the castle at the top of the bluff, but within the outer wall. "Security on the gates, and a few people patrolling the wall should be enough."

After two hours, they had a set of lists, and everyone had taken responsibility for a particular aspect of the fête. Even Beverley had volunteered. It would be his task to find and look after the judges for the competitions that were a feature of Mr. Whittington's lists—best jam, largest bull, fastest runner, strongest man, and the like.

Alaric was running the actual contests. His job was to make sure the contest spaces were pegged out and set up, that contestants found the right space at the right time, that the contests were run fairly, that the prizes were on hand for the judges to hand out after they'd selected the winner, and that he'd arranged everything else required for things to run smoothly.

It came as a relief to him, and no doubt to everyone else, that they were only expected to organize and oversee. And even most of the organization was already done. The army of servants and volunteers who would act under their direction had already been working on this for months. Alaric would make sure to ask for their advice at every turn.

With that in mind, he had some calls to make, some at the castle, and some down in the town.

AS HE MOVED around the castle on his errands, Alaric kept an eye out for carvings of roses. At some point during the previous day, it had occurred to him that mansions had walls inside as well as out. If the rhyme referred to a piece of wall or ceiling decoration, then a carved, or perhaps painted, climbing rose should lead him to the other parts of the clue.

But he realized before long, the problem was not finding roses. The problem was that the castle seemed to be full of them, and he couldn't see how any of them fitted the rest of the rhyme.

The search had to take second place to preparations for tomorrow's fête. He and the other suitors had met yesterday evening, and again this morning, to report on progress and problems. Even Howard and Beverley were pulling their weight.

Howard had, with the help of Claddach's groundsmen, located the marquees, tables, and other items that would be used to set up stalls and had checked them off against the list of stallholders. He and the butler—probably mostly the butler, but Alaric didn't fault Howard for that—had selected the grooms and footmen who would be their labor force and written a schedule for what needed to be done tonight and then tomorrow morning to set the stalls up.

Beverley had been interviewing judges and had ridden out immediately after the meeting this morning to visit the remaining experts on his list.

Alaric also had a list and had been talking to some of the same experts to make certain he knew exactly what each contest comprised and how it worked, so that he could carry out his tasks.

It wasn't the fête that bothered him, or even his search for something that would help him figure out the second clue. It was that Bea had partnered Fairweather into dinner, had played the piano after dinner with Howard to turn her pages, and had gone riding with Meadowsweet this morning.

When Alaric asked to escort her for a walk in the garden, she had refused. A polite refusal, but still! Had he offended her? Been too pressing in his attentions? And yet, he had been certain she returned his growing affections.

"Sir!" It was Colyn, his borrowed valet. "Sir, you must come with me. I will show you where the pall-mall alley is."

"The pall-mall alley?" Why did Colyn want to show him to the pall-mall alley?

"For the game, sir," Colyn said.

Oh. That's right. Colyn had mentioned it this morning with a list of other activities that Lady Claddach had organized for the house guests. "I thought I'd skip the game," Alaric replied.

"I think you should play, sir," Colyn told him, his eyes intent, as if trying to send him a message he would not put into words.

Alaric narrowed his eyes, a suspicion occurring to him. "Is it a trial, Colyn?"

Colyn didn't reply—he just stared at Alaric with pained eyes.

"Am I straining your loyalties, man? Very well, I won't insist on an answer." Though his refusal to answer was answer enough. "Show the way, then, Colyn. Pall-mall is a trial? I wonder what he is testing for?"

The questions were for himself, but Colyn replied, "It was to have been boxing, but Lord Claddach ordered the change yesterday afternoon. No one knows why."

"Just as well," Alaric said. "I doubt I'm up to a boxing match just yet. Mind you, I haven't played pall-mall in years. I have no idea how I'll fare."

Lady Claddach was dividing the participants into teams of two as they arrived at the alley. It had been built on a terrace, with one long side formed by the side of the hill into which the terrace had been cut and a high wall on the other side. Bench seats had been built into the slope above the terrace, so spectators could watch the play. "Half of you shall play in the first set," she said, "and half in the second. Then the top players of each set shall play in the third. Ah. Mr. Redhaven. There you are. You shall be paired with Miss Bryant."

Alaric had automatically sought out Bea when he and Colyn arrived. She, it seemed, was paired with her cousin Beverley.

Alaric took some comfort in the fact that she didn't look happy about it. He walked over to where Miss Bryant was standing with Miss Radcliffe and Dashwood. "Miss Bryant. Miss Radcliffe. Dashwood. Miss Bryant, I trust I do not let our partnership down. It has been at least three years since I last played the game."

"Christina is pretty good," Miss Radcliffe claimed.

Alaric bowed to his partner. "I shall do my best," he promised.

They were in the second set, so they walked up to the benches to watch the first. The players with their mallets began at one end and took turns to hit their balls toward the other. Each hit counted as a point, and the winning pair would be the one with the lowest number of points.

The run ended when all of them had put their balls through the iron ring at the end of the alley. It was suspended on a long rod four feet above the ground, and the end of the run was delayed as one of the players had to make five attempts before finally succeeding in putting his ball through the ring.

They then played back up to the first end, where another iron ring waited. Each set would comprise five runs, and the scores for each run would be added together to create the final score for the set.

Servants moved along the benches with drinks. Most of the older members of the house party were watching the game, too, but Lord Lewiston and Lord Claddach were supervising the servants who were keeping score down on the court.

During the second run, Alaric was watching Bea, so he missed when Beverley hit his ball into Howard's, but he turned at the gasp. A ball shot backwards, farther from the ring, ending up against the wall where swinging the mallet made for an awkward shot. Beverley's ball ricocheted from the impact, landing closer to the ring and right in front of it.

"An excellent roquet," Miss Bryant noted. "Beverley is well-placed for his next strike, and Howard will have trouble getting away from the wall."

Beverley's next strike—his prize for the roquet—sent his ball soaring through the hoop, making him the first to complete that run, and he lounged against the wall out of sight waiting for the others, with Howard coming last.

Beverley made two more roquets in the next run, even though the second one, on Fairweather's ball, was mere spleen, since it didn't win him an advantage. Quite the contrary, since the partnership of Fairweather and Miss Howard teamed up to roquet him in return. This time, Beverley and Bea were the last two to complete the run, since the other pair targeted her ball, as well.

"Beverley has good mallet skills," said Miss Bryant, "but he is not a good player. He is not working in concert with his partner. He has forgotten that, in pairs' play, the overall score is what counts."

"Also," Miss Radcliffe commented, "the second roquet in that run was not necessary, and Fairweather and Miss Howard have punished him for it. And poor Bea, too, whose only fault was being assigned as his partner." Alaric could only agree. Again, he wondered what this trial tested. It would be interesting to see what Lord Claddagh revealed.

Chapter Eleven

I N THE NEXT two runs, Beverley fought back with vicious roquets aimed simply at disrupting one or the other of the two who had declared against them. They responded, and Bea ignored all three of them and simply played on.

At the end of the set, Beverley stormed out of the alley, and was not seen again for the rest of the day. The other seven players came up to the benches. Alaric and the others playing the second set made their way down the steps at the side of the slope to take their places in the alley.

There were three pairs in this set rather than four, and so the runs went more quickly. It took Alaric most of the first run to relearn how to hit the ball at the right spot and with the right amount of force to send it where he wanted it to go. After that, he made three tries at strikes that would lift the ball through the hoop.

In the next three runs, he improved by leaps and bounds. He finished the third run in fourth place, and the fourth in second, behind Miss Bryant, his partner.

In the fifth, he was blocked in. He had one more strike before he was within range of the ring, but Dashwood's turn came after Alaric's, and his ball landed just a few inches from Alaric's and between Alaric and the ring. Alaric would have to jump his ball over Dashwood's, and would not make the ground he needed to finish in two strikes.

He needn't have worried, since Miss Bryant, when it came to her turn, roqueted Dashwood's ball from Alaric's path, leaving her own ball neatly positioned for a second strike which took her through the ring. "Well played, Miss Bryant!" he commended her as he took his turn. "I'm thankful Lady Claddagh paired us together."

Miss Bryant and Alaric finished the fifth run first and second. They waited and watched while the others finished and then waited some more while Lord Lewiston and Lord Claddach consulted with the servants who had been counting strikes. The other players came down from the benches to listen to the verdict.

Alaric and Miss Bryant were the third of the top four pairs, so they were up again. Alaric was dry, though, after the previous set. He was pleased to see footmen with jugs of cider and glasses.

Bea was playing, too, but not with Beverley. Their partner-ship had come in fourth equal with another pair, and the highest scoring partner in each pair went through into the third set.

It was a hard-fought but fast-paced set. Each pair worked as a team, clearing way for the other when necessary. Nobody bothered with revenge roquets, focusing their effort instead on getting their balls through the rings in as few strikes as possible.

Alaric had one horrid moment when Miss Bryant needed him to clear Bea's ball from her way. He met Bea's eyes but could read nothing in her face. With a gulp, he accepted that the game required him to honor his partnership with Miss Bryant. He knocked Bea's ball to the side of the alley and cast Bea an anguished glance. She smiled in return.

To his astonishment, when the winners were announced, Alaric and Miss Bryant had the lowest point count. They had won.

BEA HOPED THAT partnering Beverley for one set would satisfy her father. She certainly did not need any more time to confirm her opinion that Beverley would make a terrible husband for her and a dreadful lord for Claddach.

She decided she had had quite enough of suitors for the afternoon. A quiet voice inside her suggested that she'd make an exception for Alaric, but since her agreement with her father made time with him impossible, she would check the ballroom.

Her mother and father were hosting a dinner party after the fête, and dinner would be followed by dancing. Bea was in charge of the preparations.

In the ballroom, a team of servants was cleaning under the direction of the housekeeper. She saw Bea arrive and came to report. "The flowers and greenery are in buckets in the corner, my lady. We shall put them out in pots at the last minute. We have set the green withdrawing room up for cards, and the cupid room for supper. The musician's gallery is furnished with chairs and music stands. As soon as we have finished cleaning this room, we shall put up the cloth drops and set out the furniture—chairs and small tables in conversation groups at this end of the room, as you requested, and chairs around the space left for dancing at the other end."

The drop cloths, which Bea and the other lady guests had painted during the first week of the house party, showed garden scenes. There would be one behind each conversation group, with large tubs of flowers and greenery framing the base of each cloth.

Bea looked along the room to the musician's gallery at the far end. And froze. Didn't the carving around the gallery include roses? She would have to wait to confirm her memory. The housekeeper was keen to show her the preparations so far, and Bea allowed herself to be conducted through the games and supper room and the ladies' withdrawing room, which was being set up in a parlor a few doors away from the ballroom.

Once she had expressed her appreciation and thanks, she said,

"I will just, if you have no objection, walk around a little more. If that will not disturb the preparations?" The housekeeper waved away her concern and Bea was free to check her supposition.

They had finished the cleaning while she had been busy with the housekeeper and were now putting up the first of the painted drops. Bea drifted to the far end of the ballroom, trying to look as if she had no particular destination. The musician's gallery was lit by only a single small window, and the ceiling was lost in shadow. But she had a clear view of the wooden paneling that rose the full height of the ballroom at this end of the room.

From the other end of the ballroom, she had not been able to clearly see the ornately carved pillars that rose from the ballroom floor on both sides of the gallery, but here they were. Roses. A beautifully carved climbing rose, leaves, vine, and flowers winding up the pillar to arch across the top of the gallery.

Better, if she did not mistake the matter, the ceiling of the gallery was painted with a moon and stars—a silver moon and golden stars.

She would check, but first she would examine the carved panels that fronted the gallery's balustrade. The sun was setting, and soon there would not be enough light to make them out.

There were four of them, and the rose appeared on them all. A man and a woman—both very young. In the first, they were dancing. The second showed the same couple in an embrace on a balcony. The next scene was one of farewell. The girl was waving from the balcony on one side of the panel, and in the distance, someone rode away. In the final panel, the girl lay apparently dead, surrounded by roses. After a few moments' thought, she identified the Shakespearean play from which they came. *Romeo and Juliet.*

It remained only to check the ceiling up in the gallery, which was reached by a set of steps off a small passage she accessed through a door hidden in the paneling.

Yes. She had been correct. Moon and stars looked down on roses, for a tendril of the vine reached into the gallery on both sides.

She needed to tell Alaric. Bother. She could not take him aside somewhere they'd not be overheard without sending her mother into spasms nor go for a walk with him without breaking her promise to her father. In any case, it was nearly time to dress for dinner.

She'd have to send her information through her maid to his valet, and hope Alaric got the message.

WHEN COLYN CAME to help Alaric dress for dinner, he also brought a message. "Lady Beatrice said to tell you, you should look at the minstrels' gallery in the ballroom," he said.

Alaric wanted to rush off and look straight away. The answer to the second clue. It had to be. He allowed Colyn to tie his cravat just so. "It would be better with a tie pin," Colyn commented.

"Perhaps," Alaric agreed. "But I am still very much beholden to my host for everything I wear." Would he hear from his father soon? It had been more than a week since he'd written. He would dearly love to have even a few pounds to give vails to Colyn and the footmen who brought the water for his bath.

Best of all would be if his father sent the trunks he had stored in the family attics when he left for Brazil. Alaric had sent a second letter, once he decided to enter the trials, explaining about the trials—and the prize—and asking for his trunks. But that letter had only gone five days ago.

"There, sir. You are ready," Colyn declared. "You have thirty minutes. Do you wish me to show you where the ballroom is?"

"Thank you," Alaric replied. It was not a place he had been to in his clock hunt, so he needed assistance finding the room expeditiously.

Colyn left him at the door to the ballroom, which was a hive of activity, with servants hanging cloths to drape from the wall, setting out chairs, and attending to two enormous chandeliers that had been dropped to floor level. They were setting new candles in the sconces and polishing each individual crystal.

The woman who was housekeeper came to meet him. "Mr. Redhaven? Is there something I can do for you? Shall I direct you to the drawing room?"

"I am here to see the minstrel gallery," Alaric explained. "I trust I shall not be in your way?"

The housekeeper looked dubious, but she said, "Of course not, sir. We are nearly finished here for the night." She stepped out of his path.

The climbing roses that framed the gallery certainly fitted the rhyme. But what of the moon and the stars? He borrowed a lamp from a nearby group of servants who had finished hanging their drape, which proved to be a cloth painted with a semblance of a garden.

One of the servants directed him to the stairs he needed, and he soon found the ceiling up in the gallery was painted with a night sky. The silver moon and golden stars shone on roses. Back downstairs again, he tried to make out the panels along the front of the gallery. He would have to return in daylight, for the details were too shadowed for him to determine their subject.

As he stood there, the servant who had given him the lamp came to retrieve it. "Did you find what you were looking for, sir?" she asked.

"Yes, thank you. Except I cannot make out what the panels are about," he replied.

"The *Romeo and Juliet* panels?" the woman said. "They are very beautiful. They were carved for this ballroom, you know. My great uncle was the carver."

She pointed up at the first panel. "They meet and dance." Then to the second. "He climbs to her balcony." The third. "He is forced to leave." And finally, the fourth. "She lies, apparently dead. Of course, after that, he kills himself and then so does she." She sighed. "Such a tragedy. We had players here the year before last. They acted the play in this very ballroom, and Lord Claddach allowed the household staff to watch. We all cried." This time, her sigh was redolent with the satisfaction of a treasured memory.

"Thank you," Alaric said, sincerely, handing over the lamp. He had his answer. Did he have time to give it to Lord Claddach? He thanked the housekeeper, too, and went looking for the earl.

His lordship was already in the drawing room, talking to the Earl of Lewiston and Mr. Howard, the father of Arthur Howard the suitor. Alaric was frustrated, but interrupting would be rude, and would also draw too much attention. He didn't want to find himself followed by suitors who were less successful than he had been, with Bea's help, at unraveling the clues.

His chance came after dinner, when the men finished their glass of port and began to make their way to the drawing room to join the ladies. "My lord," he said to Lord Claddach, "May I have a quick word?"

"Go along without me," Claddach told the other gentlemen. "Very well, Redhaven. You have my attention."

"I believe I know the answer to the second clue, my lord," Alaric told him. Claddach inclined his head, and Alaric continued. "It is the minstrel gallery in the ballroom, my lord. The climbing rose. The moon and the stars. *Romeo and Juliet*, in fact."

Claddach raised his eyebrows. "Well done. I did not expect anyone to discover the answer until tomorrow's dancing. Come to my study after we have done the pretty with the ladies, and I shall give you the next clue."

Which meant Alaric slept that night with the third clue drifting ominously through his mind:

"A victim, he, of beauty's snare

Lost at a glimpse. Young man, beware.

Elude the trap of waters still

And ne'er forget that love can kill."

Chapter Twelve

ALARIC WENT STRAIGHT down to the fête in the morning. The previous night, workmen had been putting up the pens for the contests involving animals, and marking off a ring in which the animals could be paraded. He needed to check those, and also the areas set aside for the other contests, some of them in tents and some out in the open.

"Mr. Redhaven, sir." It was the stablemaster, looking grave and shifting his hat from one hand into the other.

"Good morning," Alaric greeted him.

"It will be if we can get this judging thing sorted," grumbled the stablemaster.

"You need Viscount Beverley, then. I haven't seen him yet." Alaric looked around. Several of the other suitors were down on the jousting grounds, checking the preparations, but he saw no sign of Beverley.

"Your pardon, Mr. Redhaven, but Lord Beverley *is* the problem," the stablemaster said.

Bother the man. What has he done now?

As it turned out, quite a lot. For a start, he had given the judges a reordered schedule of contests that didn't fit with the order Alaric had inherited, through Maddrell, from the last fête. "It makes no sense, man. Sir, I mean." the stablemaster insisted.

"What he has done is order the contests by the rank of the judges, so first up is Viscount Sugden's lady judging bonnets and then the viscount and his roses. Bonnets and roses don't get stressed waiting around, sir, and they don't need to be fed and watered, neither. Nor do they have pens that need to be mucked out, begging your pardon, sir."

To make matters worse, several judges had been called upon to judge more than one contest, and Beverley had grouped such contests, so they fell one after the other.

"It means you're going to have crowds tramping halfway round the fête and then back again," the stablemaster grumbled.

Beverley had also demanded the use of a second and even a third tent so judges who were gentry could take refreshments in a separate location from those who worked for a living, and those who were in trade or the professions were apart from servants and laborers.

Beverley, in other words, had made a right royal mess of things.

Alaric was inclined to countermand all the idiot's changes, but he'd better do things properly. "We'll fix this, Mr. Mugtin," he promised the stablemaster. "I'll get together the rest of the gentlemen, and we'll address these issues to make changes."

Luke was the suitor closest to him. Alaric called out, "Luke!"

"We need a meeting," he said, when the other approached. "Beverley has made some changes to the contest timetable that will mess up the contests. I need the authority of the group to change things back again. Can you fetch as many of the suitors as you can find? I'll do likewise, and we can meet…" he looked around and then pointed to a giant oak that grew on the castle side of the field, "there."

Predictably, Beverley was not anywhere to be found on the fête grounds, so only Luke, Fairweather, Meadowsweet, and Dashwood gathered in the appointed spot. "The contestants have all been given a time by which to have their entry ready, according to the schedule, which has also been posted in various places around the town and in the villages," he explained a few minutes later. "Also, though this is a more minor matter, the prizes are laid out in order of contest. That's apart from the issues Mugtin raised. The easiest solution is to notify the judges that we are going back to the original schedule."

"Tell them Beverley did not tell anyone about his changes, and it is now too late," Luke advised.

With the agreement of the others, Alaric figured that he had a majority. He could change the tent arrangement himself, but the big task would be to let the judges know the change of schedule, and it would be best if Beverley cooperated on that task.

"Not a snowball's chance in hell," Luke figured. Alaric was inclined to agree.

Maddrell had a copy of the lists of judges, though he warned Alaric that Beverley might have been forced to find replacements. Alaric could deal with the servants who were judges easily enough, simply by sending Colyn to find them, present his apologies, and explain the conflict.

As to those judges who were coming up from the town or in from the countryside—*ah, there's Beverley now. With Bea on his arm, more's the pity.*

"Beverley!" Alaric called. "Beverley, I need your help."

Beverley sneered at him from a distance and would have walked away, but Bea, bless her, said something that had him reluctantly changing direction. "What is it, Redhaven? You had your job and I had mine. If you have any problems, I don't see why I should help you."

Alaric kept his temper with an effort. "Someone has drawn my attention to a conflict between the schedule of contests that has been circulated to the contestants, and the one you have arranged with the judges, Beverley."

Beverley glared. "My schedule was organized to respect the most important people on the island, Redhaven. Change your own."

Nothing will be achieved by losing your temper, Alaric scolded himself. "If only I had enough time," he said. "But the contestants will be arriving according to the timetable that has been advertised for weeks, I'm afraid."

"Look here, you mutton-headed chawbacon…"

"I see the problem." Bea spoke over Beverley's angry voice. "I can only imagine how upset the judges will be when no contestants are there to present their items for judging. And imagine what Papa will say when both judges and contestants complain about there being two schedules."

Beverley frowned and shook his head, but before he could speak, "There is only one thing for it. We shall have to explain the problem to the judges and apologize for any inconvenience. There is just no way to reach all the contestants before we have a disastrous mess that will set the entire island laughing at us. Cousin, I know you will be able to present it in the best possible light."

That was laying it on with a trowel, and from the suspicious look on Beverley's face, he was not buying it. "I cannot go back on my word to Lady Stowell."

"The viscountess?" Bea asked. "She asked for the changes?"

Beverley stuck his nose in the air. "We discussed it," he said coldly. "Her concerns were perfectly valid. Next to my aunt and uncle, she and Lord Stowell are the most important people on the island. Her wishes should be paramount."

Alaric stiffened his neck to stop himself from turning it to catch Bea's eye. It was typical of Beverley that he equated rank with importance. The Stowells, as Alaric understood it, didn't even live here year-round. Their primary estate was somewhere in Lancashire, and they only spent a few weeks in Claddach a year.

"I won't do it," Beverley declared. "If you want to tell Lady Stowell she has to appear at the beginning of the fête and stay down here on the grounds for over an hour, then you do it."

He was looking at Alaric, but Bea answered. "Yes, that is an excellent idea. I shall let Lord and Lady Stowell know of the change, and you will talk to all the other judges. Thank you, Beverley."

Alaric knew better than to crow. "Yes, thank you, Beverley. You've been a brick about this."

Beverley was taken aback at the compliment. "Yes. Well, of course. We are meant to work together on this stupid fête. Well. Is that the list? I'd better get started, then. I shall be blaming you, Redhaven."

"Feel free," Alaric answered, relieved they'd brushed through without a major temper tantrum from Beverley disrupting the entire day. Beverley stalked away without another word seemingly unaware that the whole scene had played out in front of an audience of villagers and castle servants, plus most of the other suitors. Those who mattered would know perfectly well where to place any blame.

"Now all we need to do is make sure Lord and Lady Stowell know we've gone back to the original timetable, soothe their ruffled feathers, and get them here on time," Alaric said to Bea.

She gave him a smug grin. "Lady Stowell is going to be here at one in the afternoon. She is taking lunch with Mama and Aunt Lewiston, and Lord Stowell will no doubt be down by the animal pens, probably having begged a pie off one of the peddlers. He is a nice man, Alaric. We won't have any trouble with him."

Meaning they would have trouble with Lady Stowell. "I am beginning to think that you and I can conquer anything when we work together," he murmured to her. "Thank you for the direction, by the way. I have my third clue."

Her eyes lit up. "Splendid. I am so glad." She frowned and nibbled her upper lip in an uncharacteristic indecision, then apparently made up her mind. "Alaric, I must spend time with the other suitors. Papa made me promise to give you all equal attention. But I do want to hear about the third clue. Could we, perhaps, meet to wait for Lady Stowell? Just outside the inner gatehouse, perhaps?"

So that was it! Alaric's heart felt lighter to know she had not tired of him or become offended by some word or act. "At half past noon?" he suggested. "In case she is early?"

She smiled and agreed.

ONE HICCUP FOLLOWED another all morning. Alaric and Luke found themselves solving problems in every corner. Howard, who was managing the parish stalls and those raising money for other charitable purposes, complained that several visiting merchants had taken over more than their allocated space, squeezing into the places set aside for the charities.

Meadowsweet, who was meant to be managing the merchants, instead wilted under their complaints and abuse, and the pair of them came looking for help.

Alaric borrowed a measuring stick from the estate carpenter and he and Luke went and remeasured each disputed space. The encroaching stall holders grumbled, but Luke glared at them, and Alaric joked with them until the stalls were in their correct position.

A farmer bringing his prize rams into the animal pens managed to lose one between his cart and the pens. While he was searching for it, it found itself in a pen with another farmer's ewes and had covered two of them before the two owners chanced upon the activity.

The ram's owner cried theft and the ewes' owner wanted compensation for the assault.

"How did he get in the pen?" demanded the ram's owner. "The blaggard opened the gate, that's how!"

"He can't keep track of his own ram, and now he accuses me of letting it into my ewes? Why would I want lambs from that old wreck?" the ewes' owner enquired, plaintively.

"Old wreck? I'll have you know that's the finest ram on Claddach. The old blaggard is too mean to pay my fee, and that's a fact. Why else would he bring ewes in heat to the fête?"

It took Alaric and Luke a while to calm the pair down and the incident wasn't done until the ram had been dragged out of the pen and herded to its proper place. Neither Alaric nor Luke felt qualified to handle any repercussions from the stolen mating, so they told the men to put their dispute to one side in front of foreigners from the mainland, and, if they must, bring it up with Claddach's steward after the fête.

The morning flew by, and Alaric was yearning for a pie, an ale, and a rest when the stable clock struck twelve. He was meeting Bea in half an hour. In fact, if he were to wash and tidy before he met Lady Stowell, he had better hurry.

He arrived still damp but clean to find Bea already waiting for him in the courtyard. She couldn't make any more sense of the verse than Alaric, but at least they would both be thinking about it. And watching out for a tapestry or a painting with water in it.

"How are preparations going?" Bea asked, so Alaric told her about the ram. She immediately named the two farmers. "Those two are always trying steal a march on one another," she explained. "They will curse and call names and insist that they are going to see the magistrate, but next week they'll be at it again. The advantage goes back and forth, and they entertain the entire island."

Alaric laughed. "I wish I'd known that. Luke and I thought we might have a murder on our hands. How Luke will laugh when I tell him. And you, Bea? I suppose you have been as busy as we are, preparing for the guests tonight."

Lady Claddach, Alaric had noticed, spent most of her time with the ladies her own age, and otherwise in retreat in her room. It was Bea who hurried from housekeeper to cook to butler keeping the castle running. Organization for the dinner and the ball appeared to have largely fallen onto Bea, though she had some help from her aunt—her father's sister, Lady Joan, not her mother's sister, who was Beverley's mother.

"You seem to be doing it all yourself," he observed.

"Reina and Christina have been a great help," she assured him naming her two friends from the town. "So have Sarah and Ellie." She chuckled. "And today we persuaded Dorrie and Lucy, my cousins, that it would be fun to make garlands to hang in the ballroom. The other girls are all there now, either making garlands or arranging flowers. Look, Alaric, I think that is the Stowell carriage arriving."

Alaric could see it, just coming up the hill from the outer wall.

They had been strolling away from the carriageway along the wall, but they turned back to the gatehouse and hastened their steps so they could go through the arch into the inner courtyard before the carriage arrived.

They were in place before the footman opened the door and put down the steps.

"Good day, Lady Stowell," Bea greeted the lady. She was a plump, little woman richly dressed in a silk afternoon gown, fussy with flounces. She wore a spencer despite the heat of the day, and her face glowed with the heat, but she had not removed her bonnet, which, Alaric thought, must weigh a ton, given all the decoration that covered it.

"Who is that? Ah, it is Lady Beatrice. Good day, Lady Beatrice. I have come to have lunch with your dear mother. Are you here to take me to her? How sweet of you, dear."

"Lady Stowell, may I present Alaric Redhaven? He is a guest in the castle and is helping to organize the fête."

Lady Stowell fixed Alaric with a shrewd eye. "One of the suitors, are you? Who is your father, boy?"

Alaric bowed. "The Earl of Elsmouth, ma'am."

"The scapegrace who was sent to Brazil because of a fight with his brother. Over a woman, wasn't it? One hopes you have learned your lesson if you are competing for the hand of our Lady Beatrice. So odd of Lord Claddach. A contest! But I suppose, since you refused to go to let your mother and aunt present you, Lady Beatrice, you need to find a husband somehow."

Trouble with Lady Stowell, indeed. In one paragraph, she had found fault with him, the earl, and Bea. He wondered what her reaction was going to be when she learned her plans and schedule had been thwarted. Probably much worse than Bea had hinted.

Chapter Thirteen

BEA KNEW THAT Viscountess Stowell was rude, but she had forgotten quite how unpleasant the lady could be. Alaric was pressing his lips together so tightly that they were white. "Lady Stowell, Mr. Redhaven and I are hoping you can help us with a ‚ problem." There. A reminder to herself as well as Alaric that they needed Lady Stowell's compliance.

Alaric took her cue. "Yes, indeed, my lady. May we escort you to Lady Claddach and tell you all about it on the way?" He offered his arm with a courtly bow.

Lady Stowell sniffed. "Your manners are acceptable." She sounded surprised.

He remained slightly inclined, his elbow crooked, and after a moment the viscountess laid her hand on his arm. "Very well, young man, Lady Beatrice, what are you buttering me up for?"

Alaric put on what Bea assumed was his most ingratiating expression. "We have been speaking to Lord Beverley, my lady. He tells me you are the foremost lady of the island, after the earl's ladies, and the most prominent and influential of all the ladies who have been good enough to be judges for today's fête contests."

"Lord Beverley is too kind," Lady Stowell said, preening. "Although I am the third highest ranked lady on Claddach, behind Lady Claddach herself and Lady Beatrice. This is true. I suppose others do look up to me."

Bea, who was on Lady Claddach's other side as they entered the front door of the castle, said, "It is a matter of the schedule, Lady Stowell. Lord Beverley made some changes, no doubt very well thought out, but unfortunately…" She spread her hands in a gesture of hopelessness. "His ideas came too late. The contest schedule was posted a month ago, and to change it at this late stage is impossible."

Alaric spoke quickly before Lady Stowell could speak whatever indignant reply her expression presaged. "My lady, we have close to a thousand contest entries, and the entire contest area has been organized around the published schedule. I know you will understand how difficult it would be—how impossible—to find every contestant and tell them the schedule has been changed. And then, imagine the chaos, when some are working to one schedule and some to another."

Another annoyed sniff. "I suppose you are telling me I will have to judge on the original schedule," Lady Stowell grumbled.

If Alaric had directed that pleading smile at Bea, she would have given him anything. "My dear Lady Stowell, I knew you would understand. I realize how annoying this must be for you, and I admire the grace with which you are prepared to put your own feelings aside for the good of the fête. And, of course, of the orphanage and the church roof, the two causes that will benefit from the contest fees."

He looked around Lady Stowell and caught Bea's eye. "Isn't that wonderful, Lady Beatrice? You were certain Lady Stowell would set an example of leadership to the other lady judges, and you were right. With Lady Stowell prepared to make the best of the situation, who else could possibly complain? Thank you, my lady. Thank you so much."

"Thank you," Bea repeated. "It is going to make all the difference, I am certain. Lord Beverley is speaking to the other judges, and he will be thrilled to be able to tell them that you understand how important it is to accept the original schedule."

Lady Stowell looked rather dazed, and well she might. Alaric had simply assumed she would comply and left her to choose between being the gracious lady he assured her she was and showing herself to be self-centered and petty. "Well. Yes. They are such good causes, after all."

They had arrived at the drawing room door.

Alaric bowed again, and Bea curtseyed. "Thank you again," they chorused. Lady Stowell inclined her head, but one last thought made it all the way out of her mouth before Alaric could head it off. "This means I will have to wait between contests. I shall not wait with servants and farm workers, Lady Beatrice. You cannot ask it of me."

"Of course not, Lady Stowell," Bea assured her. "My cousin Beverley has a tent set up just for you and the gentry. I shall ensure suitable refreshments are waiting for you." Alaric had opened the drawing room door and was holding it for the viscountess.

"*Hmmph*," said Lady Stowell. "That will do, then. But I shall be expecting the schedule to be better organized for next year, mind."

With that final word, she sailed into the drawing room and, in the moment before Alaric shut the door, Bea could hear her saying, "Dear Lady Claddach. And Lady Lewiston, too. How splendid to see you."

"*Will* the schedule change for next year?" Alaric asked Bea.

"I should put her on the organizing committee," Bea grumbled, "and leave her to figure it out. Except we would very likely finish up without an organizing committee."

He touched her hand. "We achieved what we needed," he pointed out. "Time enough to worry about next year after this year is over. Thanks to you, Bea. You were brilliant."

"And you were charming," she pointed out. "We make a good team, do we not?"

He leaned closer. "The best." His eyes seemed to darken as

his pupils expanded.

Had his mind gone to the same place as hers? There was a simple way to find out. "What are you thinking, Alaric?"

"I am wishing I could kiss you," he admitted.

Her lips tingled and her belly felt suddenly soft and hollow. Her heart leapt for joy. She had been waiting so long! Well. A week, but it felt like longer. The answer was "yes" and "now" and "hurry." It was with difficulty that she swallowed those words to say something a modicum more sensible.

"Not here, where anyone might come upon us," she replied. "Follow me." Was she really going to do it? She was. She had been thinking about it for days, and they might not get another time when most of the servants and all the younger house guests were out of the castle, as well as Papa, Uncle Lewiston, and the other gentlemen.

Just beyond the head of the stairs was a linen closet. No one would have any reason to enter it. It was perfect for their purposes. She opened the door and led Alaric inside, then shut the door behind them.

Shelves full of household linen, sorted by type, quality, size, and color, lined both sides. Light filtered in from the direction of the back wall, which had a high round window above a table for folding linen before putting it away and a basket for anything that required mending.

Bea turned to face Alaric. Now what? She hoped he knew what he was about, for she had never before been kissed.

"Are you sure?" he asked her, his voice husky. He was certain, it seemed, for he was holding his arms out to her.

She nodded as she stepped closer to him. His hands came to rest on her waist, and he gazed into her eyes. What was he about? This was not what she had imagined. The weight and warmth of his hands on her waist felt wonderful, but it was not enough. It was not kissing. After a moment, she asked, "Are you going to kiss me?"

"I am," he assured her. "I am just deciding where to start."

Bea frowned. Surely one simply pressed their lips to the lips of the other person. Was that not the whole point? But she had no time to ask, for he used one hand to tilt her head to one side and placed a kiss on her neck, just below her ear. A shiver ran down her neck and through her body.

He kissed her again, this time on her jaw, less than an inch from the first kiss, and followed along her jaw line. Not just kisses, either. He scraped his teeth over her skin then soothed it with his tongue. By the time his kisses reached the other ear, she was plastered against him, her knees too weak to hold her up.

Then he came back across her cheek and at last reached her lips. Now he would settle his mouth over hers, as she had seen men do with their wives or lovers when they thought themselves unobserved. Good. His ministrations so far had set her whole body tingling, and particularly her womanly core. She could not wait to find out what his lips felt like on hers.

But no. The rain of kisses continued. She tried to object but could manage nothing beyond a moan. An indignant moan, but hardly a clear request for more. Still, he responded, settling his mouth over hers. It felt amazing, but she still needed something else.

He opened his mouth and ran his tongue along her lips. No. That wasn't what she was waiting for. Not quite. Then, he nipped her lower lip with his teeth, and she opened with a gasp. Alaric slipped his tongue into her mouth.

A long interlude of learning one another followed. He tasted warm, if warmth could be tasted, and sweet. When she pressed her tongue against his, he hummed with pleasure, and when she chased his tongue into his mouth, he hummed even more loudly, then he followed her back, and their tongues tangled and danced while his mouth moved and his hands held her firmly against his body, one in the middle of her back and one grasping her behind.

She had no idea how long they kissed. The need for more returned, more urgent than ever. Her breasts felt heavy and ached in a way that demanded a soothing touch, and so did that area she had been taught to ignore between her legs.

Eventually, Alaric withdrew his mouth, sighed, and moved his hand from her buttock up her back to her head, holding her in place while he rested his cheek against her hair. He was breathing heavily, she was pleased to note as she was panting, as if she had run from the castle to the beach. And back.

She stood leaning against him, waiting for her breath to settle while all the thoughts that the kiss had driven from her head came crowding back into it.

"I must go," she said at last. Her voice shook, and she was still not certain her knees would hold her up. "I do not know the time, but the girls setting out the food on the castle stall will be looking for me."

"And the contestants for me," Alaric admitted. "I ought to warn you it would have been a bad idea to remain here together, even if we could. That kiss…" He shook his head, slowly. "It was a promise of more, dearest Bea. And we cannot take more. Not without being wed. I would not dishonor you or your father. Not for the world."

A promise of more. Bea had sensed that. And while her body was perfectly willing to explore that *more* immediately, her mind knew better. "It was a beautiful kiss," she told him. "My first. I shall never forget it." She stepped backward and he dropped his arms and let her go.

His expression appeared alarmed. "Your first? And I kissed you in a closet among the linens? You deserve better than that."

"I think a kiss any better than that would kill me, Alaric," she replied.

A KISS THAT would kill her! Bea's innocent remark had Alaric thinking about what the French called *la petite mort*—"the little death." That brief loss of consciousness accompanying the most exquisite of climaxes. How he would love to bring Bea to that moment, and to watch her as she experienced her first *petite mort.*

He would have preferred to linger in the linen closet remembering their kisses. Or to go for a long walk to think about what made that kiss different to anything he'd ever experienced before. Sadly, he was needed at the fête. Anything might have happened while he was absent.

Luke had everything under control, however, though he was pleased to hand over the responsibilities to Alaric. With the increasing number of arrivals, Luke was needed to supervise those who were shepherding carriages, carts, and horses to the prepared waiting areas, and checking pedestrians as they entered at the outer gatehouse.

After that, Alaric had no time to think about anything but the contests, the contestants, and the judges. Or, at least, all the judges who did not happen to be gentry. Beverley was being diligent about looking after the upper class only. The middle sort and the working class were beneath his attention, and Alaric didn't want to make a fuss while others were around, so he got away with it, the arrogant blellum.

By the time Lord Claddach announced the opening of the fête, the grounds were already crowded. "Has everyone on the entire island downed their tools for the day to come to the fête?" Alaric wondered aloud. The people who were waiting patiently in the sun for the produce tent to open chorused a resounding, "Yes," though one woman added, "Those who can be spared."

The contest schedule and Maddrell's pocket watch were seldom out of Alaric's hand after that. He had a cadre of contest stewards—footmen, maids, and volunteers from the town—but not a minute went by without a question to be answered, a difficulty to be smoothed, an ego to be stroked. Thank goodness many of the stewards had done this before and could help out when he was stumped.

He moved from contest to contest, staying long enough to congratulate winners, commiserate with losers, and thank judges, then hurry on to the next. Beverley appeared occasionally, escorting a judge he regarded as lofty enough to merit his consideration.

In the heat of the sun, Alaric soon left his cravat in his coat in one of the judges' tents. Even so, he welcomed the moments under one of the marquees erected to shade the animals, even with the noise and accumulating smell.

Beverley was least in sight when several of the bull pens proved to be more fragile than intended, and a trio of bulls made a break for the pens holding the heifers.

Fortunately, one took exception to the romantic intentions of the other two, and while they were disputing the matter, Alaric managed to organize the owners of the bulls and a number of other islanders, sending a contingent to shore up the bull pens, and setting the others to diverting the bulls toward the pall-mall alley, with its sturdy walls.

Thank goodness for Luke! He saw what was happening and brought the men answering to him to help with the herding, so the incident was soon over, and Alaric could get back to the next contest.

When the last of the contests ended, he still was not finished, though Beverley had left with the judges who were invited to dinner. Someone had to supervise an orderly clean up, and Alaric supposed that someone would be him.

A group of three people—two men and one woman—approached him. Alaric, with an internal sigh, gave them a smile and prepared to listen. He'd met them all in the course of the day, though he'd lost their names in the flood of introductions the day had held. A church warden from the other side of the island, the wife of the island's foremost boatbuilder, and the town's mayor. The church warden spoke first.

"Well, boyo, it's a good job ye've done this day."

"Aye," said the mayor, "the job of three men." He chuckled. "Or, I should say, of two men and one woman."

"And that we know for a fact, you darlin' man," declared the boatbuilder's wife, with a broad smile. "For would'na we three have been after doin' what you did today if his lordship had'na set you to the task?"

Alaric stared at them, speechless.

"Aye, lad," the mayor confirmed. "Ye're looking at the contest steward." He spread his hands in a gesture that included all three of them.

"We've come to take over, boyo," the church warden told him.

"Ye've earned a rest, and so you have," the boatbuilder's wife said, kindly.

"Besides, ye've got a fine dinner to dress for, I understand," the mayor reminded him.

It crossed Alaric's mind to wonder if this was one of Lord Claddach's tests. Was he supposed to insist on working on till everyone had gone home? But the woman was right. If he did so, he was likely to be late for dinner.

Then Luke strolled up, with Meadowsweet and Fairweather. "Ah, good," he said, with a nod and a smile at the three islanders. "I see you've got your marching orders. Come and walk up to the castle with us."

Looking up at the path to the castle, Alaric could see others walking that path. "Howard and Dashwood have already gone," Luke told him.

It must be right, if the others were gone.

He shook the hands of each of the islanders, thanking them. "Not at all, lad," the mayor said.

"You did us a favor, boyo," the church warden told him. "First time in years I've had fête day off."

The boatmaker's wife seized him by the shoulders and pulled him down for a kiss on the cheek, which she then patted. "Thank you, Mr. Redhaven. You'll do."

He grabbed his coat and cravat and returned to the castle. Colyn was waiting for him, and there was time for a hot bath and to dress, but not much more. Alaric was not the first in the drawing room, where they were gathering before dinner. He was the first of the suitors. But no. Wait. Beverley was there, in the corner, admiring himself in the mirrored backboard of a tall whatnot.

"Cousin Beverley cannot seem to walk past a mirror." The wry comment came from Bea, who had stepped up beside him. "He is in love with himself." He met her gaze and smiled at her. The room suddenly seemed brighter and warmer.

Love. And yes, just so. I have gone and done it, he realized. *I have fallen in love with Lady Beatrice Collister.*

But then, he realized what she had just said. *Ah yes! Beverley's in love with himself.* The thought triggered another. "His love affair with himself," he repeated, out loud.

Chapter Fourteen

B EA HAD THE same idea as him. He could see it in her face as
her eyes widened and a grin spread. "Narcissus," she said,
keeping her voice low. "He fell in love with his own handsome
reflection. A victim, he, of beauty's snare...Lost at a glimpse.
Young man, beware...and then something about still water."

Alaric nodded. He was grinning, too. It was the answer to the
third clue. Now all he had to do was find the painting or statue or
whatever it was that pictured the impossibly handsome young
hunter of Greek mythology, who fell in love with his own
reflection in a pool of still water.

"I know where it is," Bea said. "I shall show you in the morning."

"Your father doesn't want—"

"Leave it to me. I will think of something."

She would, too. *My Bea can solve any problem put before her.* His
Bea? Not yet. He had to win the trials, or at least place in the top
three. And he had to convince Bea that her future lay with him.

They were interrupted by Fairweather and Meadowsweet,
the conversation became general, and then Alaric was assigned to
take one of Beverley's sisters into dinner. Even so, one part of
Alaric's mind kept thinking of ways to convince Bea he was the
right consort for the Lady of Claddach. The kiss was all very well.

No. That wasn't it. The kiss had been amazing, spectacular, world changing. But Bea wouldn't be swayed, he was certain, by further kisses, however exceptional. She was intelligent and focused, with a sense of responsibility for and to her people and her land. Kisses were nice, but hardly important to the running of an island. He would have to appeal to her mind—and especially to her sense of duty. Also, she wanted a partner. Not someone who would try to be earl in all but name, leaving her without an opportunity to use her knowledge and her acumen, but someone who would support her abilities while allowing her to be countess.

He'd rein his desire in, Alaric decided, and focus on how well they worked together. If he could, for his admiration and his desire seemed to set fire to one another—the more he respected her, the more he wanted to bed her. And that kiss had only reinforced his admiration for all her sterling qualities.

In the train of the British envoy to the royal court of Portugal in exile in Brazil, he had attended many a grand dinner. He could hold a pleasantly flirtatious conversation and handle successive courses without giving either his full attention. When it was time to turn to the lady on his other side, he did so.

In this case, she was the daughter of a man Lord Claddach called, "the biggest farmer on the island, apart from myself." He had been introduced while they were in the line to enter the dining room.

"Are you having a pleasant evening so far, Miss Kewish?"

"Yes, Mr. Redhaven," she answered, but more as if it was the polite response than with any enthusiasm.

Alaric set himself to find a topic that would relax her and encourage her to talk. "Were you at the fête, today? It was very crowded. I did not know the island had that many people!"

"I was," she answered, and then confided, "I saw you there. I had a rose in the contest for best bloom."

"Did you, indeed? Let me think. The lady who won was from the other side of the island. A neighbor, perhaps?"

"It was Mrs. Stean from our village," she said. "Hers was very lovely, was it not? She was the one who first made me interested in growing roses, and she has been so supportive. I did not expect my rose to beat hers, but I am proud to have been a finalist."

"That is why your name sounded familiar," Alaric commented. "I heard it read out. I do apologize, Miss Kewish, for not remembering."

"I daresay you heard a great number of names today, Mr. Redhaven," she replied, making his excuses for him.

"Tell me about your rose," he said. "Is it very difficult to grow them?"

That was all it took. She chattered away cheerfully, until she suddenly realized she had been doing all the talking. "But Mr. Redhaven, you cannot be interested in all this."

"On the contrary," he replied, honestly. "I love to listen to people who are truly knowledgeable about their topic. I have learned a great deal that way. Witness tonight. I had no idea that roses bloom more reliably on Claddach if they are grown on a certain root stock."

He chuckled. "I cannot say when that will become useful, but if it does, I shall be sure to remember you, Miss Kewish, and be grateful."

She gifted him with a sweet smile. "You are kind to say so. However, it is surely time for you to tell me about your driving passion. I am sure that you will be interesting, even if it *is* horses."

Had Howard, who was on the lady's other side, been prosing on about his horses again? "I do appreciate a good horse," Alaric admitted. "I would not call it a driving passion, though. Perhaps I have not yet found mine."

A fortnight ago, he would have said firmly that it was the land, and all the many skills and activities to do with getting the best from the land. Now, Bea Collister had moved to first place in his scheme of things. He wasn't going to say that to a complete stranger, though.

"I have recently arrived at the Isle of Claddach," he told her. "I was in Brazil learning how to be a diplomat, but I wasn't very good of it."

"Isn't diplomacy about charming people?" she asked. "You seem charming to me."

"Ah, but you are excellent company," he replied. "Tell me more about Claddach. You live on the other side of the island, I believe."

They conversed amiably until Lady Claddach stood to signal the end of the meal, and Lord Claddach stood too. "Dear guests," he announced, "we gentlemen shall not take our port here at the table tonight but shall accompany you ladies to the ballroom. I, and I might add, my wife and my daughter, expect every gentleman to do his duty. And, you will be pleased to know, port shall be served in the ballroom. Onward, ladies and gentlemen."

It was a pleasant evening, Alaric mused as he readied himself for bed, much, much later. He would have preferred to have been less tired when it began, but he thought he had acquitted himself well enough.

His experience in the diplomatic service had included dancing with every available wallflower and flirting with every elderly matron. He had practiced both skills tonight, until his feet were sore, and his face hurt from so much smiling. But he had been rewarded. Bea had granted him a dance and had gone in with him to supper—for which he had been well and truly ready after several hours of dancing.

And tomorrow morning—this morning, rather, for it was hours after midnight—she was meeting him in the garden to show him the statue of Narcissus. During supper, she had whispered his instructions for the morning. He was to meet her just outside the inner gatehouse, early, once the sun was above the horizon, but no later. He hoped the statue was in a private place. He would love to steal another kiss. While keeping a tight rein on his appetites, he ordered himself, sternly.

BEA WALKED THROUGH the garden with Alaric in the early morning light. Long ago, when *Cashtal Vaaich* had been the refuge for the whole island, what was now garden had been kept bare of everything except blades of grass. Any invader who made his way past the outer wall would find himself exposed to every archer and spear thrower on the walls above.

Cashtal Vaaish in those days had earned its name—Castle Death—for it had been death to approach it with hostile intent.

Vikings, Irish, Scots, Welsh—all had tried their luck, not once but many times. The Lords of Claddach and their warriors sat in their high castle, and in the hill fort that preceded it. They left the invaders alone, until one of the notorious storms of the Irish Sea swept through. Then, under cover of the rain and wind, the men of Claddach would attack and win back their land. Any who lived would be given a choice. Swear fealty to Claddach or die.

Only two men had ever taken the island, and both by marriage to the only child of the Lord of Claddach. The first had been a Norman knight, Turstin Fitz Waundrile. He had persuaded his wife to swear fealty to William II of England in return for being named countess, with her sons to be earls after her. From that day on, any invader risked facing English might, as well as Claddach's own men and the temperamental weather.

The second was Jamie McAllister, who'd married the second Lady of Claddach in the fifteenth century. His surname, anglicized to Collister, remained the family name today. If Bea became Lady of Claddach, she would be the third countess in the seven-and-a-bit centuries since the first.

"The gardens were laid out in the seventeenth century," Bea told Alaric, "after the restoration. There were gardens in Stuart times, but they were ripped up and the trees chopped down when the thirteenth earl feared invasion during the civil war. During the wars with Napoleon, we had plans to strip the grounds again. I am glad they were not needed."

"I am, too," Alaric agreed. "Your gardens are lovely."

"Papa and some of the earls before him brought back statues

from Greece and Rome after their grand tours. It is one of those we are going to see." They were making their way around the castle. The path wound through trees on the edge of a sunken garden that bordered the inner wall. And here were the steps that led down into the garden.

"Was this the moat?" Alaric asked.

"A dry moat. My nurse said bears were kept in it, or sometimes, she said, wolves. Papa said it was more likely to be guard dogs."

"A pack of hungry guard dogs would do a good job, I imagine, if anyone made it up the hill this far."

"We investigated flooding it," Bea told him. "If the French invaded. The spring further up the hill, on the other side of the castle, would fill it in a couple of days, Papa calculated. But the head gardener said the ground drains too freely, which is why it is not a pond instead of a garden."

She turned a corner into the little garden within a garden she was looking for. "In spring, this garden is full of narcissus. The flower, that is. But I think that is what you are looking for."

She pointed. The statue was of a naked man. He was leaning over to peer into a pool, with a knee on the pool's wall, and the opposite foot on the semi-circle of paving that bordered the wall. The pool was against the outer side of the dry moat, and water trickled down through ferns, lichens, and mosses to fall into the pool, but the disturbance was all on one side. Directly beneath the statue's marble gaze, the water was still.

The garden was still in shadow, since the sun was not high enough to shine its rays into this declivity, but in broad daylight, Narcissus would be reflected against the background of the sky. "Echo is peeping around the rock at the back of the fountain," Bea told Alaric. "There. See?" The rocky backdrop to the pool was even darker than that pool itself, but she could just pick out the shape of the poor nymph who wasted away to just her voice, yearning for the man who could not look away from his own reflection to discover she existed.

"How on earth," Alaric asked, "did your father expect us to find this statue hidden away here in the dry moat? Or have we got the wrong answer? No, this is it. It all fits, Bea. The trap of beauty's snare. Love can kill. That might be a number of stories. But still waters?"

Bea considered his question. "He did not object to me helping you," she pointed out. "Perhaps one of the tests is whether you gentlemen ask for help. I will say, before you ask, that you are the only one to ask me, but any Claddach servant—indeed, any number of Claddach's people—will know the artworks as well as, or even better than, me."

"I believe it," Alaric agreed. "I'd swear the island folk were taking notes all day yesterday. During the steeplechase, too. Do you remember that your father arranged for us to come across a distressed woman and her cart?"

"Yes, and disqualified those who ignored her," Bea commented. They shared a look of understanding. It seemed to Bea that Alaric leaned closer to her as if perhaps to kiss her but then he took a step back and looked down at the moat.

"I shall go to your father and name Narcissus as the answer to the third clue," Alaric said. "Have you noticed that so far, they are all love stories, of different types? Unhappy ones. I hope that is not your father's message!"

"We shall have to see where the other clues lead us," Bea told him. He looked at her again and he seemed to struggle with himself before he stepped close once more.

"Bea," Alaric asked, "May I kiss you again?"

She answered him by lifting her face to his and their lips met. It was even better than the last time, now that she knew what to do. The kiss—or rather, kisses—spun on and on, and she never wanted them to end.

During their first kiss, he had held her close to his body, but only his lips had moved. This time, his hands roved, sliding under the coat she wore to brush gently over her skin, to cup and stroke her breasts.

She knew where this was heading, and she wanted more. For long, exquisite moments, her body clouded her mind, and she could see no reason not to take what she wanted, but her mind was screaming at her about duty and Claddach. Perhaps Alaric had a similar struggle, for just as she managed to recapture the lost reins of her desire, he lifted his head and his hands stilled. Their eyes met and held. This time, she didn't want to look away; she could stare into his gaze forever, she decided.

"We must stop," he said.

"I know," she told him.

He did not immediately release her. Just as well, for the strength only slowly returned to her legs.

"Just to be clear, Lady Beatrice Collister," he said, "I *am* courting you. Trials aside, I can imagine no greater happiness than being your husband." He kissed her nose.

Bea didn't know what to say. She smiled instead and stepped away. "We should return to the castle," she said. They walked back through the sunken garden, hand in hand.

It was all very well to say, "trials aside," but the reality was she had promised to choose her husband from those who completed the trials. Of course, Alaric, to her mind at least, was one of the front runners. Still, she wasn't going to break a vow over a kiss. She owed Claddach her responsibility and that meant choosing the right man to be her earl.

Bea had guessed at some of what the trials were meant to disclose. Organizing ability, courage, sportsmanship, determination, kindness, courtesy, ethics, imagination, the ability to work with others. All important qualities, she agreed. But would Papa find her a husband who could love her?

Which led to the question: Did Alaric love her? People, men especially, married for all sorts of reasons. And love might not be enough. She sometimes wondered if her own parents still loved one another. Her mother spent her time with other fashionable ladies, gossiping and carrying out light flirtations with idle gentlemen. Her father was absorbed in his duties to Claddach and to the House of Lords.

Even now, when Papa had been told that his time on earth was limited, Mama seemed more interested in being with her sister. Not that Mama knew about Papa's illness. Papa had made Bea promise not to say anything, because he did not want Mama to worry, but surely, she could see for herself that Papa was not well?

Bea had never forgotten the conversation four years ago, when she was eighteen. Mama had been campaigning for months to have Papa force Bea to go to London for the Season. "The London marriage mart is no place to find a husband of real substance," he had declared one day.

"But Claddach," Mama had said, "I found you in London."

Papa's response had been a sigh. "Leave Beatrice alone, Mary," he had said. "She is young yet. And when she is of age to marry, we shall find a way for her to meet men who will be up to her weight."

"Up to her weight, indeed," Mama had objected. "Men are not horses, Claddach." But she had stopped bothering Bea about London and husbands, beyond the occasional wistful comment.

It would be easier if men were horses. One chose a stallion for a mare based on breeding lines, conformation, performance, temperament, and current progeny. Bea sighed.

"A penny for your thoughts," said Alaric.

"A fleeting memory," she replied. "Not worth repeating." They were nearly at the door that would let them unobtrusively into the castle, and those were the first words they had spoken since he announced that he wanted to be her husband.

"The trials will be over in a few days," she said. "I believe you will among those selected by my father as suitable for Claddach. I..." she hunted for words for a moment, settling on, "I am glad. I do not feel it right to make any commitments while the trials continue, but Alaric, I have helped no one else with their clues. I have allowed no one else to court me."

There. But what would she do if he did not love her? For Bea was very much afraid she was falling in love with him.

Chapter Fifteen

A LARIC FELT LIKE crowing, but he could not, of course, show Bea the disrespect of sharing her revelation with anyone else. Not even Colyn or Luke, who were the nearest he had to friends on the Isle of Claddach.

He parted from Bea at the foot of the stairs and went to her father's study. The earl was probably there already—he seemed to be an early riser. And sure enough, when Alaric knocked on the door, the earl's voice told him to enter.

"You again," said the earl. "Have you solved the third clue, Redhaven?"

"I believe I have, sir. The verse is about Narcissus, and possibly also Echo. Though mostly Narcissus. The statue of Narcissus is in the sunken garden, staring into a pool, and Echo is there, too."

"Ah," said the earl. "That was where you and my daughter had been when I saw you coming back through the courtyard."

Does Claddach have eyes everywhere? But that was a silly question. Of course, he did. "Yes, my lord," Alaric admitted.

"And was it you or my daughter who solved the clue?" the earl asked.

"Both of us." Alaric's lips twitched into a grin at the memory. "At the time, Lord Beverley was admiring himself in the mirrors of the whatnot in the drawing room."

That surprised Claddach into a bark of laughter. He and Alaric exchanged an amused glance.

"Lady Beatrice did show me the statue, though, sir."

"Nothing wrong with that," said Claddach. "Everyone who finds it will have help from someone. It is not something people are likely to chance on. I suppose you want your next clue?"

"Yes, please, my lord," Alaric said, wondering if the earl's tolerance of his cheek would extend to telling him who else had solved the third clue.

Claddach pulled out a drawer and removed a folder. Alaric was startled to see his own name on the front. The earl pulled out a folded sheet of paper, much like the ones that held the previous clues, and handed it over.

"Your fourth clue, Redhaven. The answer to the question you are too polite to ask is yes. You are still the leader in the treasure hunt. No one else has solved the third clue. If you plan any more early-morning excursions with my daughter, or excursions at any other time of the day or night, you will oblige me by including a chaperone. Enjoy your breakfast, young man. You might mention to the other suitors that I will see you all in the entry hall at ten o'clock."

Did his early morning spy also see our kiss? Alaric bowed toward Bea's father. The man who would be his father-in-law if all went well. Suggesting a chaperone could just mean that the earl had been young himself, once. Either way, his suggestion was fair, but also kind. The earl seemed to like him. Alaric vowed to do everything he could not to let the man down. "I will, my lord." The earl inclined his head and then turned his attention back to his desk.

Alaric stopped by a window on the stairs to read the clue.

"To save his liege requires a fee—
"A loyal man, he must agree.
"His bride he finds a dear delight.
"Choose wisely. Day? Or dark of night?"

Another cryptic verse. Nothing immediately occurred, but at least he knew—or at least he *thought* he knew—that the answer would be a set of lovers. Narcissus didn't count as a set, but he was still a lover. Chuckling at his own rambling thoughts, Alaric hurried on up the stairs to leave his outdoor coat in his bedchamber.

Colyn was there before him, and his eyes lit up when he saw Alaric. "Mr. Redhaven. Ye're to go out today, sir. Lord Claddach is after givin' all the suitors a list of tenants to visit. And this evenin', the gentlemen are to entertain the ladies."

"Thank you, Colyn. That explains why Lord Claddach wants to see us all in the entry hall at ten. I have my fourth clue, Colyn." He waved the piece of paper. "No idea what it means, yet."

He read it to Colyn, who commented, "Sounds like the boyo in the verse has to get married to rescue his lord? Lucky fellow gets a bride he likes." He shook his head. "I couldn't say more than that, sir."

A man who marries a woman he loves to save his lord, and after that has to make a choice between day and night. *I know that I've heard a story like that.* But try as he might, he could not call it to mind.

EACH OF THE suitors had been assigned a gig with a groom to drive it. The back was loaded with baskets for the tenant families they were to visit. They had been paired with a lady each, and Alaric found himself escorting Miss Radcliffe.

Bea was with Meadowsweet. Alaric followed them with his eyes, and then recalled his manners and looked at Miss Radcliffe instead. "We have five houses to visit," he said, handing over the list he had been given. "Do you know the families at all, Miss Radcliffe?" *Might as well take advantage of local knowledge.*

"Two of them," Miss Radcliffe answered. "They have children at the school my mother supports. And another by reputation."

From her tone, Alaric guessed the reputation was not good, and she confirmed it when she said, "The husband is a drunkard, and the children are wild, though my mother says the wife does the best she can."

The groom had been given the route, it seemed, for he did not ask for directions but drove down the hill from the castle and turned left, away from the town. They stopped first at the home of one of the families Miss Radcliffe knew through the school, where they were greeted cheerfully and invited in, "For Da will be that cross if he does not see ye, Miss Radcliffe, and the gentleman, too. One of Lady Bea's suitors are you, sir?"

Alaric bowed as he said, "I am. I'm the one who was shipwrecked on your beach, ma'am. Redhaven is my name."

"Ma'am," the woman giggled. "As if I was a fine lady. Come along inside, sir. Lucky you were to come off alive, Mr. Redhaven." The front door opened directly into a small but clean and tidy sitting room. The woman of the house raised her voice as they entered. "Da, here's that pretty Miss Radcliffe come to see ye, and Mr. Redhaven, too, he that was washed up on the beach."

"Da" was sitting right next to the fire and, despite the warmth of the day, was wrapped in blankets so that nothing showed but his hands and face. He raised a scrawny hand and displayed a gap-toothed smile. "More dead nor alive," he quavered.

"I was, yes," Alaric told him, raising his voice in imitation of their hostess. He put the basket he had been carrying on a low table and squatted down on his haunches, so that his head was more on a level with the old man's. "But I am well again now."

"Fine doings up at castle, eh?" the old man asked.

"Fine doings," Alaric agreed. "Most nights, the ladies sing for us, or play the piano. Tonight, it will be the turn of the gentlemen to entertain. What should I do, do you think? I am not a great singer, and I cannot play the piano."

"Dost juggle, lad?" The old man asked, and made a wheezing

sound that Alaric figured, after an alarmed moment, was a laugh.

"One ball at a time," Alaric answered promptly. "If that." Miss Radcliffe and the woman had disappeared, taking the basket with them.

The old man wheezed another laugh. "Ye'll have to tell a tale, then," he said. "Tell it me, lad, and I'll give 'ee a report."

Alaric laughed and complied, making a story out of a hunting trip hosted by the Portuguese Court, that the British delegation had attended. He was just completing the story with the words, "...chased by the alligator," when the man's daughter and Miss Radcliffe returned.

"Da" was cackling so hard that it set him coughing, and his daughter had to thump him on the back before he could say, "Tell 'em that one, lad. I nigh wet meself, and so I did. Tell 'em that one."

"Miss Radcliffe and Mr. Redhaven need to go now, Da," their hostess shouted. "'Ee, but he enjoyed your visit, Mr. Redhaven," she added in a more normal tone, as she ushered them out of the house.

"It was nice of you to entertain Mr. Whittle while I chatted with his daughter and grandchildren in the kitchen," said Miss Radcliffe to Alaric, as they drove away.

"I hope," said Alaric, "if I grow to be that old, someone will visit and tell me stories of far-off places and make me laugh."

"'I nigh wet meself, and so I did,'" quoted Miss Radcliffe in an uncanny imitation of the old man's tone, and then blushed bright red. But he laughed to let her know he appreciated her skills of mimicry, and she should feel no shame.

Miss Radcliffe was not the staid demure cipher she appeared on the surface!

On the next two visits, they were met by children, who hovered politely but impatiently as Alaric lifted the basket from the rear of the gig and carried it inside for the woman of the house, who had been attracted by children's shouts.

At both houses, Miss Radcliffe talked to the mother while

Alaric did his best to entertain the children. The first house was easy enough. The boys who greeted them had abandoned a game of knuckle bones when they arrived. After receiving a biscuit from the basket, they were happy to usher Alaric outside and let him join their game.

He hadn't played since he was a boy himself, but the skill quickly returned, and when Miss Radcliffe emerged from the house, he was showing them some of the tricks he had learned years ago, when he used to play with Tarquin and the stable boys.

He was more at a loss at the next house, where they ran to daughters. However, he worked on the principle that even such small morsels of femininity would respond well to being asked what they wanted to do, and soon found himself being taught how to skip. His efforts—exaggerated to amuse his audience—had them collapsing with laughter, until they took pity on him and "taught" him to make daisy chains instead, so that he was wearing a crown of flowers with Miss Redcliffe emerged from the cottage.

Some thought teased at him throughout the visit, and as they drove away, it coalesced. "What do women want?" he declared.

Miss Radcliffe must have thought the abrupt question was intended for her, for she answered, her voice crisp. "It depends on the woman, Mr. Redhaven. Is this about Bea?"

He shot her a smile. "Indirectly. It is a legend from the court of King Arthur. Sir Gawaine and the Loathly Lady. The knight goes on a quest to find out what women want. Now all I need to do is to find a statue or a painting that illustrates the legend." In the legend, the knight was offered the answer to his question, in return for which he promised to marry Dame Ragnall, a spectacularly ugly lady.

"Oh, I can tell you that," Miss Radcliffe replied. "That is, if a tapestry will do? There is one in the little parlor on the second floor of the Tudor tower. It has three panels. Gawaine and his ugly bride, with his friends all mocking him. Gawaine and his lovely bride in the night, where she explains that the curse that made her ugly is half broken, so she can be beautiful for half of any twenty-four period, but ugly for the rest. She tells him to choose. In the third, Gawaine has his beautiful bride on his arm, out in the light of day, and his friends are all amazed and envious."

Yes, that was the story, and an interesting selection by Lord Claddach.

"Thank you," Alaric said. "You know about the treasure hunt?"

"Yes. Bea told me. I take it you have just figured out one of the clues."

Alaric nodded. "With your help, Miss Radcliffe." It had to be the answer to the riddle for in the story, the woman, Dame Ragnall told Gawaine "Their own way," meaning women want their own way. On his wedding night to Dame Ragnall, Gawain discovered she wasn't ugly but had turned into a spectacularly beautiful woman.

Asked whether he wanted to spend his nights with a beauty or show his lovely wife off to his mocking friends, Gawaine remembered, "What do women want?" and told Dame Ragnall to make her own choice. His choice to let *her* make the decision broke the rest of the spell, and she remained ravishingly beautiful day and night.

So, Alaric decided, when asked what do women want? He would answer, "to make their own choices." It was a lesson worth remembering. And, it reminded him a bit of Bea, a woman who certainly knew her own mind and who would always want to make her own choices.

He mused on this as they drove into a little fishing village. "The next house is Eamon Gorry's," Miss Radcliffe disclosed.

She sounded tense, and Alaric looked at her more closely. "The one with the drunkard father and the overworked mother?" he asked.

"That is it. You are a good listener, Mr. Redhaven."

Alaric managed not to shrug, which would have been ungentlemanly, but he was uncomfortable with the praise. He merely paid attention. People were more interesting when one paid attention.

"Are we likely to have trouble?" he asked.

"That depends on whether Gorry is at home, and how much he has had to drink," she replied. She then looked him up and down, as if assessing his strength and size. "He would be a fool to take you on, Mr. Redhaven. You are at least half as big again as him, and twice as fit. If he is rude and belligerent, I shall rely on you to deal with him. Bullies attack the weak, and you are certainly not weak!"

She appeared to be half joking, but Alaric had dealt with drunkards before, and did not discount the risk. "If he is rude and belligerent, keep behind me, Miss Radcliffe."

As they pulled up outside the cottage, they heard bellowing and things breaking. The groom turned to face them, frowning as he said, "Better we move on, Miss and Sir."

"The children will need their basket," Miss Radcliffe protested.

A woman's scream from inside the house settled the matter as far as Alaric was concerned. "Look after Miss Radcliffe," he ordered the groom as he leaped down from the carriage. He couldn't stand by while a woman was being abused.

Inside the cottage, a red-faced man loomed over a little boy who was standing between him and the sobbing woman in the corner. As Alaric burst into the room, the man swept the boy to one side, throwing him into the wall. The boy let out a loud shriek, and the woman surged to her feet and took a step toward the child.

Gorry lurched toward her, his arm raised, and his fist clenched. Alaric caught his fist and twisted the arm up behind the man's back. "Enough," he said. He ignored the string of abuse coming from Gorry to watch Mrs. Gorry kneel beside the child.

She turned her head to glare at her husband. "Ye broke his arm, ye sodden devil." She'd been hit in the face. Her nose was still bleeding, and both nose and one eye were already bruised and puffy.

"Little brat should'na have come 'tween a man an' his wife," grumbled Gorry. He tried to break away, and Alaric jerked his hand higher up his back, so he whimpered and stopped struggling.

Mrs. Gorry ignored them both, crooning to the boy, "Dinna try to move it, Padeen. Ochone, ochone."

"We will fetch a doctor for Padeen," said Miss Radcliffe from the doorway. "As for you, Eamon Gorry, what did the earl tell you about keeping your hands from your wife and children?"

"Besom," Gorry hissed at her. "Ain't no one got the right to come 'tween man and wife."

"We'll see about that," said Miss Radcliffe, carefully skirting around the edge of the room to stay clear of the bully. She knelt beside Mrs. Gorry and examined Padeen. "It is a bad break, Mr. Redhaven. Will you send the groom for Dr. Bryant?"

"And what do we pay with, Eamon?" Mrs. Gorry demanded, turning on her husband. "Ye've drunk the rent money. Aye, and the food money, too."

"A man has a right—" began Gorry, but Alaric twisted his arm until he turned and then forced him, stumbling, from the cottage, so that Alaric could send the groom on his errand without releasing Gorry.

"And once you've sent Bryant," he commanded, "see the magistrate, and tell him that Gorry has beaten his wife and broken his son Padeen's arm."

"A man has a right," Gorry mumbled.

"Aye, Mr. Redhaven," said the groom.

Chapter Sixteen

ONCE A COUPLE of constables had collected Gorry, Alaric held Padeen still while Dr. Bryant set his arm, and meanwhile Miss Radcliffe collected the four other children, a boy and three girls, all smaller than Padeen. The smallest could barely toddle after the others, and sometimes the biggest girl picked her up and carried her. They emerged from hiding around the cottage, and Miss Radcliffe coaxed them into helping her to take ingredients from the castle's basket and turn them into supper.

By the time Dr. Bryant had seen to Padeen and inspected Mrs. Gorry's injuries, a delicious smell was rising from the pot on the trivet near the fire.

"Earl will send him away, my Eamon," Mrs. Gorry said, suddenly. "Off Claddach."

"And he should," said Dr. Bryant. "This is not the first time I've patched you up, Mrs. Gorry."

"He were a good man once," Mrs. Gorry insisted. "Afore he started with the drink." She looked at her son and her eyes grew hard. "Last week, he slapped Cissolt so hard a tooth flew right out of her head, poor *cailin veg*. Aye, and it's not the first time he has hit Padeen or punched him, and so it isn't."

"He hits our Mam," said the smaller boy. "When I'm a wee bit bigger, me 'n Padeen are going to hit him so hard he'll go away and ne'er come back."

"Shush now, Dolen," said his mother. "The earl will send Da away. And what will become of us, I dinna know."

Padeen's eyes were clouded by pain and the spot of laudanum the doctor had given him, but he piped up. "We'll be right, Ma. You'll see."

They left the family eating the dinner Miss Radcliffe and the children had made. Miss Radcliffe had promised she and Lady Beatrice would call again the next day, to help Mrs. Gorry make a plan.

"Though as far as I can see, they will be better off with Gorry gone," she told Alaric as they drove away. "Mrs. Gorry has a good job, but Gorry lost his as a fisherman because he could not be relied on. I believe Gorry spends Mrs. Gorry's wages as fast as she can earn them. He is supposed to be supervising the children, but he ignores them. Padeen and Cissolt look after them when Mrs. Gorry is at work, while Gorry drinks. I would like to see them, all but the baby, in school. Perhaps now, Mrs. Gorry will agree."

They were heading straight back to the castle, having sent the groom to deliver the last basket with their apologies. As it was, they would be late for dinner, but it could not be helped. And Alaric had given next to no thought to entertaining the ladies this evening. What on earth could he do?

BEA HAD BEEN paired with Ambrose Howard for the tenant visits. Probably just as well, for Mr. Howard just stood around exuding arrogance and superiority, and said nothing. That left Bea to talk to the tenants, which suited her. Howard was useful for carrying the basket and little else, she decided.

And then, on the third visit, she discovered Mr. Howard's outward appearance was merely a mask, behind which he hid that he was completely out of his depth talking to farm laborers and their wives.

This household comprised three generations—the couple, their seven children, and the husband's parents. Howard, as usual, carried the basket into the house, demanded to know where he could put it down, then retreated to stand by the fireplace and glower at the room.

Perhaps the littlest of the tenants, a wee girl not yet walking, did not notice his expression. Certainly, it was far, far above her head height, and focused on the room at large, rather than her in particular. The tassels on his boots were much closer to her level. They were rather grand—lush bunches of gold and silver thread, hung from gold cord so they swung briskly when Mr. Howard walked.

The baby shuffled forward on her bottom, closer and closer. Bea watched from the corner of her eye, ready to intervene if Mr. Howard frightened the little girl. He didn't seem to notice. She settled perhaps two feet away, gazing at the tassels. Mr. Howard stamped his heel and the tassels swung. The little girl smiled.

The first time, Bea thought it was a coincidence, but then he moved again, both heels, one after the other. The little girl giggled. Mr. Howard didn't appear to be paying her any attention, but a smile played at the corner of his lips, and he set up a little jiggle with both heels.

Ambrose Howard is a fraud. How much of the behavior she had abhorred in him came from awkwardness with people?

The little girl shuffled closer, one inch at a time, and Mr. Howard continued to swing his tassels for her delight. When she was close enough, she put out a hand and one pointed finger touched the nearest tassel. She snatched her hand back and giggled again.

Mr. Howard momentarily lost control of his smile. It spread across his face until he was able to impose control over it again and force his lips to—almost—straighten.

The baby's mother noticed what her child was doing and said, "Marlo, leave the gentleman be."

"She is not bothering me, ma'am," Mr. Howard intoned, his voice cold and lofty. The father, though, swept the little girl up into his arms, and she wailed a protest.

Bea was sorry to see it, and Mr. Howard remained mute for the remainder of the visit, but when they were leaving, the father put his daughter down, and Mr. Howard caught her eye and then shook a leg at her.

"You haven't done this sort of thing before," Bea stated, as they headed to the next house. "Tenant visits, I mean."

"I don't know what to say," Mr. Howard blurted. "One talks about one's horses and one's tailor. Or a hunt or... What does one say to a farm laborer? Or his wife!"

Mr. Howard's horror at the mere idea could not have been worse if he found himself visiting a village full of cannibals on a tropical island.

"The weather is a universal topic," Bea suggested. "Or the wellbeing of the children, perhaps?"

"Hmmm," said Mr. Howard.

At the next two houses he made an effort. Stilted and awkward, but even so, an effort. She was feeling much more kindly toward the man by the time they arrived back at the castle. Especially since he didn't bother her with the insincere—or perhaps awkward—flattery of the sort he'd tried in the early stages of the house party.

Actually, he had bothered her very little in the past week. Was he more comfortable with her, or had he lost interest? Perhaps the answer lay in the way he hurried to help her cousin Dorrie when they arrived back at the stable yard at the same time as Dorrie and Mr. Meadowsweet. If he had transferred his interest to Dorrie, it would certainly suit Bea!

She washed and dressed for dinner, and came down to the drawing room, where she chatted with Christina, who had been out with Mr. Fairweather. Mr. Howard, when he appeared a few minutes later, made a beeline for the Hetherington sisters.

The other houseguests gathered, one by one, joining the

conversation as they waited for dinner to be announced. Not Alaric. Nor Reina, either. They had not arrived by the time dinner was announced. Indeed, it was halfway through the first setting before Reina finally appeared, stopping at the foot of the table for a quick word with Mama, who waved her to her place a few seats along the table next to Mr. Maddrell.

Alaric slipped into the room quite ten minutes later, also stopping to talk to Mama. He shot a quick grin at Bea as he seated himself opposite her, and applied himself to the serving dishes nearest to him.

He was just in time, for the footmen—after a moment's hesitation resolved by an instruction from Mama—began replacing the first setting with the second. They must have wondered if they should wait for the late guest to eat what was on his plate.

Bea was burning with curiosity. What made him late? Him and Reina? Mama would not tolerate speaking across the table, and the ladies either side of him—Dorrie Hetherington on one side and Sarah Howard on the other—did not ask him.

She had only to wait until the end of dinner. She was able to speak to Reina as soon as they were together in the drawing room. "What happened to you and Mr. Redhaven? Problems?"

"Gorry," Reina replied. "He was beating Mrs. Gorry. We arrived just as Padeen tried to stop him, and Gorry broke the boy's arm."

"Oh dear." Bea had had her own altercations with Gorry. He was mean when he was drunk, and he was always drunk. "I hope Mrs. Gorry has finally had enough."

"I think so. Now he has started beating the children. Apparently, he hit Cissolt, too, a few days ago. Your Mr. Redhaven stopped Gorry and held him so he could do no further harm. And he sent for my father and the constable. He was wonderful, actually. Mrs. Gorry says the earl threatened to exile Gorry for his next offense?"

"Yes. I hope Mrs. Gorry won't want to go with him," Bea said.

"I told her you and I would visit tomorrow, to help her make a plan. I think if she knows she will have work, and the children will be safe and cared for, she will stay on Claddach and let Gorry go where he will."

Bea nodded. "Perhaps we can finally get the older children into school. Now, who might be able to take the little ones during the day?"

They talked for several more minutes, pulling Christina into the conversation. The three of them were accustomed to cooperating on matters concerning the welfare of the families in the care of their fathers.

Bea was called away by her mother to pour the tea, but the day—and the problems of the Gorry family—were a good reminder of the true reason for this house party. The people of Claddach depended on the castle in so many ways, and her choice of husband would directly affect their wellbeing.

This evening, the suitors had been given the task of entertaining the ladies. Lord Luke Versey and Mr. Meadowsweet went first. Mr. Meadowsweet played a guitar while Luke sang several plaintive ballads in a pleasing tenor. Sir Henry Dashwood's contribution to the evening was to declaim a rather long poem in which horses featured prominently.

Mr. Howard gave them a juggling act, first with five and then six balls, and then with four objects offered by his audience—a snuff box, a hip flask (empty), a quizzing glass, and a fan. Mr. Howard had hidden depths!

Beverley read a passage from Mr. Coleridge's "Rime of the Ancient Mariner." He was followed by Mr. Fairweather, who took his place at the piano, and gave them two lovely Bach sonatas.

Finally, it was Alaric's turn. It suddenly occurred to Bea that he would not have had time to prepare anything. What was he going to do?

"My ladies, my lords, gentlemen," Alaric said, bowing to the company. "I have been awed by the display of talent this evening.

I face you with some trepidation in light of your many accomplishments, but dare to offer you that most humble, yet ubiquitous of fireside offerings, a story."

With that, he launched into the story of the White Hart, the story of a white deer that appeared at the wedding of Arthur and Guinevere, and of the knights who followed it, and what happened to them.

He bowed to the enthusiastic applause his narrative deserved, and Mama declared that fresh tea had arrived, while Papa asked who would prefer a port or a brandy. "Oh, by the way," he said. "Tomorrow, gentlemen, you will be helping to move the castle's bulls."

There was a stir among the gentlemen, a couple of them exclaiming in alarm and others smiling.

Mama poured the tea this time, and Bea carried around the cups, and at last was able to greet Alaric for the first time since the morning. "Were we right?" she asked. "Was it Narcissus?"

"It was. And I've solved the next one, too. I have made you a copy." He handed her the piece of paper, folded small enough to pass to her unseen. "Miss Radcliffe can tell you the answer. She told me where the tapestry was, and I went to see it before dinner." He bent slightly closer. "I've told your Papa and he is going to give me the next clue at the end of this evening," he murmured.

At that point, Mama called Bea away, and she did not have another opportunity to speak with Alaric that evening.

Bea was pleased he had solved another clue. She really was. She wasn't at all disappointed he had done it without her. If he had asked Reina for her advice while they were off visiting the tenants, he had every right to do so. It would be petty of her to feel otherwise.

And there she was, arguing to convince herself, and not succeeding. She went up to bed at evening's end with a persistent sense of dissatisfaction she did not want and did not feel entitled to. She was disappointed in herself.

But the feeling lifted when her maid Eunys handed her a sealed note. "I don't know if I should give ye this, my lady. A note from that there Mr. Redhaven. Colyn Mugtin guv it me. Lady Claddach'll have my head if'n she hears."

"She will not hear it from me, Eunys. It is nothing to worry Mama. Just a poem that Mr. Redhaven promised to copy out for me."

And that was true, she discovered, for when she opened the note, it was a copy of yet another verse.

"She keeps the hearth, defends the home.

"He far across the seas does roam.

"Which is her lord? The bow's the test—

"Revealed, triumphant, still the best."

He must have hurried straight up to his bed chamber when Papa gave it to him and written out the copy. It didn't make sense to her. Not yet, at least. And neither did the third clue—the one he had passed to her in the drawing room.

She looked forward to discussing them both with him tomorrow.

ALARIC HOPED THEY didn't make too early a start on this bull herding business. If he could, he'd like to spend some time with Bea—perhaps make up a group to go for a walk in the garden, thereby circumventing Lord Claddach's edict that Bea eased up on the time she was spending with him.

He was disappointed to find she had already ridden out with Miss Radcliffe. "They are visiting Mrs. Gorry," Miss Bryant explained. *Well.* Alaric could be glad of that, anyway. He decided to spend a bit of time walking around the castle, examining paintings and tapestries in the hopes that something made sense of the latest verse.

However, he had not gone far when a footman stopped him

with a message. Lord Claddach wished to see him immediately, in his study. He hurried downstairs, wondering what his lordship wanted. Something to do with Gorry, perhaps?

When he stepped inside, he first noticed Lord Claddach's severe expression, and then the earl's visitor. The man stood at the window, his back to the room, but Alaric knew him anyway. He stepped forward with a smile and a glad greeting. "Tarquin!"

His brother turned, a look of such loathing and disgust on his face that Alaric stopped in his tracks, his hand falling away.

"Redhaven," said Claddach. "Be seated, please. You too, Stavely. Redhaven, Viscount Stavely has made a serious allegation against you. I am giving you the opportunity to speak in your own defense."

"He admitted it," Tarquin insisted. "I told you."

Alaric looked from his brother to the man he hoped to soon call father-in-law, and then back again. "I do not understand. What allegation? If this is about Eloise, it was her choice, and anyway..."

Tarquin lunged at him, yelling imprecations. Alaric grabbed at Tarquin's hands in time to stop them closing around his throat even as his brother's velocity knocked him and the chair he was in backward onto the floor.

Chapter Seventeen

"STAVELY!" LORD CLADDACH roared. "Sit down!"

Tarquin slunk back to his seat and Alaric picked himself and the chair up, keeping a cautious eye on his brother. What was wrong with the man?

"Redhaven," said Lord Claddach, "do I understand that you claim your former betrothed, now your husband's wife, consented to being bedded by you?"

"He forced her!" Tarquin insisted.

Alaric was about to resume his seat. His knees gave out and he landed in the chair with a thump. "I never touched her!" he said, hotly. "Bedded? She would not even let me kiss her."

Tarquin swore again, quite vilely, then said to Lord Claddach, "He lies. My wife told me…"

Alaric stared at Tarquin, aghast. "How can you think I would do such a thing. Tarquin!" He felt bereft all over again, the loss of two years ago repeated and made worse.

"You admitted it," Tarquin insisted. "The day of my wedding. I asked you why you did it, and you said it was Eloise's choice."

With a determined shake of the head, Alaric denied that charge and corrected it. "You asked me why I broke it off with Eloise," he said. "I told you I didn't. After she met you, Eloise informed me she did not want to marry me, and then a week later, the pair of you announced your betrothal."

Tarquin's face worked, as if he was fighting to contain an angry response.

"Can you remember the exact words you said, Stavely?" Lord Claddach asked.

With a frown, Tarquin admitted he was not certain. "Something like, 'I know what you did to Eloise. How could you, Alaric?' That's more or less what I said."

"That sounds right," Alaric agreed. "You wanted to know why I jilted her, but I didn't."

"I wanted to know why you raped her," Tarquin roared. He looked as anguished as Alaric felt.

"I didn't!" Alaric found himself roaring in return as a slew of emotions—anger, fear, sadness, disgust, betrayal—washed through him. He fought to gain control and to remain civil in spite of them, but he could not keep back the words, "And if she says I did, she lies!"

Tarquin dived for him again but slunk back to his chair when Lord Claddach bellowed. "Gentlemen, we are going to go nowhere if the pair of you keep making accusations. Now, Stavely, I take it—and I apologize for the indelicacy—that your wife came to her marriage bed—or, from the sounds of it, her pre-marriage bed—not intact."

His cheeks red, Tarquin nodded. "I asked her. I thought she and Alaric might have anticipated their vows, as she and I were doing, though only by a day. I was not blaming her, Lord Claddach. I just wanted to know if any child might be my brother's."

"And she told you your brother had forced her."

"She did, my lord. And she is not a liar!" He glared at his brother. "Still, I couldn't believe it. My own brother. My twin! Then, Alaric confessed."

Lord Claddach sighed. "I think we have determined, Stavely, that your conversation with Redhaven might possibly have been misunderstood on both sides."

"Yes, but…" Tarquin trailed off when Lord Claddach held up a hand.

"Up until that point, would you have expected such behavior from your brother?"

"Never," Tarquin declared. "It was against everything I knew of him." Tears started to his eyes, and he grimaced as he tried to suppress them. "It broke my heart, to think he was not the man I believed him to be." He shook his head again. "But she was forced, my lord. She was… I will not discuss it, but it has taken a long time and much patience to… She was forced. If not Alaric, then who?"

That was the question. And why would she blame Alaric? That lie had cost him his brother's love. It had sent him into exile, and into a life he didn't want and wasn't good at. Alaric had never complained but he knew he'd never been the same since, lost in a world without the one person he had always been able to depend on—his twin.

"She said straight out that she had been forced by your brother?" Lord Claddach asked.

"Ye…" Tarquin trailed off. "No. You must understand that she was distressed, sir. Weeping so hard I could barely make out what she was saying. I asked her if she had been forced—for she was… Well. Never mind that. She admitted it, and when I demanded to know who, she said my brother."

Alaric, who was staring fixedly at his brother, straightened. "*My* brother? Or just 'brother'?"

Tarquin frowned and then paled as he leapt to his feet. "That sodding bastard!"

"Bebbington," Alaric said, rising more slowly. The Viscount Bebbington was Eloise's stepbrother, and a more controlling conniving person Alaric had never met. He had put one obstacle after another in front of Alaric. Eloise had begged Alaric to run away with her, but in the end, he had managed to persuade Bebbington to approve the betrothal, and they had traveled to Alaric's father's estate to see to the agreements.

There had always been something odd about the way Bebbington behaved with Eloise—and the way she had behaved with him.

Tarquin was pacing in the way he always did when agitated. "Gad. She begged me not to leave her there, and I wouldn't listen. I left her at Bebbington's estate! I must get back to the Wirral Peninsula. Claddach, I take back everything I said about my brother. It wasn't him at all! When does the next ferry leave?"

Lord Claddach stood too, and so did Alaric. "Who do you have to guard your back?" Alaric asked. "Bebbington is a piece of work, and he might not want to give Eloise up, even to her husband."

A shake of Tarquin's head was answer enough.

"I am coming with you," Alaric decided. "Lord Claddach, I beg you to hold me excused for long enough to get my sister-in-law away from her brother."

"Bebbington," said Lord Claddach. "He asked to be included in this house party. I would not give a dog to that man, let alone my daughter. The next ferry is not until this afternoon, Stavely, and it goes to Liverpool, so you would still need to cross the Mersey. Take my yacht to Birkenhead. She is berthed at Dara, in the north of the island. Redhaven can direct you. I shall also send two footmen with you. I shall send instruction to the stable to prepare a carriage." He smiled, as if at a private thought. "Redhaven, can you drive a carriage?"

"Yes, my lord," said Alaric, mystified.

"Make it four footmen," said Lord Claddach. "You can leave the carriage at Dara. Someone there will make certain it gets back to me. When you have Lady Stavely, sail directly back to Bailecashtel. Stavely, you and your wife must join us for the last of the house party. Your brother may need you. I shall expect the three of you for dinner."

ALARIC HAD NO time to do more than throw a couple of items in a bag in case of delays and ask Luke to give a message to Bea. But when he told Luke that he and his brother were going on a rescue mission to bring Lady Stavely to Claddach, Luke insisted on coming too.

"Bebbington cozied up to me my first Season in Town," he said. "I found I was getting in too deep and had to ask my brother Thornstead to bail me out. Then Thorn explained that Bebbington tried to compromise my sister Barbara during her first Season. Apparently, Father told him that, if he came within a mile of any of my sisters ever again, Father would destroy him. So, he came after me, instead, and I fell for it. Please let me come. It never hurts to have a Versey on your side."

After that, Alaric went to Miss Bryant, instead. "Please let Bea know I shall be back as soon as I can, and that I wouldn't leave at all if it wasn't important," he said.

The carriage was ready. Alaric took his place up on the driver's perch, with Tarquin on one side and Luke on the other, while the footmen crowded inside. "It's a one-hour trip across the island," Alaric told Tarquin, "and at most, three hours to Birkenhead. From there, we can hire horses to take us to Bebbington's estate. We shall be there no later than three in the afternoon, perhaps even by two."

"My carriage is at Birkenhead," Tarquin said. "We'll take that to Bebbington's and back."

"We'll reach Claddach by six," Luke commented, with satisfaction. "In time for dinner. Ellie will barely have time to miss me."

After that, Alaric concentrated on his driving, and on the route. He was not taking the long way to Dara that he'd traveled on the steeplechase, nor could he go over fields or along paths only wide enough for a horse. He had asked the stable master for the fastest carriage route, and the landmarks by which he would know the turns.

Tarquin and Luke had fallen into conversation. Alaric was

leaning forward over the reins, so their words were passing behind him, and when his total focus was not needed for a tricky piece of driving, he heard what they were saying without really listening.

Luke was describing the marriage trials. "So, we are up to eight, with four to go," he said. "Today, we were meant to be moving bulls, but Alaric and I already did that, at the fête. If Lord Claddach counts that, we have already passed that trial."

"Then you and my brother are rivals for Lady Beatrice's hand?" Tarquin asked.

Luke laughed. "Not really, for several reasons. First, the goal is simply to finish the trials without being disqualified by Lord Claddach. Since we do not know what will get a man disqualified and what will allow him to pass, influencing the outcome is out of our hands."

"How peculiar," said Tarquin.

"Shrewd, I think," Luke replied. "He is not just looking for a husband for his daughter but a caretaker lord for Claddach. She will inherit the lot, including the title. She and her husband will be parents of the next earl. Whatever his criteria might be, I think the trials are designed to show us for who we really are."

Tarquin made a considering noise before making the non-committal remark, "I see. And your other reasons?"

"Second, Lady Beatrice will make the final decision, from those who are successful in the trials. Or, she may choose none of us—but I can tell you she shows a marked preference for Alaric. And third, I have asked Lady Eleanor Fairweather, another guest at the house party, to be my bride, and she has said yes, subject to her father's approval. So, while I want to finish the trials because we Verseys don't give up once we've started something, I am not a suitor for Lady Bea's hand."

The remark about asking for Ellie caught Alaric's attention, though it came as no surprise. "Congratulations, Luke. She is a wonderful lady."

"She is," Luke agreed. "Exquisitely lovely, graceful, kind,

sensible. She says her father will agree, since I am a Versey. If she is right… But if she is not, I shall do anything…"

Alaric was certain that, if he could spare the attention to look, Luke would be staring into mid-air with a besotted expression on his face. But he was negotiating a tricky corner, and he gave all his thought to that, even as Tarquin joined in with his congratulations to the lucky prospective groom, and his reassurances that a son of the Duke of Dellborough, even a third son, must be acceptable to the somewhat ramshackle earl who had fathered Martin and Eleanor Fairweather.

They covered the distance to Dara in a little over sixty-five minutes, Luke taking the reins for the second half, to find that the groom sent to ride cross-country had arrived before them. The inn was ready to receive the carriage and horses and the captain of the yacht had sent for his crew.

"He will be ready to cast off in ten minutes, sir, he says," the groom told Alaric. And he was.

After that, there was nothing to do but stay out of the way of the crew. "The wind is right to give us a good run to the Mersey, my lords," said the captain. "I shall have you in Birkenhead in good time, never you mind."

"Claddach seems like a pleasant island," Tarquin said to Alaric, as they sat out of the way in the owner's cabin. "Out of the way, and I daresay it is isolated by storms fairly frequently, but the farms appear well cared for, from what I saw, and the town looks prosperous."

"I have been impressed," Alaric agreed. "I have talked to a lot of Claddach's people, between the steeplechase, the fête, and the tenant visits. The earl is a fair but firm lord. They love their island, and they love Bea. 'Lady Beatrice,' I should say. It would be a good place to live, I think."

"And what of Lady Beatrice?" Tarquin asked. "In Town, they say that Claddach keeps her at home because she is unmanageable—and unmarriageable, even with her dowry. The suitor trials have caused quite a lot of gossip, as you can imagine."

Luke burst out laughing. "I see the heavy hand of Beverley and his mother behind that gossip," he said. "Lady Beatrice, unmarriageable? The suitors the earl gathered would argue otherwise. Three relatives of dukes, one earl's son? Even Dashwood is a baron. Landless, it is true, but that was one of Claddach's criteria."

"It was? The gossip notes that the trials have attracted only those without an estate, and mostly without a title," commented Tarquin.

"You spoke of Lady Beatrice's dowry," Alaric said. "The thing is, she doesn't have a dowry—or not what most people understand by the word. She will be countess in her own right. She is already Lady of Claddach in all but name because her mother takes little interest. She needs a husband who will make her, her lands, and her people the center of his world. That's why her father invited younger sons. And that's what Beverley and his mother do not understand. *Willfully* choose not to understand, for Claddach has made it clear enough."

"Ah. I see why you are so interested," Tarquin said. "You love the land. Could you love the lady, too, do you think? Marriages are better, I believe, if husband and wife are at least friends."

That prompted another burst of laughter from Luke. "I rather suspect that you have it the wrong way around, Lord Stavely."

"I am in love with Bea," Alaric admitted, "if that is what you are driving at, Luke."

"Have you told her that?" Luke demanded.

"Of course not. She is not looking for a love match, but for a practical arrangement with someone who can be her consort. I have been trying to prove to her and her father that I can be the man she needs."

Tarquin and Luke exchanged a look, and Tarquin said, "Admittedly, I have not met Lady Beatrice. Still, I think she would like to hear the words. I know Eloise needed to hear them."

"Ellie, too," Luke agreed. "Especially if Bea is beginning to love you. She certainly favors you ahead of anyone else."

Might they be right? But Bea had not said anything. Besides, would it be fair? If he were not one of Lord Claddach's selections, wouldn't it be worse for Bea if she knew he loved her? That is, if she loved him, too. Alaric shook his head. "It isn't the right time," he told the pair of them. "She has agreed to choose one of the suitors who successfully completes the trials, with her father's approval whether she loves him or not. Who is to say I shall be one of them?"

"Lady Beatrice, possibly," Luke answered. "You seem to think the earl will make the selection without her, but he certainly involves her in all the other decisions regarding the earldom and its holdings. Why not this one, which so nearly concerns her?"

"I had not thought of that." Alaric was much struck. What Luke said made sense. And it was true that Bea liked him. She would not have let him kiss her if she disliked him.

"If she means that much to you, why did you insist on coming with me?" Tarquin demanded. "You should have said. I would have understood."

"And let you face Bebbington on your own? I thought I had lost you, Tark. To find out it was all a mistake..." He turned away from the others so they would not see the tears in his eyes and coughed to clear his throat before he spoke again. "I don't have so many brothers I can afford to stand by and let one be killed, Tarquin."

"I *do* have four brothers," said Luke, "and I wouldn't let any of them go on their own to face Bebbington, either. Not even if it meant disappointing Ellie."

Tarquin grasped Alaric's shoulder in a tight grip and gave it a gentle shake. His own voice was husky when he said, "We have to get you back by the end of day, then." He shook Alaric one more time and forced his voice to light humor. "I can't have my brother missing out on becoming Lord of Claddach."

"Consort to the Lady of Claddach," Alaric corrected. "It matters, Tarquin. Bea inherits as countess. Her husband's role is to support her."

"That is…" Tarquin trailed off, shaking his head. "It wouldn't bother you? Taking second place to your wife?"

"I don't see it that way," Alaric insisted. "It won't work that way. Not with Bea." He thought of a parallel. "Does Eloise take second place to you?"

"Eloise has her own place," Tarquin said, immediately, "and when I need her support or she needs mine, we talk about it."

Alaric raised his eyebrows at his brother. *See?*

"I see your point," Tarquin said. "It still seems unnatural to me, but if it is what you want…"

"Bea is what I want," Alaric told him. "I have never met anyone like her. Even if she didn't have Claddach as part of her dowry, I'd love her." He shrugged. "I don't know if it will be as straightforward as I expect, but the fact is that Bea comes with this… package. The Isle of Claddach, the title of countess, the expectation that she will rule, not her husband. I cannot have Bea as my wife unless I accept the package. So, I do."

"Then let us rescue Lady Stavely and return to Claddach and the trials," said Luke.

Chapter Eighteen

B EA AND REINA went out early to visit Mrs. Gorry. The poor woman had had a disturbed night, with Padeen in pain and unable to sleep, and two of the children suffering nightmares in which their father was beating them. She was exhausted but determined.

"I can't have Eamon back, Lady Bea. But he is my husband. The law says I cannot stop him from moving back in, from beating me, from beating the children, from getting another child on me. What am I to do? If I went to my family, my father would send me back to Eamon, though I think my brothers would help me. But I don't want to leave my friends and the children's friends. I have a job here, too. Who is to say I could get work again? Especially work that lets me have time if the children need me. What am I to do?"

"I will talk to my father," Bea told her. "I think you can apply for a separation on account of his violence. I am certain Dr. Bryant would stand witness to the injuries to the children. You would need the magistrate to appoint someone else as guardian of the children—someone you trusted. You would retain custody, Mrs. Gorry, but someone else would have the legal right to stop Gorry from taking the children away from you. Perhaps your father, or one of your brothers."

Mrs. Gorry narrowed her eyes, thinking. "Would your father do it, my lady? Gorry is not going to come after the children if your father stands for them."

It would be the ideal solution. "I will ask him," Bea said. "At the moment, you are safe. Gorry is locked up, and he is not going anywhere before he comes up before my father to explain why he should not be exiled."

Back at the castle, she and Reina joined the rest of the house party in the drawing room, where Papa was about to tell the men about the exercise ahead of them. They would be moving the estate's stud bulls from one pasture to another. It was a small herd—only five bulls—but they were the Isle of Claddach's own breed. Small for cattle, hardy, and clever.

The Claddach cow was gentle of disposition and gave copious quantities of rich milk. The Claddach bull's character, by contrast, was surly at best and downright dangerous at worst. Still, if they worked together as a team and obeyed the instructions of the herdsmen, the suitors should be able to manage with little difficulty.

Papa raised a hand as a signal to be quiet, and the room hushed. *But, wait a minute.* Where was Alaric? Luke, too, was missing.

Even as she had the thought, Fairweather spoke up. "Redhaven and Versey are not here, my lord. Shall we send a footman to let them know the meeting is about to start?"

"They are gone," Beverley sneered. "Redhaven's brother Viscount Stavely came to fetch him to face justice for raping Lady Stavely back when she was engaged to Redhaven. I don't know why Versey went with him."

There was a burst of comments. Bea didn't listen. She was having trouble catching her breath and her head was spinning.

"Silence!" Papa raised his voice. It had the desired effect. Everyone fell silent.

"Lewiston," Papa said to Bea's uncle, "I am distressed to have to inform you that I cannot like your son. He tries to cause trouble. He listens at doors. He spreads malicious gossip. He treats other people with disrespect. He does not act the part of a gentleman."

Beverley's mother began a protest. "Well, I never…"

However, her husband said, "He is, I will acknowledge, a disappointment. I think his cousin would be the making of him. Beatrice my dear, I do hope you will have him."

"I will not," Beatrice said, absently. Her mind was still absorbed in Beverley's accusations.

Beverley added his voice to Aunt Lewiston's, both of them decrying Bea's unwomanly determination and Papa's foolishness.

"Enough," Papa said, with some force, and again, the room fell silent.

Beverley was the first to speak. "I only speak the truth," he said. "Stavely did say that Redhaven r… forced Lady Stavely. I heard him."

"You were not in the room," Papa said, "so I must suppose you had your ear to my study door and were forced to move away before you heard the rest of the discussion. Since you have repeated the accusation in front of others, I shall explain that the accusation Beverley overheard was retracted when Lord Stavely realized he was mistaken. Redhaven and Versey have gone with Stavely—voluntarily—to assist with a family matter. They will return by this evening. I have excused them from the bull run and instructed them to be back for dinner."

"You have favored Redhaven from the beginning," Beverley accused. "He should never have been part of the trials, with his terrible reputation. My aunt agrees with me, do you not, Aunt?

Mama looked embarrassed and began shifting restlessly, avoiding everyone's eyes, while she sought something to say. "Well, Beverley, dear, there are different ways of looking at such things, and taking one thing against another…"

"I shall be the arbiter of who is suitable and who is not," said Papa, sternly. "All you need to know, Beverley, is that you are not."

"I withdraw my suit," Beverley declared. "I wish nothing further to do with you, with Claddach, or with your daughter." On the final word, he swung around on one heel and left the room.

"Good riddance," said Papa.

"I have never been so insulted in my life!" Aunt Lewiston declared.

Papa pressed his lips together as if he was swallowing the first words he came to mind. Bea would love to know the retort he was refusing to vocalize.

"Oh, Dorothy," Mama said to her sister. "Don't take on so."

"Your daughter will die an old maid, Mary," Aunt Lewiston insisted. "You mark my words." She marched off after her son.

"Oh dear," said Mama, looking between Bea and her father. "Now look what you have done." And she ran off after her sister.

"Are you sorry to lose your cousin as a suitor, daughter?" Papa asked.

"No, Papa. But did Lord Stavely really accuse Mr. Redhaven of... *that?*"

Papa said that Lord Stavely had accepted he was mistaken, but he must have had a reason for the terrible accusation, must he not? Bea had trouble believing that Alaric would leave with his brother if such a matter still lay between them. What had really happened?

Papa was not minded to be helpful. "You can apply to Mr. Redhaven for further information. For now, we must move on to the bull herding." He pointed to the chief cattle herd, who was waiting quietly in the corner. "Gentlemen, you will go with Mylechreest, here. He will tell you what you need to do." He went to follow the gentleman from the room, but Bea placed a hand on his arm.

"Papa, Mrs. Gorry is anxious to separate herself from Gorry. By law, and with the children given into her custody, and into the guardianship of a man she trusts. Will you help?"

Papa nodded. "The young men will be at least half an hour

sorting themselves out, and perhaps another half hour doing the moving. I have a few minutes, Bea. I shall ride down into town on my way to the bull pens, and see what Gorry has to say for himself."

But when the constables went to fetch Gorry from the cells, he was gone. How he had escaped, no one knew, but the constables soon found that he'd taken his former employer's fishing smack from the harbor, and that he had a passenger. People who had been on the harbor walls at the time swore that the passenger was Lord Beverley.

TARQUIN, ALARIC, AND Luke decided to leave the footmen with the carriage rather than precipitate a fight by arriving in strength. Perhaps Bebbington would be sensible about the matter, though they doubted it, since their approach to the estate had been interrupted when a young woman had stepped out in front of the horses calling, "Lord Stavely!"

It was Eloise's maid. She told them she had been turned out of the house and told her mistress would no longer require her. Certain her master would return for his wife she had been waiting in the bushes since late morning.

Bebbington would not see them, and his butler tried to shut the door in their faces.

When they were refused entry, Tarquin pushed past the butler and stood in the entry hall, calling for Eloise. His shouts brought Bebbington out of his study. "She is not returning with you, Stavely. Get off my lands before I have you thrown off."

Alaric and Luke moved up beside Tarquin. Bebbington's eyes widened and then narrowed. "Redhaven. You are not welcome here. Nor is your friend. Watts! Summon footmen to have these intruders removed."

The butler looked alarmed but left through an unobtrusive

door.

"You have no legal right to keep Eloise from her husband," Alaric told Bebbington, "and if your footmen lay hands upon me and Versey, here, we shall sue you for assault."

"Eloise!" Tarquin shouted at the top of his voice. He was rewarded by a loud clatter and the sound of screaming. No. Not screaming. Words, in a high-pitched voice.

"Help! Tarquin! Help!"

Just that, and then silence, but Tarquin was already leaping up the stairs, two at a time. Alaric and Luke followed. Bebbington did not—presumably he was waiting for reinforcements.

At the second-floor landing, Tarquin stopped, looking at the doors that led from the stairwell on three sides. "This floor, or the next?" he asked.

Alaric shook his head. He didn't know. They would have to search each floor and fight off the footmen he could hear muttering down in the entry hall.

"Eloise!" Tarquin shouted again and had his reply. Another large crash and the sound of a voice swearing mingled with a shriek of pain.

"This way." Tarquin pulled open the door between them and the source of sound, into a passage with closed doors on both sides. Behind them, on the stairs, the thump of feet indicated that the footmen had overcome their reluctance to tangle with three members of the aristocracy.

As Tarquin hurried down the passage, listening at each door, Alaric removed a pike from a display on the wall. Luke must have guessed his intention, for he pulled the ties that held back the drapes on either side of an alcove. They worked together to tie the handles of the door leading to the stairwell to the pike, which was long enough to stretch the width of the door frame.

Just in time. They had no sooner finished tying and tightening the rope than someone began pulling on the door on the other side.

"There will be other stairs," Alaric said to Luke.

Tarquin had heard something at one of the doors, for he was kicking at it with his booted foot. Alaric came up beside him, and at the count of three, they both hit the door at the same time. It burst open. Despite the seriousness of the situation, Alaric felt a surge of joy at working in unison once more with his twin.

Eloise was inside, struggling in the grip of another woman. The sudden entrance of Tarquin and Alaric had the captor losing her hold, and Eloise threw herself into Tarquin's arms. "I knew you would come for me. I told my brother."

"I am sorry," Tarquin told her. "I should have listened to you."

"Time for apologies later," said Alaric. "We need to get Eloise out of here."

"My maid," Eloise said. "They took her away. I have to rescue Maisie."

"Maisie is safe," Tarquin assured her. "She waited for us outside. She is in the carriage."

Luke had opened the window and was staring out. "We can get out this way," he said. "We'll need to tie the sheets together. Alaric, can you get the door shut again? And locked?"

Alaric had been keeping an eye on Eloise's jailor, but she did not seem to be intending any hostile moves, so he turned his attention to the door. They'd burst it open without breaking it, and it took Alaric a matter of moments to turn the key in the door to free the latch, shut it again, and relocate it. "Help me move that chest in front of it," he ordered the jailor. She cast a wary glance at the other two men then complied.

Just in time, for there was a thunderous rattle of knocks on the door. "Purston! Open up. Is my sister safe?"

Eloise was climbing out of the window, her face white. Luke had gone ahead, and Tarquin was helping his wife. Alaric frowned at the woman—apparently her name was Purston—and he put his finger to his lips.

"Purston!" came another shout.

"You'd better follow us, Mrs. Purston," Alaric told the jailor.

"Bebbington is likely to take his anger out on you."

Purston surprised him then. When she began to shout back through the door, Alaric made a move to clap his hand over her mouth to gag her but stopped when he realized she was trying to deceive Bebbington to keep him from realizing that the brothers were already in here with Eloise. "How do I know it is the viscount?" Purston demanded through the door. "You could be the villains after my lady, pretending to be Lord Bebbington."

She nodded to Alaric and whispered, "You go first, m'lord. I'll follow."

"Thank you. Follow and we'll take you to Birkenhead. We'll give you some money to get away."

She curtseyed. "Thankee, m'lord. I'd be right grateful. I've no love for them as women and no wish to help them."

Alaric wasted no more time ducking out the window to climb down the sheet. It wasn't far. The window looked out over the roof of a lower part of the house, and the other three were already on their way across the roof to the edge where several trees grew close to the house. They were the outliers of a wilderness that stretched all the way to the road where their carriage waited.

As he sprinted after them, he heard a shout, and looked back. They had been seen from another window, and the man there was calling out to others! Mrs. Purston was almost to the lower roof. He didn't wait for her but followed the others. Eloise froze on the edge of the roof, but Luke held out a hand from the closest branch of the oak and Tarquin murmured to his wife and lifted her, holding her out over the gap until she reached a hand for Luke's and a foot for the branch, and was safe.

They scrambled together out of Tarquin's way, and by the time Alaric reached the edge, Tarquin was helping Eloise down the trunk. Alaric took the leap and followed, scrambling down the tree as fast as he could, to join the fight he could hear below him.

Above, the tree shook as Mrs. Purston followed.

Two footmen were trying to stop the escape. Luke was

fighting one of them. Tarquin was holding the other off but was hampered by his refusal to let Eloise go. Alaric grabbed the man and threw him into the one Luke was fighting, and they went down in a tumble of arms and legs.

Luke began to relax, then stiffened again as he saw Mrs. Purston descend the tree.

"She's with us," Alaric told him. Tarquin and Eloise were already running, hand in hand, into the wilderness.

Mrs. Purston had picked up a fallen branch, with which she thumped the two footmen on the head, one after the other. They subsided into a heap. Luke's eyebrows shot up, but he said, "Very well. Let's go, then."

In moments, they were in the carriage, a little squeezed for room, with the footmen holding on wherever they could to the outside. They headed back to Birkenhead where the yacht awaited.

Except, when they got there, it was to see the yacht sailing away down the Mersey.

Chapter Nineteen

"BEST GET YOURSELF and Eloise out of sight," Alaric advised Tarquin. "Bebbington might follow us, and he is the local viscount. At best, he'll make an embarrassing fuss. Luke and I shall see if we can find out what has happened to the yacht, and we'll make inquiries about the ferry."

Tarquin and Eloise walked off to a nearby inn, surrounded by footmen.

It was Luke who thought to speak to an elderly gentleman sitting on a bench, smoking a pipe, and watching the harbor. He must have been there for hours, for he remembered Luke, Alaric and Tarquin arriving on the yacht, *Sea Mist*. "You, sir, and the other gentleman, there," he said, "and the gentleman who just escorted the lady into the inn."

What luck to find such a keen observer. It made the old man's day, too, to have Alaric and Luke hanging on his every word.

"Yes, indeed, I saw the *Mist* leave. Such a beautiful vessel. Fine lines. The Earl of Claddach's, I believe. She's been berthing here quite often recently, as the earl's lady and her sister have friends in Birkenhead."

"She is a lovely ship," Alaric agreed. "We came over from Claddach on her and expected to return this afternoon. We were surprised to find her gone." That was putting it mildly.

"That explains why the captain was arguing," said the gentleman. "It was that young pup, Beverley. The earl's nephew. Thinks a lot of himself, that boy. He must have demanded the captain take him somewhere. Back to the island, perhaps?"

"Beverley!" Luke's tone made the name into a profanity. "What was he doing here?"

"Putting a spoke in our wheel, clearly," Alaric declared. "More to the point, how did he get here? There was no ferry until three this afternoon, and it cannot be more than a quarter to three now."

"Ah, well, it could be the young viscount came in on a fishing smack," said the gentleman. "He came along the quay from where the fishing fleet docks, and he had a rough-looking fisherman type with him. Fellow pointed out the *Mist* and then went into the tavern, there. I haven't seen him come out, so I suppose he is still there."

"Sir," Alaric said, "could we persuade you to come into the tavern with us and identify him?"

Alaric offered the elderly man his arm, and all three of them crossed the road to the tavern, where the observant gentleman very quickly found a man sitting in the shadows hunched over a mug. "That is him. That is the man who directed Lord Beverley to the *Mist*."

Alaric recognized him immediately. "Gorry," he said.

They saw the gentleman back to his bench. Alaric told Luke, "He will recognize me straight away as the man who called the constables on him for breaking his son's arm." With that, Luke took on the task of talking to Gorry. He went back to the tavern and Alaric sat with their new friend to watch the boats.

The old gentleman had some questions. "Please tell me if I intrude, sir, but I sense a story. I am burning with curiosity. Is Lord Beverley the villain of the piece? Is that unprepossessing fellow in the tavern? How did you come to be on Claddach, and why are you so anxious to return? Are any of you suitors for the hand of the earl's daughter? His trials are the talk of the county, and we are all agog to know what is happening. And who is the lady your friend whisked away into the inn? She was not with you on the yacht, so where did she come from? Now you can tell me to mind my own business, sir."

Alaric laughed. "I will not do that, sir. I shall start by introducing myself. I am Alaric Redhaven, and yes, I am an aspirant for the hand of Lady Beatrice Collister. So is my friend, Lord Lucas Versey. Though I daresay he is not as keen on the lady as I."

The gentleman inclined his head. "I am Thomas Oxton. Sir Thomas, if we are being particular, but since I have passed the reins to my son, I do not bother much with such details."

"It is a pleasure to meet you, Sir Thomas," Alaric said. "The other gentleman you saw is my brother Viscount Stavely, and we came to Birkenhead to meet his wife and to take her with us to the island. The trials are the reason we need to return quickly. Versey and I have been given leave for today but must be back tonight.

"As to Beverley, he is also a suitor in the trials. Whether he is a villain remains to be seen. I last saw Gorry, the man in the tavern, on Claddach being taken away to await the magistrate's pleasure. I have no idea why Beverley or Gorry would be here in Birkenhead."

Sir Thomas chuckled. "To cut you out, Redhaven. You and your friend Versey, who is, I imagine, one of the Duke of Dellborough's whelps."

"And here he comes," Alaric said, not without relief. Sir Thomas might be old, but he was still sharp.

Luke crossed the road and came up to them. Alaric said, "Sir Thomas, may I present Luke Versey. Luke, this is Sir Thomas Oxton. I have just been telling him we are suitors in the trials. Apparently, everyone on this side of the water is just as interested in them as those on the island. He understands why we need to get back."

"Beverley has done his best to make sure it doesn't happen

tonight," Luke told them. "He paid Gorry to bring him across from the island. Gorry put a lot of words around it, but in essence, Beverley found him at the harbor about to steal his erstwhile employer's fishing smack, and came along for the ride."

"Stealing a boat? Gorry's keen to tighten the noose around his own neck, isn't he?" Alaric commented.

"Gorry reckons he was just taking back his own," said Luke, with a grimace. "Seems the fisherman who owns the boat bought it off the gambler who won it off Gorry."

"Then felt sorry enough for Gorry's family to hire the disgusting excuse for a husband and father to work for him."

Luke nodded. "Only to fire him for persistently turning up drunk or failing to turn up at all. 'It's not right. A man has a drink or two to keep him warm, and next thing, he's thrown off his own boat.' According to Gorry, everything that has happened to him is somebody else's fault."

"I know the sort," said Sir Thomas. "What of the yacht, Lord Lucas?"

"Gorry recognized you on the yacht, Alaric. They were close behind us when we landed, and Gorry blames you for his arrest. He suggested to Beverley that the sea trip to Brighton would be quicker and pleasanter than the coach trip to London. Beverley was only too pleased to try to stop you from getting back to the island by Lord Claddach's deadline."

"Do either of you gentlemen know how to sail a fishing smack?" Sir Thomas asked.

"I've done a little sailing in my brother's pleasure yacht," Luke admitted.

"I am a complete novice," Alaric conceded, "but I can follow instructions."

Sir Thomas hoisted himself to his feet. "Hmm. We can't have you drowning on the way over. We'll have to see if we can do better than that. Come along, gentlemen. We are going to arrange your transport back to Claddach."

❯❯❯❯❮❮❮❮

BEA SPENT THE day fighting off a bad mood. The men—those who were left—went off to move the bulls and returned triumphant and pleased with themselves. They did not seem to mind that Papa had given Luke and Alaric credit for already completing that particular trial when the pair retrieved the errant bulls at the fête.

Indeed, they were full of praise that the two men had managed on their own, though from what Bea had heard, a host of commoners had helped.

Bea could not bring herself to care. Or, rather, she cared too much. Alaric was gone and Bea was—she would admit it, if only to herself—Bea was out of sorts.

She was pleased Beverley was gone. She was not so delighted that Aunt Lewiston had reacted by retreating to her bedchamber with the drapes drawn and Mama in anxious attendance.

"I wish Mama would not do whatever Aunt Lewiston asks," she said to Aunt Joan.

"Lady Lewiston is the older sister," Aunt Joan said. "Your Mama has obeyed her all her life. You know that I love your Mama, Bea, but even her greatest devotee could not call her a strong-minded lady. Not like you, my dear. But then, my brother is strong-minded enough for two people, so I dare say she is happy doing what makes him happy. As long as her sister is not nearby. Poor, dear Mary. She must feel as if she is being pulled in all directions, between Lady Lewiston, my brother, and you, Bea."

Which was all very well, but when Aunt Lewiston was around, Bea did not much like her mother. Nor did she much like her remaining suitors, all four of whom seemed to have taken the absence of Alaric, Beverley, and Lord Luke as their opportunity to spend the afternoon making an impression on her.

She was being unfair again. At least two of them were attempting to make an impression on other ladies in the house party—Mr. Howard on Cousin Dorrie, and Mr. Meadowsweet on Sarah Howard. Also, Papa's secretary, Mr. Maddrell, and Reina appeared to be close to making a public declaration of the attachment everyone around them had been aware of for some time. Certainly, they made no attempt to hide their interest in one another.

Perhaps it was the budding romances around her that had her snapping at Ellie when that besotted damsel assured her, "Luke and Alaric will be back by dinner time, Bea."

"They can come and go as they please," she retorted. "I certainly have no control over their movements."

Despite her denials, though, she did expect Alaric to come back. When six o'clock came and went with no sign of him, she was as disappointed as Ellie, though unlike Ellie, she did not allow herself to droop and look downcast.

"Reckon somethin's delayed them, my lady," said Eunys, as she helped Bea dress for dinner. "He'll be back, though. Powerful fond of you, is Mr. Redhaven."

Not so powerful fond, however, that he refused to run off to the mainland at one word from his brother.

"I daresay he will return in his own good time, if he wishes to do so," she told Eunys.

She knew she was being unfair. She had no idea what their errand was, and how necessary Alaric was to its successful conclusion, and it was unreasonable to blame Alaric for not telling her where he was going when she was away from the castle when he left.

They had still not returned when night fell. She lay awake, at one moment wondering if Alaric was in trouble, even perhaps injured, and the next moment certain that he had lost interest in her and her father's dumb trials. Had he gone, never to return?

One of Claddach's sudden storms began to buffet the castle and Bea knew for certain. Alaric would not be returning tonight.

Chapter Twenty

ALARIC AND HIS party had been delayed in Birkenhead when Bebbington arrived, demanding the release of his sister. He had made such a fuss that those witnessing the altercation insisted on taking the matter before a magistrate. And the magistrate was out of town, and not expected back until after dinner.

They ate in a private parlor at the inn, none of them—except for the footmen—hungry. Alaric and Luke arranged for them to be fed in the public room, and when Alaric checked on them, they announced themselves well satisfied. Bebbington refused to stay, saying he would eat with friends and return later.

The magistrate, when he eventually arrived, dealt with the matter quite simply by asking Eloise. She immediately claimed Tarquin as her beloved husband and accused her brother of attempting to ruin her marriage for his own purposes. She even wept a little when she explained how much she missed her son.

Bebbington was clearly shocked. He left the magistrate's house, muttering about ungrateful sisters and betrayal.

"He did not expect you to stand up to him," Alaric observed.

"I never have," Eloise said, simply. "But I love Tarquin, you see."

"I am proud of you, my darling," said Tarquin. "You were very brave."

"Your brother will say too little, too late," said Eloise, sneaking a peek at Alaric.

Alaric, who had been angry with Eloise for years, found he had no resentment left for her at all. He had never been in her shoes, but he could imagine that, if one had been abused and bullied since one was a small child, and told that it was for love, it would be hard to trust. "I say you were very brave, sister," he said, and felt adequately rewarded when both Eloise and Tarquin beamed at him.

Back at the harbor, the fishing boat captain Sir Thomas had found to help them was itching to leave. "We're cuttin' it right close," he said. "I dinna want to be out on the sea after full dark."

"Too close?" Tarquin asked. "I know you need to return tonight, Alaric, but I don't want to risk Eloise…"

"Neither do I," Alaric agreed. "We are not going to make dinner, Tarquin. If we cannot get there safely tonight, we'll have to go in the morning."

Tarquin looked worried about that, too, and well he might. Who knew what Bebbington might try next?

"*Ee*," said the captain. "We'll do it right fine, good sirs. But mind you, we need to leave soonest."

"We are ready," Alaric declared. It remained only to be ferried out to the smack in a rowboat, and within fifteen minutes, they were underway. With the captain and a crew of two, Alaric, Tarquin, and Luke were also doing duty as deck hands, with the help of some of the footmen.

"If the wind holds," said the captain, "I'll have ye back in Bailecashtel well before sunset." This close to midsummer, the sun was up until ten o'clock, which was in three hours.

The fishing smack held few comforts, but Eloise and her maid did not complain. They sat where they were told and tried to stay out of the way.

It was Eloise who noticed the boat that was following them.

"Just goin' the same way as us," the captain assured them, but Eloise was afraid it was Bebbington, coming after her. Tarquin didn't mock her belief, and Alaric noticed that several of the sailors were also keeping a wary eye on the boat.

"They'll not catch the *Peggy-Rose*, m'lady," one sailor told Eloise. "She handles like a dream. Just a puff of wind, like we've got tonight, and we'll fly all the way to Claddach. If the wind holds."

The wind did not hold. In fact, it died entirely halfway through the journey, and then a fog came up out of nowhere.

"Isn't that just like herself," said the captain. "She's a ticklish bit of sea, this one. One minute a storm, the next a fog and not a breath of wind. Keep a sharp look out, lads. Gents, I should say. We should be well clear of any rocks, but she's a tricky one, and that's for sure."

Twice, a slight breeze came up—enough to ruffle the sails, but not to fill them even when the captain ordered this rope pulled and that one loosened. Each time, the fog cleared just enough to see the other boat. Each time, it was closer.

The second time the fog cleared, a man could be seen standing up in the prow of the other boat and shaking his fist. "It *is* my brother," Eloise told Tarquin. Alaric was staring at the other sailors. One looked remarkably like Gorry. Then the fog rolled back between the boats, though the *Peggy-Rose* was afloat under a patch of sky, where the clouds were stained pink by the rays of the setting sun.

"Cap'n, look at they clouds," said one of the sailors, indicating the skies to the left of the direction they were heading.

"Damn me," said the captain, then bowed to Eloise. "Beggin' yer pardon for me language, marm."

"Is it a problem, captain?" Tarquin asked.

"I'll not lie," said the man. "I'd be right happy to be in Bailecashtel, with a mug of beer in one hand and a pie in the other, but there. If wishes were horses, then beggars would ride, as the saying goes. Here's the thing. That's a storm, or at least a squall. It'll bring us a wind, coming straight at us from Bailecashtel. Now I'm not sailing straight into a squall, but I can use the wind to take us out of trouble and bring us safe to Dara, and that's what I plan to do, not being wishful to risk the *Peggy-Rose* or your lady."

He pointed in the direction of the other boat. "If they're wise, they'll do the same."

Even as he spoke, a gust of wind buffeted the boat and set the calm sea tossing. The captain shouted some commands so fast that Alaric had no idea what he'd just been ordered to do. Fortunately, the sailor next to him told him which line to grab and pull, and in moments the boat had turned and was speeding at perhaps a seventy-degree angle from its previous direction.

For several minutes, Alaric had no time to look for the other boat, and when he did, it was not visible. The wind had whipped the fog to shreds, but the fast-gathering clouds, the setting sun, and the rain that came with the wind meant the patch of sea they could see around them grew smaller by the minute.

There followed a tense, scrambling, clawing, tugging interval of time, filled with the groan of ropes, the howl of the wind, and the slapping of waves on the fast moving, bucking hull of the boat. Alaric did what he was told and tried his hardest not to think about the last time he'd experienced one of the Irish Sea's storms.

Then one of the sailors let out a glad shout. "The signal fires on Dara Sea Wall!"

The captain corrected their course and sailors did complicated things with the lines and sails, until Alaric could see, through the gloom, a fire on either side of them as they sailed into Dara Harbor.

"Any sign of Bebbington and the other boat?" Tarquin asked. But the boat did not follow them into the harbor, nor did it appear in the time it took for them to anchor, come ashore, and arrange for the anchorage with the harbormaster.

Things nearly turned pear-shaped again, when the harbormaster sent for the justice of the peace, for the *Peggy-Rose* had been reported stolen. However, when Alaric introduced himself and explained how they came to be bringing the stolen boat back to Claddach, the justice said, "I thought I recognized you, Mr. Redhaven. You did a grand job running the contests at the fête. Shouldn't you be at the castle, wooing our Lady Bea?"

Which led to more explanations and ended with Alaric, Tarquin, Eloise, and Luke being invited to spend the night at the justice's house. "And we shall give you a good sendoff bright and early in the morning, and so we will," said the justice.

Tarquin escorted Eloise to the justice's carriage, but Alaric and Luke took a moment to say farewell to the crew, and to thank them again. Alaric pressed a pouch of coins on them, glad that Tarquin had thought to share what he had brought with him.

"Sir, we've been paid for the voyage," the captain protested. "And for our ferry fare home in the morning."

"But not for your costs at the inn tonight," Alaric pointed out. "Have a good meal and a drink or two on us and thank you again."

"Aye, we'll drink a blessing on you, sir," the captain agreed.

"We would be grateful for it," Alaric said. He was not sure whether their trip had been cursed—since so much had gone wrong—or blessed—since they had avoided disaster over and over.

The thought occurred to him again the following morning, as he stood on the bank of a swollen river, looking at the ruins of the bridge they had intended to cross.

"It was meant to be a simple journey there and back again," he commented to Tarquin.

"It has turned into a bit of an odyssey, hasn't it?" Tarquin replied.

Alaric stared at him. That was it!

"She keeps the hearth, defends the home.

"He far across the seas does roam.

"Which is her lord? The bow's the test—

"Revealed, triumphant, still the best."

Odysseus and Penelope. Surely. Clue solved! When he returned from his long voyage to find his wife besieged by suitors, and she agreed to marry the one who could draw her husband's mighty bow. Odysseus, in disguise, was the only one to succeed.

Now all Alaric had to do was return to *Cashtal Vaaich* and find the image of the pair of them.

BEA'S SLEEP HAD been restless and disturbed. She woke heavy-eyed to the news that the suitors were attending the horse fair in the village of Duncarrick today, with instructions to buy a carriage horse for a lady and a horse suitable to pull a plow for the home farm.

"The ladies are not required to attend, my lady," Eunys told her, "but can if they wish."

A horse fair. It might be better than drooping around the castle all day, waiting for news of Alaric.

"My riding habit, please, Eunys. And let the other maids know to tell their ladies I will be going to the horse fair, and they are welcome to ride with me or come by carriage, if they wish to attend."

An hour later, they all rode out—the four remaining suitors, Bea, Ellie, and the Hetherington sisters on horseback, and Mrs. Howard and her daughter, Lady Dashwood, Aunt Joan, Reina, and Christina in two curricles, one driven by Mr. Maddrell and the other by Mr. Whittington.

Papa and Lord Lewiston must have been up early, for they were already at the fair when the castle party arrived, as were servants from the castle, who were setting up a tent to provide shade, and in it chairs and refreshments.

The men went immediately to examine the horses on offer. The fair had also attracted peddlers, and Bea led the ladies toward the area where they had set up their stalls. Time enough to admire the horses when the auctions started.

Buying a horse was nearly the last trial. The very last was an interview with Papa.

Alaric and Luke had missed the horse buying. They had missed moving the bulls and driving a carriage, too, but Papa had decreed they had completed the first task on the day of the fair, and they had driven a carriage to Dara yesterday, so that would count, as well.

Papa had been testing the suitors for courage, common sense, prudence, and teamwork. That had been easy enough for Bea to work out. What did buying a horse tell him about the suitors? An eye for a good horse, she supposed. An even better test than the steeplechase of the sense not to be taken in by a showy animal with more flash than substance. What else? The ability to negotiate? A sense of ethics?

Alaric would pass, she was certain, if he were here. But he was not. Would Papa disqualify him from the trials because he was not back when he said he would be? Surely not without listening to him. But that was *if* he came back. Would he?

Did she want him to?

Her heart said yes, and it also said no. No, because he had hurt her by leaving. But surely, he had had a good reason?

The debate continued in her mind as she chatted with her friends, admired ribbons with her cousins, and exchanged commiserations with Ellie, who was as worried about Luke as Bea was about Alaric. Worried, only. Ellie did not seem to be beset by the same doubts as Bea. She was certain Luke would return and was imagining all the dire circumstances that might have delayed him.

"Luke loves me," she told Bea in an undertone, though the others were totally absorbed in the antics of a monkey that was dancing to the tunes played by a man with an accordion. "He wants to marry me. He is coming back."

Does Alaric love me? He kissed me. He wants to marry me—or, at least, so he said. But does he love *me?*

And when had Bea decided that she wanted love? She had

agreed to the trials—had told her father she would choose one of the successful contestants who met with his approval. "Love will come," Papa had promised her. "Marry a suitable man, and love will come."

I want what Ellie and Luke have—what I think Reina and Maddrell are developing, but I want it with Alaric.

There. She had thought it, and now it could not be unthought.

"Of course, he will come back," she told Ellie, remembering how Luke looked at Ellie when they were together.

"And Alaric will be with him," Ellie assured her.

Neither of them mentioned that perhaps something had happened to both men, especially with the storm the night before, but Bea could see that knowledge in Ellie's eyes, and Ellie must have understood that Bea was thinking it, too. She squeezed Bea's hand. "Come," she said. "The auctions are starting. Let us go and watch."

Chapter Twenty-One

AFTER A COUPLE of hours, the men had completed their purchases, and had also imbibed more than a few jugs of ale to lubricate the negotiations. They were pleased with themselves and just a little loud and brash in their self-congratulations.

When Aunt Joan announced that the *Cashtal Vaaich* servants were serving an al fresco lunch, Bea was happy to retreat to the shade and relative privacy of their tents. Perhaps some food would help to soak up some of the alcohol.

She was seated off to one side, with a good view of the road leading into the field where the fair was just winding up, and so was the first to see two men riding at a gallop along the road toward the fair. By the time they turned off into the field, Bea was almost certain she knew their identity. "Ellie," she said, "look there."

Ellie took one look and beamed. "Luke is back."

That's what Bea had thought. The riders were Alaric and Luke, and they were fast approaching the tent, though they had slowed their mounts to a walk as they wove between the people who thronged the field.

Alaric's eyes met hers and he held her gaze as he dismounted. He stepped toward her, leading the horse.

"Mr. Redhaven and Lord Lucas Versey," Papa said. "I assume

you have a good reason for your late return?"

"One obstacle after another, my lord," Luke replied. "That is the short answer. We can give you the full details whenever you are at leisure." His eyes looked past Papa to seek out Ellie.

Alaric had not looked away from Bea, but now he turned to Papa and said, "We brought my sister-in-law safely away. She and my brother are at the castle. There are matters you should know, my lord, but they are not urgent." He frowned slightly. "Not anymore."

"Have we missed the horse trading?" Luke asked.

Papa's smile was slight, but it was there. "I do not know," he replied. "I do not recognize this pair. Borrowed?"

"Purchased in Dara," Alaric explained. "We had to put in there last night because of the storm, and we were in a hurry to return to the castle."

"Tell me about them," said Papa, stepping out of the tent to approach the horses. Alaric, with one last longing look at Bea, obediently began to explain the points of the horse he was leading, while Luke stood by, making cows' eyes at Ellie.

Bea's heart was singing. Alaric was back. He had been delayed by one obstacle after another, but he had overcome them to return to her. His eyes declared his continued interest, and perhaps more. Perhaps a warmth that was merely desire. But perhaps it was the love she yearned to inspire in him. And what a fool she would be if she did not make a push to find out.

ALARIC WAS NOT too late, thank goodness.

Sir Henry Dashwood was inclined to be offended that Lord Claddach was prepared to credit Luke and Alaric with the three trials they had missed. For the bull herding, that frantic action on the day of the fête had been counted. For the carriage riding, which had apparently been yesterday, Lord Claddach pointed out that Luke and Alaric had been first, driving Alaric's brother from one side of Claddach to the other.

And now the good earl was accepting the two horses that the men had purchased in Dara. There had been four, in fact—one for each of them. The footmen were coming back by carriage.

Including Eloise among the riders—though she could hardly have been left with her maid and the footmen—had slowed them down, too. Eloise was not a confident rider, and Luke and Alaric had felt it essential to stay with the couple. After all, Bebbington might still be out there somewhere, washed up on Claddach. Gorry, too.

The trip was so slow, they probably would have been better to have bought or hired a second carriage, if there had been one to be had. *Well.* No point in repining about impossibilities. And it was just as well, as it turned out, for now Alaric had passed all the trials so far. Eleven trials! Could that be true? *Well.* Ten, and the treasure hunt, which he had not yet completed.

Perhaps Odysseus was the last clue?

I haven't told Bea about Odysseus. She was still sitting in the same place he'd seen her when he turned in at the gate—off to one side of the tent, a little aside from the others. Three of the other ladies had been with her. Ellie, who was now admiring Luke's new horse, and Miss Radcliffe and Miss Bryant, who had left their seats to go to the tables where Claddach's servants were serving food, and who were now chatting with Maddrell and Fairweather.

Alaric took his chance and the seat next to Bea. "I have so much to tell you, Bea," he said. "But first, how are you?" *Did you miss me?* He was afraid to ask.

"I am well, thank you, Alaric." She was looking at her hands, then she looked up and met his eyes, and her own seemed to be asking a question, though perhaps not the one implied by her next comment. "Your trip was not without incident, I gather."

"I should have been back last night," he admitted. "I would have been, but Beverley went off with your father's yacht. Then

Viscount Bebbington, Eloise's brother, tried to have us arrested, and when we finally managed to get on the ocean, a storm came up, and we had to divert to Dara."

"You took such a risk!" Bea exclaimed.

"How could I not?" Alaric told her. "I had promised your father. I had promised you, in the message I gave Ellie. I could not be back by dinner last night, but I am here as soon as I could be."

There it was. Her smile. The smile that made his heart grow two sizes too big for his chest. "I am glad," she said.

"I realized what the fifth clue meant," he told her. "Tarquin, my brother, suggested we were like Odysseus, thwarted at every turn."

"It is the rhyme!" Bea declared, after a cautious look to see that the others were all absorbed with their own conversations. "Odysseus and Penelope. Alaric, there is a frieze in the picture gallery of scenes from the Iliad and the Odyssey, and one of them is of Odysseus drawing his bow, with Penelope and her loom, and the suitors all looking horrified." She chuckled. "Having one's husband shoot them all is not something one can do with unwanted suitors in this day and age."

"Am I a wanted suitor?" Alaric dared to ask.

She had no time to answer, for Lady Dashwood came hurrying up, her son beside her. "Dear Lady Beatrice," she gushed, "what are you doing all by yourself over here? Henry has come to keep you company, haven't you Henry?"

Their private moment was over, but Alaric was content. Lord Claddach had accepted them back into the trials. Bea wasn't angry with him. Both had agreed to wait for a fuller explanation.

As they prepared to ride back to the castle, Bea found a moment for another private word. "The picture gallery is on the first floor. From the main stairwell, turn east and go through the double doors. At the far end of the passage, turn right into a salon. The doors on the other side of the room let into the picture gallery. Meet me there at two o'clock."

They were interrupted by Dashwood again. He brought Bea's horse, leading it with the reins gripped close to the bit, so that the mare was objecting, sidling sideways and rolling her eyes.

"Your horse, Lady Beatrice, though she's a bit feisty for a lady, isn't she?"

Bea held out her hand for the reins, her eyes snapping. "You are holding her too close and pulling on her mouth, Sir Henry." She softened the rebuke, adding, "Thank you for bringing her to me."

The horse had calmed immediately under its mistress's tender hands, one on the reins and one on its neck. Bea said a few gentle words to it. "There you are. Good girl. Good girl."

Sir Henry, who had bristled at Bea's criticism, was looking around, frowning. "There isn't a mounting block, my lady," he pointed out.

"Mr. Redhaven shall toss me up," Bea decreed, and Alaric took his cue, bending to offer his linked hands to her boot.

One of Claddach's servants had taken his horse for water and food, and now led it to him, and soon the entire party was on its way back to the castle, leaving the servants to pack up the tent and all that was in it.

Bea rode next to the curricle containing her friends from the town, and Alaric took a place as close to Bea as he could, given that Dashwood had the same idea.

Dashwood had the coveted position when they were approaching the castle. The earl rode up next to Alaric. "I will hear your fuller explanation when you have had time to wash and change, Mr. Redhaven. I assume you will bring your friend Versey and your brother. Perhaps Stavely's wife, too, if you consider it appropriate. Two o'clock. My study."

"Yes, sir," Alaric replied. *Damn.* The same time as Bea had set. "Sir? It might be helpful if Lady Beatrice was also there. She has a right to know what took me—me and Luke—away when we are committed to the trials."

Claddach responded with a piercing look and a single nod.

"Very well," he said.

Alaric hoped Eloise did not mind.

He went up to the bedchamber the Stavelys had been assigned. Tarquin opened the door to their room. "Oh. Alaric. Come in."

It was a two-room suite. Eloise was reclining on a sofa in a little sitting room, and Alaric could see the corner of a bed through the door into the next room. "Alaric. Did Lord Claddach forgive you for arriving late? Did Lady Beatrice?"

"Provisionally," Alaric told her. "We have been granted a pass in the three trials we missed, since they were all things we've done on the island—catching bulls, driving a carriage, and buying a horse. He wants a fuller explanation, though. So does Bea. That's why I came. Tarquin, he wants to meet us at two o'clock. Eloise, you too, if you wish. Bea and Luke will be there, too."

Eloise paled. "Do you have to tell them about Bebbington and... you know."

"Sweetheart," Tarquin told her, bending over her and taking her hand. "Lord Claddach guessed at the same time as Alaric and I did. We shall not need to talk about it, will we, Alaric?"

"We can just say that Bebbington wanted to keep you from leaving, and Tarquin, Luke, and I had to rescue you," Alaric agreed. "But Eloise, I would like your permission to tell Bea the truth. She is, I hope, going to be my wife—your sister. She will not blame you, I know. Indeed, she might blame you if she does not know the truth. For jilting me." Was it unfair to say that? But Alaric thought it was true. When he had mentioned Eloise and Tarquin at the horse fair, Bea had made a caustic comment about forgiveness and his years of exile.

Eloise grimaced. "I am so sorry that I lied about you forcing me, Alaric. Or, at least, failed to correct Tarquin when I realized what he had assumed. It was wicked of me."

"We understand, darling," Tarquin assured her. "You did not know me well enough to know I would not blame you. Bebbington is at fault—for damaging your ability to trust as well as the other."

"You did what you thought you needed to," Alaric said, dutifully. He was determined not to hold a grudge, and he truly did not want Eloise to keep apologizing, which she had been doing at intervals ever since they'd extracted her from her stepbrother's clutches.

This time, she explained. "I should have told the truth," she insisted. "About falling in love with Tarquin, and about what my brother had done to me. Bebbington was threatening to ruin you if I married you, and you didn't deserve that. Besides, I didn't desire you, Alaric, though I could see you desired me. I didn't think I would ever desire anyone. And then you introduced me to Tarquin, and I discovered I was not as broken as I thought. I knew my brother would be no match for the heir to an earl. In any case, it would not have been fair to marry you, feeling as I did about Tarquin."

"I should say not," Alaric admitted. "You did the right thing. And you do not need to keep apologizing, Eloise. You would have told the truth if you had been able. It has weighed on your conscience all this time, you said. If you feel you need punishment, you have had enough."

It was true, he realized, the last of his grudge dissolving. Eloise had done her best in a bad situation he was blithely unaware of at the time, though surely the signs had been there. Neither he nor Tarquin were the least surprised when they guessed, after all. Had he desired Eloise? He supposed he had, but what he remembered feeling for her was only a shadow of what he felt for Bea.

Mostly, he had wanted to protect and shield Eloise, dimly sensing she needed a defender, like a half-fledged bird with a damaged wing and predators lurking.

Come to think of it, that had been part of Delphine's attraction too. She had seemed to need rescuing when he met her, though in her case, it was a calculated ploy.

Not Bea. He could stand side by side with Bea, and what a

marvelous thing that was!

"I shall tell Lady Beatrice myself," Eloise announced. "I need to do that, Tarquin, so do not argue. Alaric says she can be trusted, and I trust Alaric. Alaric, will you let me tell Lady Beatrice? She won't think me a disgusting wanton, will she?"

Ah, poor Eloise. Among her stepbrother's sins had been convincing her that his abuse was her fault for tempting him, and he was only giving her something that, deep down, she really wanted. Alaric was glad it was Tarquin and not him who had had to deal with the aftermath of Bebbington's appalling actions.

"Bea will understand that Bebbington is a twisted, cruel monster who preyed on an innocent he was bound to treat with kindness and respect by family loyalty and gentlemanly duty," Alaric insisted. If she was the lady he believed her to be. "She will be on your side, Eloise, as are we."

"Then I shall come to the meeting with Lord Claddach," Eloise decided.

"Are you sure, my love?" said Tarquin. "We can do it, Alaric, Versey, and I. None of us will mention Bebbington's unspeakable motives."

Eloise was sitting up, toeing her feet into her slippers, and reaching for her shawl, which was draped over the arm of the sofa. "I am sure, Tarquin," she insisted.

The three of them met Luke on their way to Claddach's study, and inside, they found Bea was with her father.

"My dear," said Claddach to Bea, "this is Lord Stavely, Redhaven's brother. And, I take it, Lady Stavely?"

Eloise and Bea dropped curtseys to one another. "Welcome to *Cashtal Vaaich*," Bea said.

"Thank you for your hospitality," Eloise replied. "And thank you, Lord Claddach, for allowing my husband and brother, and their friend, to use your yacht when they came to my rescue."

"I am pleased to welcome you to Claddach, Lady Stavely," said Claddach. "Unharmed, I trust?"

"Unharmed," Eloise confirmed, with her gentle smile. "My

THE TRIALS OF ALARIC

stepbrother did not hurt me, but he declared his intention of turning Tarquin away, and keeping me imprisoned." Her eyes filled.

"They were not going to prevent me from reaching my wife," Tarquin declared.

Luke chuckled. "Tarquin walked right past the butler and up the stairs, and Alaric and I followed."

"Then Alaric blocked the door, and we climbed out the window," said Eloise. "Tarquin had the carriage waiting. Fortunately, my brother had turned my maid out of the house, and Tarquin and Alaric had already found her."

"So, we left for Birkenhead," Alaric commented. "So far, so good."

Claddach turned his attention to Alaric. "My yacht is back in Dara, I suppose?"

Alaric grimaced. "No, sir. While we were at Bebbington's estate, your nephew Lord Beverley commandeered your yacht and its crew. His declared destination was Brighton. I cannot tell you where your yacht is now."

"Beverley!" Claddach's eyebrows had shot up at Alaric's words, and they now dropped again, drawing together fiercely over his eyes. "Lewiston needs to do something about that son of his, and so I will tell him. That was one of the obstacles you mentioned, I must suppose, Redhaven."

"Yes, my lord. Beverley had sailed to Birkenhead with Gorry, who had stolen a fishing smack, so we thought we'd bring it back to its owner at Bailecashtel. A townsman we met at the harbor helped us find a captain and crew, but before we could set sail, Bebbington turned up with a justice of the peace."

"The swine," said Tarquin. "But Eloise was very brave. She stood up to him and told the justice she wanted to come with me, and that Bebbington had been holding her against her will."

Luke took up the tale. "But by the time we set sail, we had already missed your six o'clock deadline. We would have made it to Bailecashtel before full dark if the storm had not come up. It blew us off course, and so we sailed to Dara instead."

"Pursued by Bebbington and Gorry," Alaric added. "Or, at least, so we believe. The fishing smack following us did not make it to Dara, but they may have come ashore somewhere else."

"Then this morning, several of the roads we wanted to use were closed with floods or slips, so it took us a long time to cross the island," Luke explained. "I was wondering what else could possibly go wrong, but here we are, my lord. Returned as promised, and with Lady Stavely. Late, it is true, but my lord, we did try!"

"Well, Bea?" Claddach asked his daughter. "What do you say? Are they forgiven?"

"They are, Papa," Bea declared. "And Papa, Alaric tells me that he has solved the fifth clue in the treasure hunt."

"Close to, at least," Alaric amended. "I know the topic, and Lady Beatrice has told me where to find the *objet d'art* implied by the last two lines."

"Indeed?" Claddach asked. "Then, young man, you had better repair to that location immediately. I take it, daughter, that you were about to ask me if you could take a walk with Redhaven here? You may, if Lord and Lady Stavely go to play propriety. And Versey, Lady Eleanor would undoubtedly enjoy your company. I believe she was intending to repair to the music room."

"Thank you, sir." Luke sketched a brief bow to the two ladies and left the room. Alaric offered his arm to Bea and inclined his head to Claddach. "Thank you, my lord."

"The portrait gallery?" Bea asked.

"The portrait gallery," said Alaric.

"I take it," Tarquin murmured to Alaric, as they followed the ladies into the portrait gallery, "that my part is to distract my wife so you can kiss Lady Beatrice."

It was good having his twin back. Tarquin had always been the friend who knew what Alaric was thinking before he spoke. The breach between them had healed, and he felt whole again. Winning the next clue had to be a priority, but Tarquin was quite right. Alaric would take any opportunity to kiss Bea.

Chapter Twenty-Two

WITHIN AN HOUR, Alaric had satisfied both priorities, and was well-pleased with life.

After the portrait gallery, Eloise and Bea went off together, Eloise pale and determined. Alaric visited the earl's study, and Tarquin returned to his bedroom suite to wait. Alaric joined him once he had the longest and most confusing verse of them all.

The sixth clue made no sense at all, yet. But he had to solve it and so he would. It was the last in the treasure hunt, the earl said, and there was only one more trial. An interview of sorts would be held tomorrow. "A test of understanding," said Claddach. Whatever that meant.

Alaric had until that test to complete the treasure hunt and win the treasure, when the only treasure he wanted was Bea. Her smiles, her incisive remarks, her kisses, her loyalty to those she loved, her kindnesses, and her kisses. *You have already said kisses,* he reminded himself. But it bore repeating.

"Did Lord Claddach give you the next clue?" said Tarquin.

Alaric had forgotten his brother was even in the room. He had been in a daze since the portrait gallery, where Tarquin and Eloise had disappeared into an alcove and Bea and Alaric had celebrated finding the Odyssey panel they needed with an embrace.

None of Alaric's previous experiences had prepared him for kissing Bea. It was all consuming. He could have kissed her, just kissed her, and touched her breasts, for hours. Even though he wanted more—wanted everything—he wouldn't dishonor her. Not when he had not yet been given the right.

And somehow, it didn't matter. Kissing and cuddling had always been a preliminary—to be given the necessary time, since women enjoyed the culmination more that way—but only a stage in the journey to what he really wanted. With Bea, it was different. He wanted her kisses. He wanted her embraces. They satisfied him, thrilled him, in a way that had nothing to do with the physical. He would rather have a single touch of her hand than to bed the most skilled courtesan in all the world.

In fact, even thinking of some of his previous experiences felt wrong. In his heart, he was Bea's, and she was his. No other woman would ever do. Not ever again.

When he had told Tarquin that, his brother had nodded. "You love her, and you want to make her your wife, your own. Naturally, every other physical encounter pales by comparison."

It was true, and even if he had been of a mind to deny it, the evidence was clear. He loved Bea.

"The clue?" Tarquin asked.

Alaric dragged his mind from Bea's soft lips and firm curves. "Sorry."

Tarquin grinned. "You are in love, and if I must repeat myself half a dozen times, so be it. The clue?"

"Yes. The clue." Alaric had it clutched in his hand. He opened it and read it out loud.

"The hidden doors the secret keeps

"Till opened by uneasy sleep.

"Where knights once watched for pirates bold

"Discover, man, the secret gold.

"Learn from our verses, if you're smart.

"The trove you seek is Claddach's heart."

192

"I do not understand any of it," said Tarquin, taking the paper from Alaric and scanning the words as he spoke. "No. It doesn't make any more sense to me when I read it myself. Were they all like this?"

"Not really," Alaric said, then reconsidered. Some of them had seemed impossible, at least at first. "Or perhaps. They have all been hard to interpret. If this one refers to a famous love story, then I have no idea which one. Well. Perhaps Bea has an idea."

"You know it is a good sign, don't you, when the lady you are trying to win is helping you to do so."

"I think she has decided I am the best consort for Claddach," Alaric confided. "After all, it was for the island's sake that she agreed to choose from those who succeeded in her father's trials."

"Yes, but surely falling in love with you changes that," Tarquin argued.

"In love?" Alaric said. "She is attracted to me, Tarquin, but she is not in love. At least, I do not think she is. She hasn't said."

Tarquin sighed. "I suppose you haven't told *her* that *you* love her. Why not, Alaric?"

"I do not want to burden her with my feelings."

His brother shook his head, but if he had more to say, he didn't speak it, for the door opened, and his wife entered, her eyes damp and shining, but her smile broad.

"Alaric, your Lady Bea was so kind," she said. "I am quite forgiven, though I do not deserve it after the wicked things I allowed Tarquin and your father to believe. She said, if you have forgiven me, Alaric, when you were the one most sinned against, then that is all to be said about the matter."

She stepped into her husband's waiting arms. "She said she quite understood why I was afraid to say anything, and she is glad that Tarquin is such a wonderful person. Tarquin, she said I was not a sinner, but that I had been sinned against."

"That is what I have been telling you," Tarquin told her, kissing her hair.

"Is she downstairs?" Alaric asked.

"Yes, in the green parlor. Refreshments are going to be served, but I said I needed to wash my face."

"I will see you soon then," said Alaric, and hurried downstairs, giving the couple their privacy.

BEA HAD NEVER admired Alaric more. Poor Eloise! But poor Alaric, too, to have been accused of such a dreadful thing and to have his own brother and father believe it. How wonderful he was to not only forgive his sister-in-law, but to immediately volunteer to help his brother rescue her.

Even so, her conversation with Eloise had unsettled Bea. It was not jealousy. Eloise had said quite enough for Bea to be certain that the lady was head over heels in love with her husband. But Alaric must have loved her once. He had asked her to marry him. He had been jilted in favor of his brother. Did seeing her again bring back all that pain?

"Bea?"

Bea blinked at the sound of her name, and realized she was sitting in the parlor with the other young ladies and ignoring them all in favor of thinking about Alaric.

"I apologize, Ellie," Bea said. "I was distracted for a moment. I did not mean to be rude."

"She is thinking about Mr. Redhaven," said Cousin Dorrie, and she and her sister giggled.

"Why should she not?" Reina asked. "He is handsome, clever, kind, and attentive."

"He is also the front runner in the trials," Christina pointed out. "He and Lord Lucas, but we all know Lord Lucas only has eyes for Ellie."

"In fact," said Cousin Lucy, "with my brother gone, Sir Henry Dashwood doing so poorly in the trials, Lord Lucas disqualifying himself by falling in love with Ellie, and Ambrose Howard making up to Dorrie, it is just as well Mr. Redhaven is so gorgeous, Bea. I would not want to have to choose between Fairweather and Meadowsweet. No offense to your brother, Ellie."

"Mr. Meadowsweet has also expressed an interest in another lady of the house party," said Sarah Howard, with a smug smile.

"Oh my," Dorrie said. "Another one drops off Bea's list."

Lucy smirked. "A choice between Fairweather and Redhaven is no choice at all, especially now that Mr. Redhaven is reconciled with his brother. What do you think, Dorrie? Is Mr. Redhaven still in love with his brother's wife?"

Aunt Jane, whom the sisters had clearly forgotten, observed, "Dorothy's conversation has been bordering on the vulgar, young ladies, but Lucy has just slipped over that border. Another topic if you please."

"You asked me a question, Ellie," Bea reminded her friend.

"I did? Oh yes. I asked about the plans for tomorrow."

Papa planned to interview each of the leading aspirants for her hand, but Lucy was right. The list was down to two at most. There was no reason why the rest of the gentlemen could not join the ladies for an excursion. Having them out of the house would also give Papa time for a rest, which he must have needed after the exertions earlier in the day.

"Would you care to visit the ruins of St. Benigna's Abbey? Those who wish to sketch could do so, and there's a hermit's cell part way up the nearby hill, for those who would prefer to walk up to see the view. We could take a picnic."

The door opened and Mr. Howard walked inside. "So, this is where you have hidden yourselves," he said. "Fairweather? Meadowsweet? The ladies are here."

Dorrie began telling the gentlemen about the visit to the abbey ruins, and then had to start again when first Luke, and then Alaric arrived. Lord and Lady Stavely joined them a few minutes later and were the next to hear of the planned expedition.

After that, it was all repeated to Mr. and Mrs. Howard and

Lady Dashwood, who had been walking in the garden, then to Mr. Maddrell and Mr. Whittington, and finally to Papa and Lord Lewiston.

"An excellent idea," Papa told her. "However, I shall need Mr. Redhaven and Mr. Fairweather during the morning. Perhaps they can join you in time for lunch?"

That was it then. The final trial and only two of them left. Bea presided over the tea pot, but her mind was on her trial, which was still to come. How would she turn Mr. Fairweather down? She had no experience with proposals, either refusing them or accepting them. More importantly, how would she find out whether Alaric loved her?

Papa was pouring drinks for those who preferred something alcoholic, attracting most of the men to the large sideboard, but Alaric came to sit beside her. "Bea, I have the next clue, and it is the last," he murmured, his voice too low for others to hear. "Can we meet somewhere so I can show it to you? Perhaps the portrait gallery?"

She found herself thinking about how to divest herself of all the other guests and her aunt, so she could have another of his mind-altering kisses. No. Not an hour ago, they had agreed to wait until the trials were over. His eyes dropped to her lips, and she knew he was thinking about it too.

"After dinner," she said, her voice husky, and she swallowed before she spoke again, her voice more normal, this time. "I shall suggest a stroll in the portrait gallery. If you and I walk together with your brother and sister, or perhaps Luke and Ellie, we can stay apart from the others without attracting comment."

It was easy enough. Nothing had been arranged for the evening beyond the usual cards and the expectation that some of the young ladies would sing or play the piano. Bea suggested a walk before they settled to the evening pursuits, and most of the young people accepted. Bea noted with some amusement that Sir Henry Dashwood, having had an interview with Papa before dinner, ignored Bea and gave all his focus to Lucy.

So much for having his heart broken, but poor Sir Henry. Bea doubted Lucy would have him, or that Uncle Lewiston would allow a proposal even if Lucy were interested.

"Dashwood did not take long to shift his interest," said Ellie. "He would be better to leave the house party and try elsewhere."

"Why is that?" Eloise asked. "He is a baronet, and passably attractive."

Ellie replied, "If one lacks a high title, a fortune, or looks that are more than ordinary, one should at least practice being agreeable." Which was acerbic, but true.

"Oh," was Eloise's only comment.

"Bea?" Alaric said.

Bea looked at her friends and the Stavelys, whom she believed would become friends. "Would you please allow us a moment to discuss the last clue in the treasure hunt?"

Luke's eyes widened. "Alaric, you've solved the clues?"

"Five of them," Alaric admitted, "with Bea's help, and Tarquin's on the fourth clue. This is the sixth and last, and I don't even know where to start."

"I gave up after two," Luke admitted. "By the time I received the third, Ellie and I... Well, there didn't seem to be any point."

"Show it to us all," Tarquin suggested. "Let us see what we make of it."

It was a good idea, and Alaric must have agreed, for he nodded. "We need to make sure the others don't see us reading and ask what we have," he said.

Bea couldn't see the problem. He had won, after all, even without the treasure hunt. However, the others agreed, and moved together to mask Bea as Alaric handed her the clue.

She read it carefully and then gave it to Ellie to read. Ellie passed it to Eloise. Tarquin passed it to Luke, saying, "I have read it."

"Any thoughts?" Alaric asked, when Luke looked up from the piece of paper.

Bea spoke first. "We have watchtowers all along the coast to warn us of pirates, but the mention of knights makes me think the verse must mean one of those here in the castle."

"The one nearest the coast, I imagine," Eloise said.

"Yes," Bea nodded. "It could be the highest tower of the keep, but I think the more likely answer is one of the watchtowers at the ends of the inner wall."

"Is that where we will find the hidden doors?" Tarquin wondered.

"Possibly," Alaric agreed. "The only other clue that might be intended to give us a location is 'uneasy sleep,' which might mean one of the bedchambers."

"Let's look at the watchtowers before breakfast," Luke suggested. "What about the last two lines? By the way, the three clues I've seen only had four verses."

"All of the other clues had four verses," Alaric confirmed. "They were all about famous love stories. Romeo and Juliet. Odysseus and Penelope. That sort of thing. What is the lesson learned? Most of them had tragic ends."

"The trove you seek is Claddach's heart," Eloise repeated. "The heart of Lord Claddach? Or the *isle* of Claddach?"

Her. The answer to that part of the clue was Bea herself. Her father had made it clear from the time he began to train her as his successor that he, his predecessors, and his successors were the heart of Claddach. But perhaps the line had other meanings and, besides, Bea couldn't refer to herself as the "heart of Claddach." Alaric might believe he had to win her heart, and the truth was, he already had it.

"We shall meet by the front door in the morning," she declared. "If that suits you all? At seven?"

They agreed, and just in time, for Dashwood approached with Lucy on his arm to say they were returning to the drawing room.

Their time to conspire on the clue was over for the evening.

⇶✦⇷

ALARIC WAS NOT comfortable. His bed had always been narrow, and high, but until tonight, he had slept well enough. Tonight, it seemed as if the mattress had developed hard lumps. Or, at least, a hard *lump*.

He had wriggled around until he was able to avoid it, but as soon as he fell asleep, he shifted, and the lump woke him again. In the early hours of the morning, he gave up, lit a spill from the embers of the fire to light a lamp, and went looking for whatever had got into his bed.

After stripping off all the blankets and sheets, he had a bed base and a stack of mattresses. Very thin ones, all filled with down. No wonder the bed was so high! He had never seen so many mattresses all piled one upon another.

Finding the lump with his hand, he used the other hand to search between the mattresses. He found the object three mattresses down and pulled it out. It was a ring of keys. Two large metal keys and a small one, all of the old-fashioned sort.

"Till opened by uneasy sleep," he repeated. The keys to the hidden doors? He certainly hoped so!

Now to find the doors. Alaric remade the bed and slept soundly for the rest of the night, but the keys did not leave his hand.

Chapter Twenty-Three

WELL BEFORE SEVEN, Alaric was up and dressed. He walked through the castle, carrying his boots so he did not wake anyone else. The tallest tower on the seaward side was little used, but Claddach's housekeeper was conscientious and each room he came to as he climbed the stairs was clean and tidy. He saw no hidden doors, but then he wouldn't, would he? If they were hidden?

So, he came back down the stairs, stopping at each room to run his hand over panels and examine floorboards. Still nothing. It was nearly time to meet the others, and Bea didn't think this tower was the one in the verse, but Alaric would come back if they found nothing in the other towers.

He hurried from the tower to the main door, and found Bea, Ellie, and Luke all waiting. Tarquin and Eloise arrived before he'd had time to say more than, "Good morning." Bea nodded to the footman who was standing by to open the door, and they all thanked him as they passed out through the door and into the fresh, crisp morning that waited beyond.

"I was thinking about the verse," Luke announced. "I think we should start with the north tower. It is closest to Scotland, and by the time of the knights, Scots pirates were a great danger to English shipping. Irish pirates were more active in Tudor times, which is probably a little late for the Earl of Claddach to have knights in his watchtowers."

"It is a good point," Bea noted. "I was thinking of the Vikings, but that is a little early for knights, is it not? In any case, Vikings would most likely have come here from Scotland or Wirral in England. Even if they came from Dublin, they were as likely to round Claddach from the north as from the south."

They all looked to Alaric, who shrugged. "North it is," he said. "We have to start somewhere."

Bea had brought the key for the watchtower door. She opened it, and Alaric said, "Let's start at the top. I imagine that would be where the knights kept watch, since they could see more of the sea on the other side of the bluff from the highest point."

The others set off toward the stairs that spiraled up from one side of the ground floor room, but Bea stopped. "I had forgotten. The very top door has always been locked. For as long as I can remember."

Alaric pulled the ring of keys from the pocket of his coat. "That might explain why I found these under my mattress last night."

They all stopped to look at the keys dangling from his hand. Bea was the first to speak. "The locked door is a good sign then. Let us go and see if one of the keys is a fit." She was the first to reach the stairs, and the others followed, hurrying up them as fast as they could.

The tower had eight levels, and the stair spiraled through the immensely thick stone walls, with openings into the interior on every level. They climbed past empty room after empty room. The run had become more of a walk by the time they reached the top floor. The stair spiraled on up. "The top of the stair opens onto the roof," Bea explained. "From up there, you can see for miles. But the view from the room below is nearly as good—or, at least, it is in the watchtower at the far end of the inner wall, which is in every way the same as this one, so I do not see why the top room would be different."

"Try the key, Alaric," Tarquin said.

The second of the larger keys fitted and turned. Alaric stepped back and asked Bea to open the door. She did so, and stepped inside, followed by the others.

The room inside was unexpected. Alaric's first impression was of a blaze of color, but that was a reaction to the grey stone he had seen all the way from the ground. As his mind adjusted, the bewildering chaos resolved into tapestries, carpets, drapes, furnishings. The watch room had become a bedchamber.

No. More than a bedchamber, for a large desk resided under one window, and comfortable seats beckoned from near the fireplace. In which a fire was laid, awaiting only a flame.

It was a luxurious medieval fantasy of a room.

"My," said Bea from beside him. "I had no idea."

"Was that the hidden door?" Ellie asked. "And if so, where is the secret gold?"

"The door wasn't hidden," Alaric pointed out. "Just locked. Also, the verse says doors, not door. But the key let us enter the room, so we must be in the right place."

"Are you meant to sleep here?" Eloise wondered.

It was possible. "I think the uneasy sleep was about finding the keys, but I cannot be certain."

"Let us search," Luke suggested. "Hidden doors could be under any tapestry or behind drapes. Even in the furniture."

"Search carefully," Bea warned, lifting the nearest tapestry to peer behind it. "This must be Papa's retreat. We don't want to damage anything."

It was Luke who found it. He drew the drapes for more light and disclosed a large window on the seaward side of the tower. Here, eight floors up and on the edge of an eight-hundred-foot cliff, the builders had not been concerned about stray arrows or siege engines, or even the structural integrity of the tower since they were right at the top.

Instead, their aim had been the best possible view of the sea, and all six searchers stopped to stare out over the ocean. They had to step right into the window embrasure to do so. A wooden frame had been built to jut out over the cliff, allowing a watcher to see down the cliff to the waves breaking below and to both sides, as well as so far ahead that, in the far distance, a soft misty shape against the sky was very possibly Wales.

Heavily carved paneling lined the embrasure, and a window seat had been built under the bay of the window frame. Alaric could imagine reclining there, on the colorful cushions, dreaming as he looked out to sea.

The paneling and seat were not recent, Alaric thought. The wood was dark with centuries of polish, and to his eye, the carving looked Tudor, or perhaps earlier.

"There are cupboards under the window seat," Luke commented. "I'll check those."

Reminded of their goal, the others returned to their search, until Luke called, "Alaric! Come and look at this."

Luke was kneeling on the window seat and had piled the cushions behind him, so the carved panels were laid bare down to the wood of the seat. "I've found several cupboards that weren't obvious," Luke explained, waving an airy hand at a couple of open doors. "But once I realized they were there, I opened them easily enough. Nothing inside. But look."

He ran the tip of his finger down the paneling in a straight line, and Alaric could see it. A crack. But the wood was old and probably dry. Dry wood cracked. Luke moved his finger back to the top of the crack, stretching to do so, and ran it in a straight line toward the window. Alaric's interest sharpened. And when Luke, without taking his finger from the wood, dropped it down in another straight line, he was almost convinced.

"How do we open it?" he asked, examining the carving for something that looked like a handle.

"I've tried to twist, push, or slide all the knobs I can find," Luke told him. "I don't think that's it. I think it is locked, Luke, and one of these holes in the pattern will take your key."

By now, the others had gathered around. "Try it," Bea said.

The first two holes were not deep enough, but in the third hole, the second largest key met with a brief resistance and then turned. They waited. The panel remained stubbornly shut. Luke tried the knob—it was a carved rose—closest to the lock and this time, it turned. Still, the panel did not open.

They stared at the paneling in disappointment, no one looking more crestfallen than Luke.

"That should have worked," he complained.

"Doors," said Tarquin. "Alaric, you said it. The verse says doors. And look!" He traced a rectangle that shared a long side with the first. It extended beyond the window seat toward the room, but it definitely looked like a door. Or as much like a door as the first had.

Alaric looked at his remaining key.

"Too small," said Bea. "Try the same one again."

He looked up into her eyes and saw the same excitement in them that he felt. Then he tried the second key. This time, he found the correct hole on the first try, judging it by the position of the other. He stepped back to let Luke turn the rose on that door, and both doors popped open.

"The hidden doors," Luke said, unnecessarily.

The cupboard was empty. Alaric could not have described the depths of his disappointment, and from his friends came a chorus of sighs.

Then Eloise spoke. "Lord Lucas, were the other cupboards you opened carved inside, as well as out?"

They all turned to look at her. Then Luke reached out to stroke one of the details on the inside of the door nearest to him. His touch was almost tender, as if the carving were a baby animal or a beloved woman. "No," he said. "No, they were not."

Ellie stated the obvious, her voice full of awe. "These ones are."

Both carvings seemed more modern than the rest—the wood less discolored by time, the proportions of the scenes closer to real life. They both showed lovers. Alaric squinted at the edge of the door nearest to him, and sure enough, he could tell that the inner carved panels were applied to the doors, and not an integral part of them. Indeed, the doors were remarkably thick for cupboard doors—perhaps as much as an inch and a half.

On the left-hand door, two people in the long chainmail hauberks of medieval knights stood hand in hand. One wore padded leggings and a conical helmet with a nose piece. The other was a woman, her long gown showing under the hauberk and her plaits tied in a crown of hair around her head.

On the right, the embracing lovers were from the late medieval. Alaric guessed the era from the high-waisted gown and elaborate head dress on the lady and the hip-length doublet that showed under the robe worn by the gentleman. Their robes, capes, and hats appeared luxurious and ornate, and they were hung about with jewels.

The background of both panels showed crops being harvested, boats coming ashore laden with fish, and simply dressed people dancing.

Bea touched the nearest lady with gentle reverence. "Brede daughter of Fergus, and first Lady of Claddach," she said. She moved her hand to the knight. "Turstin son of Waudrile. Her consort."

The others stepped out of her way as she moved to the second panel. "Lulach FitzWaudrile, Second Lady of Claddach. Jamie McAllister. Her consort. The panels show the first two Ladies of Claddach and the men who loved them."

"But where is the gold?" Eloise asked.

As if light suddenly poured into his mind, Alaric knew. The secret gold of which the verses spoke was the Lady of Claddach. The two depicted, and the one beside him, who did not yet hold the title but would in time to come.

And then he suddenly understood the last two lines. He said nothing, however. How could he? To announce such a thing in public, even to dear friends, before he had told the two people who most deserved to know?

As the others discussed the images and the rhyme, Alaric realized that Bea also remained silent.

HER FATHER WAS a cunning man. Bea had always known that. Known, too, that he was proud of her. It was only today that she realized how much he loved her. She had solved the last riddle, and she was almost certain that Alaric had, too. He went very quiet, and he kept looking at her when he thought he would not be noticed.

Did he truly understand? Every few minutes he would smile, as if he were full to the top with joy that bubbled from within and had to be released, or he would burst in front of the whole house party. Or perhaps she was putting her own feelings on to Alaric.

Time would tell. She had a visit to the ancient abbey to conduct, and Alaric was off to answer her father's questions. But afterward! Afterward, if she was right about what Alaric thought and intended, she would be able to pick up all the dreams she had set aside when she agreed to choose her husband through the trials.

Afterward.

Chapter Twenty-Four

A LARIC FOUND HIMSELF on his own in the study with Lord Claddach. He had not felt this way since he had last been sent to the headmaster at his school, not conscious of any major sins but certain he was about to be lectured, beaten, or expelled.

It didn't help to remember that, on that occasion, the headmaster's purpose had been to tell him his mother had died, and he was being sent home. Claddach did not keep him waiting long but entered after only a few minutes that Alaric had spent in anxious waiting. Fairweather was not with him.

"Mr. Fairweather has gone to see the abbey," Claddach told him. "He could see no point in answering my questions. He thinks you have won already, Redhaven. Are you of the same opinion?"

"No, my lord," Alaric answered. "I am of the opinion you will not entrust the Heart of Claddach to any man who is not worthy of her, and of the island she will rule."

Nervous though he was, it pleased him to see the earl's eyebrows shoot up in astonishment. Not for long. Claddach had his expression under control again when he said, "The Heart of Claddach, Redhaven?"

"It is part of the solution to the sixth verse," Alaric explained, confident of his reasoning. "Bea—I mean, Lady Beatrice—is the secret gold and Claddach's heart."

Claddach nodded thoughtfully. "You call her 'Bea.' And yet you say you have not won?"

"I have not asked her to marry me, my lord, if that is what you mean. I will not, until you give me leave." He shrugged, trying to find the words to explain his thoughts. "It would not be fair to her, for she will not marry where you do not approve. Her sense of duty is too strong."

"Very well, Redhaven. You have answered well. Let us see what you do with the rest of my questions. First, the trials. Why did I set you to an archery contest?"

Alaric had thought about this a lot. The trials were not just a contest to narrow down the suitors. They allowed the earl, often through the servants and the islanders, to get to know the suitors. "I think, sir, you were looking at sportsmanship and focus."

"Hmmm. And the steeplechase?"

"The obvious. Horsemanship, stamina, the ability to plan under pressure. But you also set up an opportunity to cheat and an obstacle where we had to choose between the race and helping someone in need. So, I think you were testing us for integrity and kindness."

"Pall-mall?" Claddach asked.

"Teamwork, my lord. Also, sportsmanship. And whether a person would rather punish another than win."

Claddach continued through the events, giving Alaric no hints as to whether his answers were acceptable. After that, he moved to questions about farming, animal husbandry, brewing, Alaric's views on politics, family, Society, and world affairs.

Finally, he leaned back in his chair and said, "That is all satisfactory, Redhaven. Now for the treasure hunt. What have you learned from the treasure hunt?"

Alaric, who was feeling a little as though he'd been crushed to flour between a couple of millstones, took a moment to order his thoughts.

"Sir, the clues all took me to stories about love—good examples and bad. And lastly to the inner side of the cupboard doors in the watchtower, with the two previous Ladies of Claddach and their consorts. Two more love stories. Do you want to know whether I love your daughter? For I do, with all my heart. And I want you to know, if I am fortunate enough to win her, I shall spend my life in her service as her consort, and I will live in hope she shall one day love me, too."

"Hmm," said Claddach, not letting Alaric know if this answer about loving his daughter pleased him or not. "So, you found my room and the cupboards by the window seat. That is two keys, Redhaven. What of the third?"

"I do not know what the third key opens, my lord," Alaric confessed.

"Then you have not completed the treasure hunt," the earl told him. "I shall give you a clue, shall I? My daughter is, indeed, the Heart of Claddach, but that is only part of the answer. Keep looking. In the meantime, you may continue courting my daughter, Redhaven, but you do not yet have my permission to ask her to marry you. First, my boy, you must find the secret gold, which is not my daughter, though that was a good guess. Let me give you another clue: you will know it when you see it."

He paused, leaning back in his chair with his eyes closed. To Alaric, he had always seemed like a force of nature—large, vital, powerful. But for just that moment, he seemed diminished, his fires banked. Alaric had never noticed how translucent his skin was, or how it seemed stretched over bones with no flesh between.

"Sir?" Alaric asked. "Are you well?"

Claddach opened his eyes. "No, Alaric. I am not well. I am, in fact, dying—I have a cancer eating my gut. I am trusting you not to speak of this to anyone except Beatrice, who understands she shall be Lady of Claddach sooner than she might have hoped."

"I am sorry, sir," Alaric managed to stammer. "Of course, I will say nothing."

"This is why I am anxious to see my daughter married,"

Claddach explained. "And married well, to a man who is worthy of her. It is why she agreed to the trials, rather than leave Claddach and go to London, on the off chance there might be a treasure amongst all the fribbles." He straightened and seemed to shake himself. As if shrugging into a disguise, he once again seemed like the dominating man Alaric had first recognized, and he gave Alaric a stern smile. "Do not fear. My death is not imminent. I will live to see my daughter married."

"I am glad to hear it, sir. Your daughter and her consort will need your guidance. And your daughter and your wife will be distraught when you go."

The earl sighed. "I am sorry for it. I have yet to tell my wife, Alaric. It is something I must do once Beatrice is safely married."

Why after Bea's marriage? And why safely? Alaric did not feel he could ask. Or should.

"Enough of this," Claddach decreed, closing his eyes again. "I am tired, and you have ruins to explore and a picnic to attend. Go and tell my daughter that you passed your twelfth trial, Alaric. Just find where the third key fits, and I shall be happy to accept you as my son. Pull the bell for my valet as you leave."

Alaric obeyed, but paused in the doorway to say, "Thank you, sir. I will not let you down."

The only answer he received was a smile. The man who came into the room through another door—Claddach's valet—came to his master's side muttering about sick old men who thought they were twenty again, and Alaric backed away out into the passage and closed the door behind him.

The news of Claddach's ill health had shaken him. He went up to his bedchamber to change into his borrowed riding boots—Tarquin had given him plenty of money since their reconciliation but had not brought the trunks of clothes he'd asked for.

Colyn wasn't there, but Alaric managed to pull his boots on. From his window, he could see the northern watchtower. Was the third keyhole there? Or perhaps a hint to its location on the panels showing the ladies and consorts of Claddach?

He couldn't wait, and a few minutes' delay would not matter, since Bea was not expecting him. He picked up the ring of keys and hurried downstairs and outside, not to the stables but to the watchtower.

The first key let him into the room. The second unlocked the two doors. He stopped, his hands hovering over the rose catches. Should he wait for Bea? But she would be away most of the day. Wouldn't it be better to find out whatever the panels had to tell him and share that with her?

He grasped the roses.

He and Bea were to be partners. He had promised Claddach. He had promised Bea herself. He huffed a sigh. *Best to start as I mean to go on.* Reluctantly, he locked the cupboard doors. Discovering this with Bea was the right thing to do, but still, he struggled, keen to have the treasure hunt over, to win the right to propose to Bea. He turned to the window, gazing outside while he repeated to himself all the reasons to walk away now and come back later. With Bea.

Something on the rocks at the foot of the cliff caught his eye. "What's that?" He squinted to better focus his eyes. The object, whatever it was, was half on the rocks and half in the water, with the waves breaking over it to further disguise its shape. But if he was not mistaken, it was a human being. *A human body*, he corrected himself.

Alaric left the top room of the tower, locked the door, and made his way to the stable. Soon, he led a small band of grooms and groundsmen out of the castle to investigate what he had seen.

They went out through both walls and through Bailecashtel on the castle side of the river to the bottom of the cliff, then out over the rocks. Their destination was only accessible at low tide, and then only by a difficult scramble from the town side of the bluff.

The tide had turned by the time they reached the body. A few more waves and it might have been dragged back off the rocks. They were in time, though, to pull the body onto the stretcher they'd brought with them.

"Not dead above a day or two," said the stablemaster. "Nay, dinna ye look, Master. Drownded men bein't a bonnie sight."

"I think I know him," Alaric said, ignoring what the stablemaster said and wishing he didn't have to. "Yes, this ring confirms it. Viscount Bebbington. Lady Stavely's brother. So, it was him on that boat. And if it was Bebbington, it was probably Gorry. I'll need to let Claddach know. And my brother and his wife."

If the rocks had been hard to negotiate going there, they were much harder returning with the stretcher. The stablemaster's wisdom in bringing eight sturdy men became clear when the two groups of four swapped tasks, one set carrying the stretcher, and the other going ahead so the stretcher could be passed up to them, or down, or—when the sea surged between the rocks— over.

Even so, they were all winded and a little battered by the time they arrived back on stable flat ground. Especially Alaric, whose riding boots had slipped on the rocks. Between the scratches on them and the effect of the salt water, he doubted they'd ever be fit to wear again.

"Eh, lads," the stablemaster said. "Here comes the cart to take the poor boyo to the castle."

"To Dr. Bryant's," Alaric corrected, "so there is no chance of the ladies seeing the body in its current state. Also, surely Lord Claddach doesn't need to be bothered with the death of a mainlander who has died at sea from such an obvious cause. There must be another magistrate who could declare the man drowned."

The stablemaster regarded him thoughtfully. "Aye, Master," he replied, then turned to the driver of the cart, who was watching the stretcher bearers lash the body to the cart. "You heard him, Asmund. Take this here body to Dr. Bryant's. Do you want me to see the doctor, Master Redhaven?"

It *was* "Master" he was saying. With the man's accent, Alaric had been uncertain. Why "Master"? But he had more important concerns. "I've identified him. I'd better go with him to Bryant and the magistrate. Is it Mr. Radcliffe?"

"It is," the stablemaster confirmed.

Seeing the body to Dr. Bryant's place and then being interviewed by Mr. Radcliffe ate up the rest of the morning and part of the afternoon. Alaric was footsore and tired by the time he arrived back at the castle. And bewildered. The stablemaster had been only the first to call him "Master." Down in the town, most people he met addressed him that way.

As he came through one of the side gates in the outer wall, a cavalcade was entering the main gate—the house party guests, in curricles and on horseback, returning from their expedition to the ruined abbey.

Bea—he couldn't see her face under the brim of her hat, but he never doubted his identification—broke away from the rest to canter toward him.

"My goodness, Alaric. What happened to you?"

Alaric looked down at himself. He was a mess, his boots and pantaloons scraped and stained, his coat no better, his cravat long since balled up and stuffed into a pocket, and his hat left behind on an errant wave. "I apologize for my state, Bea. I saw a drowned man from the watchtower window and helped to retrieve him. I've been down in Bailecashtel telling the magistrate what I know."

"Gracious!" she swung down to walk beside him. "Someone caught in the storm the day before yesterday? Who was he? Not Bebbington!"

BEA DIDN'T NEED Alaric's confirming nod. After all, if Alaric had identified the man, it had to be someone he knew, and the house party was mostly intact. It had to be either Beverley or Bebbington. And Bebbington had last been seen sailing straight into the squall.

"Someone will need to tell Eloise," she said. "I can do that, if you wish, while you tell Papa."

"I should wash and change first," Alaric told her, with a deprecating wave at his attire. He certainly did look as if he had been dunked in the sea several times and then bashed against the rocks.

"Of course," she replied. "A few minutes will not make any difference to Lord Bebbington. Alaric, tell me, what did Papa say? Did you solve the treasure hunt?"

"Almost," he said. "I have to use the third key and find the secret gold. I was certain you were the treasure, and the Heart of Claddach. You are, indeed, Claddach's heart, he said, but that was only part of the answer. I thought I would check the doors again, to see if the Lady and Consort panels hold a clue to where I use the third key." He shrugged. "But I didn't feel right looking at it without you."

Bea's step faltered. She had assumed he had gone ahead without her, and was trying not to feel hurt, but he had stopped himself. He had waited. She smiled as she stepped out again, her heart brimming with love for her castaway. "I'm glad," she told him.

"We are to be partners," he said, simply, then reddened. "That is… I have your father's permission to propose once I find the secret gold, but you are under no obligation to accept."

If Alaric could be honest and open with her, she could do the same in return. "I intend to accept," she replied. "I love you, Alaric." From the look in his eye, he was about to seize her and kiss her, a scheme of which she thoroughly approved, except they were in the middle of the garden and most of the house party was watching with interest. She took another two strides in the direction of the inner gatehouse. "We had better find the secret gold quickly, I think."

She felt Alaric's gentle grasp on her wrist, stopping her from moving too far away. "Bea? Your father told me… I am sorry. I had no idea he was so sick."

For a moment, Bea froze in place, her vision blurring as tears filled her eyes. She did not like to think of it, but it was the truth. Her dearest Papa was fading. The blankety house party had been hard on him, but it wasn't that. He had avoided many of the events, had shut himself away in his study, sleeping on the day bed there, and appearing when it was strategic to do so.

His valet was in on the conspiracy to keep his condition a secret, and so was Dr. Bryant, of course. Even on the day of the steeplechase, he had managed to spend most of the day resting.

Alaric caught up with her, and he grasped both of her hands. "I don't know what to say," he confessed. "I cannot imagine how it feels, to be so close to a parent. And then to know you're going to lose him…"

"I have had him for twenty-three years," Bea commented. "Please God, we will have him for a few more."

"That is why I had Bebbington taken into town," Alaric confessed. "One less job for your father. And for you, for that matter. You wear yourself thin, Bea, being both your mother's deputy and your father's. I hope soon to have the right to share your tasks."

There didn't seem to be much to say to that, but Bea's heart lifted that he was willing. Yes, and that he did not mouth any nonsense about taking the burdens that were rightfully hers off her shoulders. Sharing was fine.

They went through the gatehouse, and the men on duty nodded to her in greeting. No, not just to her, but to Alaric, too. "My lady. Master."

She shot a sideways glance at Alaric, startled.

"They were calling me that in town," Alaric commented. "'Master.' Is there some meaning I don't know?"

There was, and Bea was dumbstruck once more. "The people in town, and the servants here?"

Alaric nodded. "Come to think of it, the first was Colyn, last night. What are they saying, Bea? They don't seem to be annoyed, so I don't think it is bad."

Chapter Twenty-Five

"IT IS GOOD, if a little premature," Bea confirmed. "In our tradition, the heir to the earl is given the title *Master. Master of Claddach*. We do not know about Turstin, but Jamie, the second consort, was always called by the same title. My people have chosen you as their leader and my husband, Alaric." Her eyes filled with tears again, but she smiled through them.

"Just as well you agree," Alaric commented, but his own voice was unsteady.

"They knew my mind, I suspect." Bea had no doubt of it. Her maid Eunys had been certain for days she would choose Alaric when the time came and would certainly have shared that opinion with her sisters and aunts, all of whom worked in the castle. And with her cousins in the town.

"Well then, let us pass on the news about Bebbington and then find the secret gold," Alaric suggested.

They separated at the main door, Alaric to find her father and Bea to inform Eloise. The viscountess cried. "Tears of relief, mainly," she claimed when she lifted her face from Tarquin's shoulder. "I know you would have protected me, Tarquin, but he was determined to separate us." She turned to face Bea. "He has made trouble for Tarquin. I am convinced he was behind several investors turning away from Tarquin's canal project, and two months ago, someone tried to kidnap our baby son when the nurse was walking him in Green Park. I think that was Bebbington, too. To trade for me, I suppose, for he told me bluntly, when I said that Tarquin would never let me have Wulfric at Bebbington Close, that he had no interest in Tarquin's brat."

Figuring that Eloise needed a distraction, Bea asked about the baby, and received a panegyric that ended with the viscountess in tears again, for she missed her little boy. "But we thought it best not to bring him north with us," Tarquin explained. "I would have left both him and Eloise at home, but Eloise insisted on coming."

"I did not want to bring my darling Wulfric anywhere near Bebbington," Eloise said, "but I also didn't want Tarquin to confront Alaric without me nearby. I was so afraid. I am sorry I did not just tell you all, Tarquin. What a silly I was."

Tarquin's efforts to convince his wife that he liked her just as she was did not require Bea as an audience, so she excused herself and went to find Alaric.

She met him coming up the secondary stairs, on his own. *Excellent.* "Let's go to the watchtower now."

"But we need a chaperone?" The lift at the end of the sentence made it a question.

Bea tossed her chin in the air. "Until I had allowed the others to court me and had made my choice, Papa said. I have made my choice, Alaric."

In answer, he took her hand, and they hurried down the stair, out a side door, and across the courtyard to the path along the inner wall.

Upstairs in the furnished room, Alaric gave Bea the keys. She unlocked the cupboards. They turned a rose each, their eyes on one another. Something in Alaric's eyes made Bea very conscious that they had slipped away from the company alone, without telling anyone where they were going, to a room with a locking door and a bed.

She was captured by that look—trapped as surely as if he held her in place. It took a long moment before he swallowed hard and turned to look at the inside of the doors, releasing Bea to do the same.

"Does anything stand out to you?" Alaric asked.

Bea shook her head, but even as she did, she noticed a detail that had slipped by her before. "Here," she said, putting her hand on the breast of the first Lady of Claddach, Brede, wife to Turstin, the first Master of Claddach. "And here." She moved her hand to the second Lady of Claddach, Lulach, wife of Jamie.

Alaric's eyes had jumped ahead, and he was now looking from one to the other, leaning close to see more clearly. "A necklace of some sort," he said. "A large stone or medal on a chain."

"The Heart of Claddach," Bea said. "I thought it was a legend. It is gold, they say, with a ruby in the center, both the gold and the ruby worked into a heart shape. Turstin gave it to Brede as a marriage gift, saying she was the heart of Claddach, and all would know when they saw the symbol on her chest. It was passed down by the family, but no one wore it again until Lulach. It is part of the stories, Alaric, but I never thought it was real."

"The carver thought it was real," Alaric commented. "Whoever wrote the rhyme thought it was real. But where is it?"

Bea was following Alaric's example, leaning in close to the nearest door to peer at the figures. "This fold in her cloak," she said, pointing to Brede's chest. The cloak had been carved as clipped to her armor at the shoulder, draping down behind, but at the front falling only to her breasts in graceful folds. "Does it hide another keyhole?" Bea asked. "A little one?"

"Try it," said Alaric, and Bea poked the key into the fold, looking for a hole. Unsuccessfully, but when she tried the same thing on the trim of Lulach's ornate neckline, the key slipped into place and turned.

The bottom of the carving dropped away, disclosing a shallow cavity inside the door. A cavity which contained a velvet bag.

Bea touched it. "That is not old enough to be from Lulach's

time," she objected.

"Whatever is inside is what counts," said Alaric.

"You open it," Bea decided. "If it is the Heart, then it is your place to find it."

Alaric lifted the bag. "It is a fair weight," he commented. He cupped the base of the bag and shifted his hand to feel what was inside. "A chain and something flattish," he said.

She was bouncing with impatience. "Open it," she pleaded.

He untied the strings that held it closed and tipped the contents into his hand. Gold, as bright as the day it was beaten into links and a smooth heart shape. Alaric turned the shape over to show the surface, with its central ruby and the engraving all around—workers in the fields, fishermen, people dancing—similar to the backgrounds of the panels.

"The Heart of Claddach," Bea said, her voice hushed. "But why did Papa say *I* am the heart?"

"Because you are." Alaric's voice was equally low and reverent. "You are the heart, and this is the Heart. You are the secret gold, and this is the secret gold. This is the symbol of which you are the reality. May I put it on you, Bea? Will you give me the right?"

She knew what he was asking, and she had already given him his answer. Still, something in her wanted it all. "You may propose now," she replied, and his eyes lit with laughter, even as he lowered himself to one knee.

"Beatrice Collington, Heart of Claddach and possessor of my own heart, will you be my wife? Will you allow me to stand beside you and support you and Claddach all the days of my life?"

Oh! That was perfect. A simple yes would not suffice. "Alaric Redhaven, I will. You have passed my father's trials and my own. Stand with me as Master of Claddach and master of my heart."

He rose from his knee and kissed her, then he put the chain over her head, so the Heart nestled between her breasts. Then he kissed her again.

"I love you, Bea," he said.

"I love you, too," she told him. It was some time before they locked up the cupboards and the door to the room.

WHEN BEA PRODUCED the Heart of Claddach, Eunys was as awed by it as Bea had been. Bea gave her the Heart's bag to put away. Tonight, she would wear the Heart for all to see. She asked for a dinner gown that would do it justice, but Eunys had first to study it and exclaim over it before she pulled from the dressing room a gown in dark green against which the Heart blazed.

Bea and Alaric had agreed to meet in a parlor downstairs and allow the rest of the house party to gather in the drawing room before they entered together. Bea was delayed more than she expected as servants gathered to watch her pass. Eunys must have disclosed the news and it had spread quickly.

She arrived in the parlor to find Alaric had only just arrived. He, too, had been detained by servants who wanted to congratulate him and tell him how pleased they were.

"You look amazing," Alaric said, his gaze skimming her once and then focusing on the Heart.

"You look splendid," she returned. "So, do you think Eunys and Colyn conspired?" He was dressed all in black, white, and silver, except for a waistcoat the same color as her gown.

He glanced at it, and chuckled. "Now I know what was in the message that came for Colyn while I was dressing."

"Let us join the others," said Bea holding out a hand. He took it and led the way out into the passage. They were greeted by clapping. The passage was lined on both sides by servants, who smiled and clapped as Bea and Alaric walked the short distance to the doors to the drawing room.

Two beaming footmen opened the doors and Skelly announced them: "Lady Beatrice Collister, heir to Claddach, and Master Alaric Redhaven, heir to Turstin Fitz Waudrile and Jamie

McAllister."

Conversation in the room stopped. So did Bea. Alaric must have shared the same impulse to give the servants their dramatic moment, for he stopped too at her side. He lifted her hand, so it rested on his and smiled at her before looking back into the room.

Papa walked toward them with both hands out, one to clasp Bea's free hand and one for Alaric's. His glanced at the Heart. "Well done, Alaric," he said.

"I could not have done it without Bea," Alaric answered, and Papa's smile became a broad grin.

"You'll do, young Master," he replied, then he turned back into the room, standing at Bea's side without releasing her hand. "My ladies, my lords, gentlemen, I am delighted to announce the betrothal of my daughter, Beatrice Elizabeth Maeve Collister, to Alaric Theodore Redhaven."

Mama had recovered from her shock and was at the head of the crowd coming to congratulate Alaric and tell Bea how delighted she was. "He is a fine young man," she said. "Your Papa has been telling me about how he behaved in the trials. And the Heart of Claddach! I had no idea that it was even real! Papa said he was certain Alaric would find it. Oh, Beatrice, I am so happy. Papa will see you married before…" She broke off and patted her eyes with a lace handkerchief from her reticule.

Aunt Joan put her arm around Mama's shoulders. "There, there, Mary. Claddach is still with us. We must be glad of that. Especially on this happy occasion. Bea, dear, I am so happy for you. Congratulations, Master Redhaven."

"Please," said her betrothed, "call me Alaric, Aunt Joan."

Mama allowed Aunt Joan to draw her to one side, but she remained near Papa and Bea as the rest of the house party took their turns to give her and Alaric their best wishes.

Until Aunt Lewiston approached, her face grim, her eyes blazing. "You were meant for Beverley," she hissed to Bea, and she glared at Mama. "Mary and I agreed when you were only a baby."

"*I* never agreed," Bea replied, even as Mama turned her face into Papa's shoulder.

"Your son was given his chance, even against my direct instruction," Papa responded, putting a comforting arm around his wife. Mama surprised him and Bea by turning to face her sister.

"If you had not spoiled the boy, Dorrie, I daresay he would not have given my daughter a distaste for him, but even so, he was not meant for Beatrice. I should not have gone against Claddach's wishes and let you encourage him to think he had only to reach out and the Isle of Claddach would be his." She aimed a tremulous smile at Papa. "Neither Claddach nor Beatrice would ever have allowed our island to become subject to an English earldom."

Uncle Lewiston commented, "Then we have been wasting our time here. Lady Lewiston, order our things packed. Lady Claddach, thank you for an interesting visit. Beatrice, I wish you well of your choice." His lipped curled and he suddenly looked very much like Beverley. "Elsmouth's rejected spare. When you could have had my son."

"You may as well eat your dinner, Lewiston," said Papa. "The next ferry leaves tomorrow afternoon. I would offer you my yacht, but your son commandeered it and I have no idea where he took it."

The two men stared into one another's eyes, and Uncle Lewiston looked away first. "We will take trays in our room," he informed the servants. "Dorothy and Lucy, you may stay for dinner, but make certain your maid has your trunks packed by eleven in the morning." He then offered his wife his arm and they left.

"Your mother and father won that match," Alaric whispered in Bea's ear, which made her chuckle.

Everyone else was either pleased for Alaric and Bea or too polite to say otherwise, and it was some time before things calmed down enough for Skelly announce dinner. Mama panicked a little when she realized that Alaric and Bea were not sitting together, but Papa suggested, "Lord Lucas would no doubt be delighted to sit next to Lady Eleanor, and that will leave a place beside our daughter for her young man."

Mama nearly bounced with excitement. "My daughter is getting married," she said. Papa smiled at her, but Bea noticed that he almost fell the last few inches into his seat. He was pale and had beads of sweat on his forehead.

"Papa looks unwell," she murmured to Alaric.

Alaric beckoned to the nearest footman. "Lady Beatrice and I are worried this has all been too much for the earl," he whispered. "Make certain his valet is standing by, in case he is needed."

"He is, Master and my lady," the footman assured them. "We are keeping an eye on Lord Claddach."

"Beatrice," said Mama at that moment. "Have you and Alaric discussed a wedding date?"

"Soon," said Papa. Just the one word, his face set as hard as granite. Bea sensed he was holding on to his poise and his pride by force of will.

She glanced at Alaric, trying to send him a message with her eyes.

"If it suits my lady, straight away," Alaric said.

"The banns," Mama said.

"License," responded Papa.

"We are technically part of the diocese of Bangor," said Mr. Whittington. "If you and Mr. Redhaven give me your authority, Lady Beatrice, I can visit Bangor and obtain a common license."

Alaric gave her a smile and a nod, and Bea said, "Thank you, Mr. Whittington. If we could have a word after dinner, you can tell us what you require for authorization."

"Good," said Papa, faintly. Mama frowned at him, then signaled to a footman, before standing. There was a scrape of chairs as all the gentlemen stood, too. "My dear guests," Mama said. "I must apologize. The excitement has been too much for me. Claddach, would you be good enough to escort me to my room?

Beatrice, dear, would you and Alaric take over for us?"

Bea met her mother's pleading eyes and gave her a smile and a nod. *Well done, Mama!*

Alaric picked up his glass and called everyone's attention. "Ladies and gentlemen, I would like to take the opportunity to propose a toast."

Well done, Alaric. While the guests were all looking at him, two footmen helped Papa from the room, with Mama hovering at his side.

Chapter Twenty-Six

ALARIC AND BEA were left to host the house party for the next few days. The only change to every other day so far, Alaric thought, was that he now had the right to assist Bea, who had been in charge since the party began.

Whittington's trip to Bangor went off without a hitch, despite the drizzly weather. The chaplain had offered to share the fishing boat he had hired with Lewiston and his family, but the earl decided not to leave after all.

"Father says he wishes to do your father the courtesy of staying for the wedding," Lady Dorothy told Bea. "Mother says we should stay in case Howard or Meadowsweet is inspired by the wedding to propose," said Lucy, and both sisters giggled.

Bea wanted to delay the wedding until her father was better, but Lord Claddach, Alaric, and—surprisingly—Lady Claddach all argued for it to be held as soon as it could be organized.

For the same reason, Alaric suspected. Bea as a young unmarried countess was going to be vulnerable to those who wanted to attach her lands to their own. Lewiston for one—Alaric was certain that was the reason for his change of mind. If he hadn't suspected Claddach's illness before the evening Alaric and Bea announced their betrothal, he must have heard about Dr. Bryant's visit the same evening and drawn the correct conclusion.

He and Lady Lewiston had buttonholed Alaric and Bea separately to explain why a hurried wedding would be a mistake—it would hint at a scandal and therefore damage Bea's reputation, it was unfair to Lord Claddach, who needed to rest, it didn't give Bea enough time to prepare, it meant Lord Claddach would be unable to attend.

Her cousins added their arguments. Bea should have a special gown for the occasion. Bea should be married in London, with everyone important in attendance. Even some of the house guests were recruited to the cause, though some took one side and some the other.

Only concern for her father gave Bea pause, and it took Lord Claddach himself to lay it on the line to her. "I need to see you married, my girl. Married to a worthy man and safe from Lewiston and his ilk, who might take advantage of your grief. Yes, you are of age and capable. But you are a woman, and English law is foolish where women are concerned."

After that, Bea simply smiled and shook her head at whatever anyone said against an immediate wedding.

Just a few days later, Alaric stood in the window embrasure in the room at the top of the north watchtower, watching his wife as she slept in the large bed.

His wife! His in every way now. By the promises of love they had made in this very room less than a week ago. By the vows they had made today in the church in Bailecashtel—no, yesterday now, for when he had looked through the window, he'd seen the first hint of dawn. By their joining in this bed.

The smile he had been wearing since he woke grew broader. And not just one joining, either. He would have stopped after the first glorious time, thinking his wife would be sore. But Bea would have none of it, and the second time was even more wonderful. And the third, after a short sleep.

He had woken ready to enter her again but was instead leaving her to sleep. She needed to rest, his wife. The whole island rested on her shoulders, a reality emphasized to him when he had arrived at the church to find the square packed with people who could not fit into the church, where every cleric on the island waited to witness Mr. Whittington officiate at their wedding.

She shifted, rolling onto her other side, and pulling the sheet up so all he could see of her now was her sweet curves, covered but not hidden by the sheet, and her dark brown curls.

How magnificent she had looked when she stepped into the church on her father's arm. He'd been well enough, he insisted, and no one else would give his girl into the hands of the man who had won her.

He had looked better, too, for his few days of rest. But Alaric had had no attention to spare for him beyond one quick glance. His eyes were riveted on his bride. His Bea. His busy Bea, both Queen and worker. Honey, too. His honey and his love.

Turning to the window, he gazed across the sea, but what he saw was his bride. In another gown of green, this one the soft color of sea foam. He hadn't seen it until she stood before him in the church, but he had heard about it. The craftswomen of Claddach had been working for this day for the past eighteen months, and the gown represented their loved island. It was made from the finest Claddach wool, embroidered in gold with the flowers of Claddach, and trimmed with lace made from flaxen thread grown and spun on the island.

The lace veil that had covered her head was also home grown and crafted. It had been fine enough for him to see the shape of her face. Her eyes met his and never looked away as she walked toward him. The Heart of Claddach had gleamed on her chest.

After that, the actual ceremony had seemed remarkably short. Perhaps because he had put back her veil and become lost in Bea's eyes. He had spoken his vows without stumbling, placed his ring on her finger—bought from a jeweler in Bailecashtel with money supplied by Tarquin, but he would pay his brother back once he had access to his bank again.

He remembered bits of the rest of the day. Stepping out of the church to face the roaring, deliriously happy, crowd.

Traveling back to the castle in a flower-bedecked carriage pulled by islanders, twenty at a time, in shifts that seemed to last only a matter of minutes so that as many people as possible had a turn. Listening as his brother made a speech that had him laughing and also fighting back tears, as Tarquin spoke of their lifelong friendship.

But best of all had been arriving at the tower, farewelling their escort—all the younger members of the house party, most of them now in couples—and hurrying up the steps to open the door and lock out the rest of the world.

No. Best of all had been taking Bea in his arms and introducing her to the arts of love. And what an apt student she had proved to be.

The bed creaked. Alaric turned around. Bea was sitting up in bed, the sheet still wrapped around her. She held out one arm to beckon him. "Alaric, come back to bed," she coaxed.

"I am not tired," he told her. "I thought I'd leave you to sleep."

She raised both arms in a stretch, and the sheet fell away, riveting Alaric's attention on her lovely breasts, which he had not, now he came to think of it, adequately loved last night or early this morning. If it was not deliberate seduction on her part, then she had a native and hitherto unexplored talent.

"I have no wish to sleep," she informed him. "Isn't there something else we could think of to do?"

Alaric could think of several things. "Things we've already done, or new things?" he asked.

His wife proved once again the advantage of marrying a confident, capable, independent lady. "Why not both," she said.

And Alaric covered the floor between them in four swift strides and went back to bed.

Epilogue

The Isle of Claddach, March 1822

ALARIC WAS LEANING over the rail, even as they sailed into Bailecashtel harbor. Yes, there they were. Waiting at the dock. His wife and his son. No doubt his beloved Bea had had a lookout posted in one of the castle's towers ever since she received his letter saying he was on his way home.

Bea was holding Jamie's hand, though the little boy's nurse was hovering, ready to dash to the rescue if he pulled away from his mother. Bea was not up to chasing anyone just now. In her letters, she had told him she was at least twice the size she'd been with Jamie, which was presumably an exaggeration.

Even as the ship glided into the dock, he could still not tell, for she was bundled up against the cold. It was her latest letter that had brought him home, a month earlier than intended. "It will probably be at least four weeks, and I hope the full eight weeks, so you must not rush, my dearest," she had said.

"The main goal is accomplished," he had written back. "Tarquin and Luke will see to the rest of it, with the help of their ladies. My place is with you."

Jamie had noticed him, and flung himself forward, presumably assuming he could fly the narrowing band of water between him and his father and then climb the vertical walls of the ship. To a child a few days short of two, all things were possible.

His nurse darted forward to pick him up, prompting the predictable howls of anger at being denied. Little Lord James Tarquin Redhaven had strong opinions and was not afraid to express them.

Bea moved up to the nurse's side and had a brief word with her heir, probably telling him he would be sent back to the castle if he could not behave, for Jamie opened his eyes with an anguished look at Alaric, and subsided.

They had a few more minutes to wait, while the ship was tied to the dock and a gangplank put out for the important passenger. Alaric was almost as impatient as Jamie, but at last he had his son on one arm and his wife held in the embrace of the other.

"You are home," Bea marveled, and her delight was so palpable he had to kiss her again.

"Hopefully for a good long time," he confirmed. He then had to turn his attention to his son, whose voluble conversation was largely unintelligible, though Alaric guessed the gist of it, and was able to answer as he escorted Bea to the waiting carriage, with the nurse and the rest of Bea's retinue close behind.

It was some time before they were able to discuss the matter that had taken Alaric away. When they arrived at the castle and escorted Jamie to the nursery, the little boy had to demonstrate to his father that he could jump. Alaric was too polite to comment on the toes of one foot that stayed stubbornly on the floor.

Advised it was time to sleep, Jamie insisted on showing his father a new book that his Uncle Tark had sent. Eloise had painted the simple pictures on thin slices of board cut and shaped by the Elsmouth estate carpenter and attached together with strips of leather by the estate saddle maker. But to Jamie, it was from Tarquin. Jamie adored his Uncle Tark.

"Bedtime, James Redhaven," Alaric said. "Off to bed now, and I will read you your book after tea."

Then there were servants to greet and presents to be given to

Aunt Joan and Mother Claddach.

But at last, they were in their own sitting room, and assured of privacy for at least two hours. The first order of business was pleasure. They had been parted for two months, after all. Bea was heavily pregnant, probably with twins (which was the news that had sent Alaric hurrying home), but they had explored ways and means when she was carrying Jamie, and it was nearly an hour later that they lay, satisfied for now, and ready to discuss Alaric's news.

"My father and his friends have your uncle subdued, and Tarquin and Luke and their friends are dealing with Beverley." The Earl of Lewiston had tried to use gossip and a motion in the House of Lords to have Bea declared incompetent and the victim of an unscrupulous rogue, with Lewiston himself to be appointed as an appropriate guardian of Bea, her son, and the Isle of Claddach.

"Uncle Lewiston is a scoundrel," Bea declared. "Just as bad as his son, though he hides it better. He would never have made such a move while my father was alive."

Lord Claddach had lived long enough to see his grandson, dying just a few days after Jamie's birth. The sad anniversary was coming up in a little over a week. Another reason for Alaric to be at home with his wife.

"He thought we had no idea how to wield social consequence and the power of the earldom," Alaric said.

His wife's smile was fierce. "He thought wrong. And your father stood our friend, Alaric?"

"I was surprised, too," Alaric said. "Apparently, he is the only person in the world allowed to call me a useless no-account. That, at least, was the essence of what he told me. His close relationship with the king and with all that set was pivotal in turning opinion our way. He also spoke on our behalf in the house, as did Luke's father. Having a duke on our side was a great help. Lewiston will not dare to go against them all."

"Your letters said that Eloise and Ellie also made a difference," Bea reminded him.

"On the distaff side, yes. Fortunately, Lady Lewiston is not much liked, but Eloise and Ellie are popular with the grand dames. I must remember to tell your mother that her letters also helped enormously. They soon put the lie to the claim that you are incompetent." Alaric kissed the swollen belly that contained his children and was kicked by one of them, which distracted the pair of them for a while.

"With Father squelching the notion I am a rogue," he said, when they had finished admiring her belly, their children and one another. "Lewiston had nothing left to do except claim to have been misinformed."

He chuckled. "Luke managed to drop the idea that Beverley was the source of Lewiston's misinformation. Since everyone remembered three years ago, when Beverley boasted around the clubs that you were his for the asking, it didn't take long for them to put two and two together."

"They put the whole mess down to sour grapes," Bea guessed.

"And when the king mentioned that notion at one of his levees, Lewiston confirmed it. His Majesty suggested Beverley would benefit from overseas travel. Lewiston took the hint. Beverley has left England to inspect Lewiston's interests in India."

"A pity my aunt and uncle didn't go with him," Bea grumbled.

"They cannot do us any harm, beloved," Alaric assured her. "The Duchesses of Winshire and Dellborough have decided you are their new favorite countess, and both Lord and Lady Lewiston know better than to take on such powerful ladies, let alone their husbands."

He stroked Bea's belly. "Perhaps we should ask them to be godmothers to the twins."

"If it is twins," Bea said.

Alaric looked into those beloved eyes. "What do you think? You, not Dr. Bryant. Not Christina nor Mrs. Fayle the monthly nurse. Is it twins?"

Bea nodded, looking morose.

He kissed her belly again. "Well, my darling, you promised your father more than one heir in this next generation, and you have always been committed to doing your duty."

Bea drew him up so he could kiss her lips instead. "In this, my love, as in all else, you have been devoted in your support."

"HEAR YE, HEAR ye," said the footman in Claddach livery, standing in the town square five weeks later. "The Lady and Master of Claddach are pleased to announce the birth of George Turstin Redhaven and Mary Aurelia Eleanor Redhaven. Mother and children are well. Father and older brother are delighted."

The future of Claddach was secure for another generation.

THE END

Author Notes

This story, in case you couldn't tell, was inspired by the story *The Princess and the Pea*. I hope you enjoyed what I did with it.

The Isle of Claddach is totally fictional, but I did take the liberty of using names, words, and a little bit of history from the Isle of Mann, some forty or so miles to the north. Along with some Irish Gaelic and some Scots.

The Portuguese prince regent, his incapacitated mother the queen, and their court did flee to Brazil in 1807, to avoid Napoleon's invasion. They remained in Brazil even after Napoleon was finally defeated in 1815. The king (he became king in 1816) only returned to Portugal in 1821, so placing Alaric in the British diplomatic mission form in 1818 and 1819 is not such a stretch.

The "Sir Edward" I mention is Sir Edward Thornton, who was head of the British diplomatic mission to the Portuguese court in exile from 1817 to 1820. His title was Envoy Extraordinary and Minister Plenipotentiary. All the events Alaric describes are fictional.

The game of pall-mall is believed by many to be a precursor to croquet, but it used an alley rather than a lawn. The loops at each end of the alley appear to have been about four feet off the ground. The rules vary according to source. I have assumed that the term *roquet*, used in croquet for whacking somebody else's ball (and giving the game its name), was originally used in pall-mall, but this was me taking a liberty with the possibilities and not an established fact.

ABOUT THE AUTHOR

Have you ever wanted something so much you were afraid to even try? That was Jude ten years ago.

For as long as she can remember, she's wanted to be a novelist. She even started dozens of stories, over the years.

But life kept getting in the way. A seriously ill child who required years of therapy; a rising mortgage that led to a full-time job; six children, her own chronic illness... the writing took a back seat.

As the years passed, the fear grew. If she didn't put her stories out there in the market, she wouldn't risk making a fool of herself. She could keep the dream alive if she never put it to the test.

Then her mother died. That great lady had waited her whole life to read a novel of Jude's, and now it would never happen.

So Jude faced her fear and changed it—told everyone she knew she was writing a novel. Now she'd make a fool of herself for certain if she didn't finish.

Her first book came out to excellent reviews in December 2014, and the rest is history. Many books, lots of positive reviews, and a few awards later, she feels foolish for not starting earlier.

Jude write historical fiction with a large helping of romance, a splash of Regency, and a twist of suspense. She then tries to figure out how to slot the story into a genre category. She's mad keen on history, enjoys what happens to people in the crucible of a passionate relationship, and loves to use a good mystery and some real danger as mechanisms to torture her characters.

Dip your toe into her world with one of her lunch-time reads collections or a novella, or dive into a novel. And let her know what you think.

Website and blog:
judeknightauthor.com

Subscribe to newsletter:
judeknightauthor.com/newsletter

Bookshop:
judeknight.selz.com

Facebook:
facebook.com/JudeKnightAuthor

Twitter:
twitter.com/JudeKnightBooks

Pinterest:
nz.pinterest.com/jknight1033

Bookbub:
bookbub.com/profile/jude-knight

Books + Main Bites:
bookandmainbites.com/JudeKnightAuthor

Amazon author page:
amazon.com/Jude-Knight/e/B00RG3SG7I

Goodreads:
goodreads.com/author/show/8603586.Jude_Knight

LinkedIn:
linkedin.com/in/jude-knight-465557166

Milton Keynes UK
Ingram Content Group UK Ltd.
UKHW051142031124
450424UK00019B/1103